Contents

Chapter 1

The rocky formations looped overhead, ringing the lake artfully, almost as though some gigantic, cosmic worm had sped through the place, leaving them in its wake, coiling, spiralling and basically jabbing the laws of physics in the stomach and then leaping back from its handiwork to laugh scornfully at them. In comparison, the lake that the intertwining cliffs surrounded looked impossibly *dull*- just another gigantic puddle, a blot on the otherwise picturesque landscape; and even if it was a pleasant ink blue on some days, compared to the surrounding dramatic sunsets and swooning mountains, it paled in comparison until it became a pathetic ghost.

It was therefore bizarre to the locals why this particular lake had been chosen as the site for the annual meeting of the cosmic birds. Many people had dismissed the ominous swirling clouds that usually preceded their arrival as a regular thunderstorm- right up until the first brush-like feathers began to land on the surface of the lake, forcing what tiny particles of gold were in the mud at the bottom up to the surface, and sweeping them viciously into an impossibly thin, but majestically radial, circular stage. Walls began to rise on all sides, and the colours of the supreme galactic overlord began to unfurl from them, fixed in place by hugely over-expensive and magnificently impractical golden stands, which clashed in the most confusing battle of wealth and colour incoordination ever recorded.

Then the cosmic birds themselves began to arrive, heads held high in proud indifference of the planet- which admittedly made it very difficult for them to settle on it with any dignity, as they couldn't see where they were landing. Down they came, swooping through the stratosphere surrounded by billowing clouds of ash and fire, surveying the planet with narrowed, judgemental eyes like the universally feared rulers they were, before descending with a flap of their mighty two-ton wings, which stirred up the surface of the lake and then went on to trigger some unexpected seismic activity in the nearest inhabited country. Their feathers having been expertly rearranged by humanoid servants, the rulers moved back respectfully to make way for the supreme galactic overlord to land.

The six limbs of dictator smashed into the planet with an accompanying disdainful snap of the beak, feathers spiralling left and right (but oddly not centre) before, with a brief glance of boredom at the assembled cosmic birds, their owner opened the meeting with an imperial bellow.

"BIRDS!" he bellowed, the word bounding around the mountains with a sonorous, resounding ringing that caused the few rulers with ears to flinch. "BIRDS, BIRDS, BIRDS, *BIRDS!!!!*" Spat the overlord to a storm of confused clapping. "NO!" he snapped, and instantly the stage fell silent, the applause stopping as fast as a radio being stomped on. "WE COME ALL THIS WAY, TO THIS PUNY EXCUSE FOR A PLANET, WE GRACE THEM WITH OUR DIVINE PRESENCE- AND WHAT DO I FIND THEM CALLING US?"

"Birds!" squeaked one confused wagtail.

"YES!" bellowed the overlord, raising his wings like a magnificent, moon-sized statue (which, in fairness, he probably *was* trying to replicate, given that he'd just come from Synant Gamma, a planet where they had chiselled every one of their thirty-seven moons to resemble him at the expense of ordinary gravity.) "I HAVE DESTROYED WORLDS FOR PRODUCING INFERIOR LIFEFORMS! I HAVE CONQUERED *SOLAR SYSTEMS*! AND I REACH THIS PLANET, AT THE END OF A HARD HUNDRED YEAR CONQUEST, TO FIND THESE PUNY CREATURES CALLING, US, THE MOST POWERFUL CREATURES IN EXISTANCE, *BIRDS!!!*"

"But... we are birds." The wagtail squeaked, confused, shortly before retreating into its purple and blue star-stained feathers as the overlord glowered at him.

"NO!!!" Roared the overlord. "ON ZALTAR NINE, WE ARE SUNSPLITTERS! ON WINDER X, WE ARE GALACTIC GODS! EVEN ON THE BACKWATER MULCH OF A PLANET, KNOWN AS *MELCHAR-*" there were disgusted clicks from the rulers at the mere mention of the muddy little planet. "-WE ARE KNOWN AS THE BEIGELESS, AND ON A PLANET WHERE *NOTHING* IS MORE THAN A DARKISH KHAKI AT BEST, THAT IS THE HIGHEST COMPLIMENT THAT ITS MENTALLY CHALLENGED BEINGS CAN THINK OF! YET HERE, ON THIS SPECK IN THE HEART OF OUR EMPIRE, WE ARE DEFINED, NAY, FULLY RECOGNISIABLE, BY A WORD *FOUR LETTERS LONG!*"

There was a storm of snarled agreement among the assembled rulers, and quite a few muttered, four letter suggestions of what the locals could be renamed to in retribution.

"SO!" bellowed the overlord. "WHAT DO WE DO ABOUT THIS INSULT?! WHAT SHOULD OUR JUDGEMENT ON THIS PLANET BE?"

"Death!"

"Destruction!"

"Obliteration?"

"Annihilation!"

"Implosion!!"

2

"Nothing."

At the last suggestion, the rulers looked around in confusion. The overlord had made it perfectly clear he didn't like the planet, so any cosmic bird with a fully functioning brain *should* have been making suggestions for ways to eviscerate the planet- many had read millions of synonyms for the word 'explode' in preparation to yell them at the overlord. To have someone object was unprecedented- even the overlord looked uncertain- and everyone started glancing about in a confused imitation of the cosmic flamingo. Just as necks were starting to get sore, the cosmic swan sailed forwards, trying to look dignified while nearly three hundred intergalactic dictators glowered at her, silently wondering why she had waited so long before admitting to her outburst.

"I said 'nothing.'"

"WHY IN THE NAME OF ME WOULD YOU SUGGEST THAT?!" the overlord frowned, genuinely confused.

The swan straightened, realised that her neck looked stupid when it was straight, hunched over again and repeated the process to ensure that everybody was watching her and appreciating the effort she took to look beautiful, behaving exactly like the prancing ruler of the Snowant sector she was. "We all know why we *really* came to this stupid speck. If you destroy this planet, you would destroy the migration point of the cosmic worm."

The cosmic worms were a species sprinkled throughout space, and a very odd one at that. They lived for untraceable amounts of time, could grow to the length of uncoiled asteroid belts (although only the smaller, nine foot infants visited the Earth), and spiralled through the galaxies seemingly without purpose, popping up now and then on certain planets. Earth was one such place, and had been for centuries- not that the inhabitants had ever noticed the lengthy beasts. The cosmic worms kept themselves to themselves, and, even on a subconscious level, people understand not to disturb another's privacy.

"You're only here to hunt cosmic worm?" the overlord's voice suddenly dropped in pitch, as though he was muttering more to himself than the shuffling crowd. There was a slightly guilty nodding. The overlord stared around, tried to close the great yellow orbs of his eyes in frustration, realised he couldn't because he didn't have manual control over his eyelids anymore (he'd had a fear of waking up one day and forgetting how to blink, and had installed a tiny machine to do it for him) and instead looked aggressively at the swan, eyes boring into her beak as he peered down from her ludicrous height. "WELL IF YOU WANT TO HUNT IT SO BADLY THEN *YOU* CAN GO AND FETCH IT!"

The swan groaned; 'fetching' the worm meant that she would be too preoccupied with herding it towards the other cosmic birds to snatch a bite herself. Despite this tragic turn of events, she turned to face the lake- offending the overlord would not be a wise move on her part.

The sun posed low in the sky, dragging every short light wavelength it could with it as it gracefully fell over, so that it could look as dramatic as possible by being surrounded by peach and scarlet clouds. The lake slopped away below, gulping miserably as tiny waves slapped against its bank, and dribbling pathetically as the mountains grandly overshadowed it. The swan spread her wings, still grumbling to herself that she had to be the one to miss out on all the fun, and then, with a sonic boom elaborate enough to make even the most skilful drummer weep with envy, she took off, accelerating foolishly fast, a halo of stars and blue- tinged galactic clouds expanding around her head like a space helmet, deflecting the ultraviolet rays of the Earth's pitifully common star, and the mind-melting climes of space.

She pierced through each layer of the atmosphere with ease, her hyper-evolved form accomplishing in seconds what had taken the puny 'dominant' species on Earth centuries to achieve, leaving the bubble of atmosphere and bursting free of gravity, back into the vacuum where stars span and galaxies billowed. With salivating glee, she spotted the cosmic worm- an eight-foot leviathan laboriously twisting itself out of a wormhole off in the distance, its blue and purple body blending almost seamlessly with the cosmos around it. The swan flew a safe distance away, watching calculatingly as the worm's sightless head pointed towards Earth inquisitively, before speeding towards it, dragging the rest of its body behind.

The swan sighed, almost pitying the worm for being so slow, then took off towards it, alerting the spooling giant to her presence with a well-practiced screech (the Snowant equivalent of a speech), feared throughout her quadrant, particularly on her home planet of Sandros 1, where she had destroyed the eardrums of every single being on the planet (aside from herself) during a particularly emotional Wintersday screech. It was a sound designed to both intimidate and impress, and had the desired effect on her prey back in the present. The worm pelted away, sensing the massive bundle of fear, death and feathers closing in behind it, hatred and fury swirling in the poisonous green irises of the cosmic bird.

The cosmic swan's increasingly desperate attempts to reach the worm (and eat it before the galactic overlord could) were hindered by the obligatory herding she had to do in order to drive the worm towards the lake where her fellow tyrannical rulers were waiting, stomachs snarling loudly enough to deafen any nearby humans, and only drowned out as the solo, baritone roar of the Overlord's belly coursed through the air.

The cosmic worm swerved and twisted, its magnificent coils spooling out behind it as the two creatures danced through the burning atmosphere, an eon long trail of fire spurting behind as they dived towards the mountain range, the swan's thoughts filled with complex calculations, aerodynamic adjustments and trajectory plans, the cosmic worm's mind space taken up by a popular song it had heard back on its own planet- consisting of two whole syllables it was a record breaker among cosmic worms.

Drumming his claws far below, the overlord spotted the two shapes and started flying straight up, mouth already open, wide enough to swallow the worm in a single gulp. Then the worm stopped, suddenly, simply hanging vertically in mid-air while the slightly confused swan behind it also stopped.

"What are we doing here?" the worm crooned. The swan shook her head, trying to ignore the humming tones and focus on driving the worm towards the overlord- or rather, trying to catch the worm herself before he arrived. "In this vast, cosmic blanket, who are we to decide who is the dreamer, and who is part of their dream? How can we divide the vast boundaries of space into sectors, when we can't even comprehend what lies at the very edge of our universe? Only a few can look into the abyss and survive, and, at the end of the day, are we even physically able to find this edge, trapped as we are in these limited mind-sets at the edge of the explosion that either began or ended everything? Are we mere corpses, walking in the wastelands of a universe already dead for centuries and never again populated by what may have been? Who made gravity, if nothing else could have borne the fruit that is our universe?"

"Wha-?" the swan froze, forgetting every other thought as she dangled there, trying to comprehend the worm's speech.

It's a little-known fact that cosmic worms use one single tactic to escape their many predators: befuddlement. Millennia of thought devoted, not to anything trivial like finding food or mating (processes which are unnecessary for their survival), left the worms free to think. On several occasions, while being hunted, cosmic worms confronted with their own mortality couldn't bear the thought that their theories would die with them- and so, in an effort to impart some of their knowledge to others before they were eaten, the worms found that other beings couldn't understand their philosophy well enough to multitask while thinking about it, allowing them to escape. Thus, their tactic of befuddling potential predators with mind blowing existential crises was born-

"GULP."

-which was why the Supreme Galactic Overlord had intelligently stuffed every single orifice that could receive sound with cloth to muffle the ramble and leave him free to consume the cosmic worm while every other cosmic bird froze, thinking more deeply than they ever would again. Admittedly, as with every great tactic, there had been one annoying downside- he'd been rendered almost completely deaf, which was why he had bellowed his way through the speech earlier. The worm, however, was delicious.

*   *   *

Mere hours after the cosmic birds had vacated the planet, there was a small "whumph!" as *something* within the world vanished. For a moment, there was a confused grinding of rock as liquid rushed to fill the space left behind... and then the cracks began appearing. Subterranean cracks that widened and spread, with increasing rapidity, magma widening the gashes like seawater through sandy tunnels, lapping away at the walls and melting the rock into a thick sludge. A vein, broad, sturdy and filled to bursting with molten, hell-red peridotite split. A volcano belched. The entire blue globe of the sky began pouring with orange rain; globules of heat that hissed as they landed and solidified into rock, only to be coated in an advancing deluge of more sizzling, hungry liquid, which bubbled and flowed, determinedly inching forwards, gurgling, sealing inanimate and animate alike in a stony casing.

From space, the spectacle was incredible. Three figures watched as the planet changed, from a blue, green and white marble to a rapidly browning nut, ready to burst, auburn and crimson criss-crossing the surface as the seas dried up, clouds boiled away, and, just when it seemed that the planet could do no more harm to itself... it simply fell apart, huge splinters of rock hurtling away from each other like some demented 3-D jigsaw... the moon, with no planet to hold it gradually began twisting away from the scene of destruction, moving gradually faster as though to escape the planetary graveyard. One of the watching figures whistled, softly.

"If only I'd brought a camera."

Chapter 2

Two days later, after the space dust had settled from the 'accidental' explosion of Earth and subsequent confiscation of its moon to add to Synant Gamma's rapidly expanding collection, the Supreme Galactic Overlord was having an incredibly important conversation with the cosmic hawk in the hawk's personal ship, the *Emerald Eviscerator*- a conversation so important, in fact, that neither being actually wanted to actually talk about it, for fear of making the atmosphere awkward, and had instead started furiously arguing about the best bar in the universe.

"So, you know Snowant's starting a new chain of restaurants?" the hawk said casually, massaging his mind desperately in an attempt to come up with a better pub than the Megalith Cubed bar (where the customised gravity could produce drinks that could be held and drunk without any kind of container) while he distracted the overlord with the most boring, but still relevant, topic he could think of.

"Does it serve anything except snow?"

"What do you think, it's run by Snowants!"

"Aren't they called Snowantites? Or was it Snowantiens?" The overlord shrugged. "I'll have to ask the swan."

"To be entirely honest, I don't think even she understands the plurals, whatever she says. So, what about Draconis?"

"Oh nice. Now this is getting interesting." The overlord rested his elbow on his large wing for a few moments, scratching his chin with a free hand.

"See? Have you *tried* their Supernova shakes?" the cosmic hawk grinned triumphantly.

"Before they were copyrighted by Starbucks? Yes."

"Seriously? When was that?! And more to the point- **how** did that pathetic coffee franchise even pull it off?" The hawk shook its head disbelievingly. "Couldn't you have them eviscerated or something?"

The overlord shrugged. "Some entities are beyond even my power. Besides, they aren't exactly pathetic, they've covered half of the spiral galaxies. Speaking of which... you're not going to like this, but I can beat Draconis."

"Oh *really*?" the hawk narrowed his eyes sceptically. "Tell you what, you beat Draconis, I'll take you to this miracle bar for a drink. Whatever you want, paid for by *me.*"

"One word. Revlar."

"Oh no." the hawk's already large pupils widened as he finally grasped what the overlord was about to say.

"Two words- Bar Aquila."

"Dammit!"

The overlord chortled, realised the word 'chortled' would make him sound like a grandfather, and guffawed instead. "You owe me a drink my friend!"

"For the love of..."

"HA!"

The hawk jumped in alarm. "Galex...!" (He pronounced the Supreme Galactic Overlord's name in the old Starswallower tongue; Gal-ex.)

"I WIN!" The Supreme Galactic overlord leapt to his claws, spread his wings just wide enough to hit the cosmic hawk in the head, and then smugly took off out of the ship's pointless airlock. Well... pointless for the galactic overlord and the cosmic hawk reluctantly following behind it, (who could survive in the vacuum of space) not so much for the legion of the hawk's loyal soldiers, who, upon discovering that their leader was missing, panicked and drifted through space for many months, before finally staging a rock concert that devolved into a coup d'état when the space pirates crashed it and detonated the- wait, I'm getting off track.

Planet Revlar, and indeed much of its galaxy, was surrounded by a thick film of alcohol- meaning that anyone or any*thing* attempting to land on the planet would have no choice but to become intoxicated to do so. The permanent inhabitants of the planet went around with livers stronger than concrete due to their constant exposure to the ethanol cloud, and had received a universal ban on buckets after the local law enforcement discovered how often people went around selling the rain to tourists. The practise, apart from ruining the economy, had begun to affect the water cycle.

The overlord smacked his underling on the back and hauled him across the neon pink grass into a small, classy establishment named Bar Aquila, after the constellation that Revlar was situated next to. Despite its relatively modest size, it was the most popular bar on the planet which, given that there were about a billion other bars capitalising on the atmosphere of the giant world, was saying a lot.

The line stretching out in front of it consisted of most of the planet's population, both sentient and not-so-sentient (some inconsiderate billionaires had sent robots to hold their places in the line), and was so long and thick that it visibly formed the planet's equator, coiling over oceans, boats, the backs of whale-like beings, through crowded cities and drunken warzones filled with wailing Vikings (don't ask) and finally right back to the bar several times over, making the planet look as though it was wearing a giant belt, with the bar forming a chunky yet fashionable buckle. The people in the middle of the line had stood for nearly their entire lifetimes just to sit in the bar, the waiting list was so long that people's great, great, great grandparents had booked in advance centuries before, in order to ensure that their great, great, great grandchildren were able to drink there... and even when you *did* get into the bar, the prices were in the millions.

Still, certain people that the owner really liked (or his great, great, great grandfather had liked) were able to bypass the queue entirely, being snuck in through a side entrance by a Cellbuster 5000 touting pile of muscles that served as Bar Aquila's sole security guard. (Not that any other guard was needed; the muscle was so well trained, that it could end any potential bar fights with a single, well placed tap on the target's upper middle back. This would snap the unruly patron into a state of complete, near instant paralysis and allow the bouncer calmly throw them through the nearest window.)

So, based solely off this information, you may be wondering- why would *anybody* go to this kind of trouble just to get into a bar?! And secondly- why would people waste their lives and fortunes on a few drinks? To which I will calmly reply, while I remove my clenched fist from the nearest flat surface, one- because it's **BAR AQUILA**, the most respected establishment in this entire sector, and two- advertising is usually just cleverly worded rubbish. In this case, the advertising is more honest than most of the universe's political and geological information- not to mention ingredients lists. The advertisement is just five words, five perfect, mind changing, perspective-rewriting words, which have drawn trillions of species across the solar systems towards it for centuries. And no, I'm not going to simply tell you what the advertisement consists of now, nor will I let you skip to the end and just find out there. Perhaps I'll slip it in somewhere random. Maybe it'll be in a piece of expositional dialogue in a few pages, possibly on a bounty hunter's butchered beermat, abandoned in a warzone, maybe in a slightly different font in the very next sentence! But I can tell you in all certainty, it isn't worth the wait. This'll build pointless suspense, trust me.

Chapter 3

Bar Aquila is sort of like a reverse Tardis, in that it looks smaller on the inside (and does exactly what you'd think it *would* do based on its appearance). The carpet is the type of swirly crimson pattern that nobody would ever put anywhere but in a pub (or possibly on a bus seat), and the tables and chairs are all made from gold encrusted Balogany wood- the single most improbable wood in the galaxy, as the trees *always* grow into the shape of furniture, making them all the more expensive, and likely to be made extinct in the next thirty seconds. Constantly.

The clientele were a mixture of every conceivable species in the universe- from the stony faced, battle scarred, moss coated Gargantuan slumped over a shoebox- sized glass of some golden, glooping liquid at the bar, to the cackling, nail high living sparks that dived into their poisonous green shot glasses then out again with a whizzing sound like a deflating balloon. There was a brown- haired humanoid sharing a sphere of violet, fizzing fluid with a black and purple, six-limbed, dragon-like creature and even, sitting by himself at a dark corner table, his star- filled face full of misery, an Obligon; a species from the very edge of the known universe who lived on a planet in a constant state of flux due to its tenuous position between two lazy black holes. It was one of the universe's million mysteries why the planet still hadn't been ripped apart- and even if the Obligons knew, they were simply too depressed to tell anyone.

The smiling bartender, who was essentially just a pile of grey and orange glowing rock, similar to cooling magma, ushered the two tyrants into the bar, slipping the two billion hertz check he'd been handed into his specially tailored suit, before removing a small universal translator from the same pocket, inserting it carefully into his hearing orifice and, in a soft voice more suited to a vicar than an anthropomorphic pile of magma sludge politely asked, "May I get you two gentlemen a drink?"

"Can we see a menu?" the overlord smiled aggressively. There was a short pause while the bartender waited for his translator to... translate, then he nodded and glided away over the carpet. Galex glanced at the globules left behind by the creature in slight distaste, made a mental note of all the mistakes it had made- asking for their orders *before* handing over the menu, not upgrading his translator to reduce the time needed for translations, calling HIM 'sir' instead of 'your highness- then decided that it wasn't worth detonating him *just* yet. He was probably new to his job.

Having reached this conclusion, the overlord leant calmly back in his chair, hands behind his head, wings shoved unceremoniously behind him, claws drumming incessantly on the plump carpet, and breathed in the alcohol-rich atmosphere deeply. The cosmic hawk, seated across the table from the overlord, shuffled uncomfortably and, glancing around tensely, muttered, "Please don't order anything too expensive, Galex."

"HA!" barked the overlord loudly. Several people around him spilled their drinks, and the dragon- like creature gave him a rather nasty look as it gingerly lifted its volatile sphere of purple liquid off the floor. The humanoid next to it stepped back and watched with an almost satisfied expression as the sphere burst, showering their drinking partner in the fluid. "I did not just fly through about a thousand meters of alcohol to be told not to get drunk by *you*." On the last word, the overlord poked the cosmic hawk's head aggressively.

"Look, Galex, there may well be bounty hunters in here. Don't draw attention to yourself!"

"Don't try to discourage me. Discouragements are stupid."

"Is that... even a word?" the cosmic hawk frowned, making a mental note to install a bigger electronic dictionary in his head.

"I dunno, I'm drunk. You either have amazing ideas that you remember and become insanely rich for, or ideas that make sense when you're drunk, then lose all meaning when you become sober, look at your holopad and see it's filled with messages from some dignitaries who want you to stop raiding their planet's cheese mines or whatever."

"What?"

"The point is being sober is overrated." The overlord grinned happily to himself, pleased to have seemingly won the argument, then greedily grabbed the drinks menu from the bartender and scanned it furiously, ignoring the five digit prices and happily ordering a miniature volcano. A childish novelty at its core, but a perfect example of a good drunk idea, almost certainly thought up by an intoxicated geologist. The hawk, deciding that, with Galex on his table, he was already bankrupt so there wasn't anything else to lose, shrugged and ordered a pint of Revlarian beer, which, to the 'connoisseurs' of the universe, may sound unadventurous enough until you realise that he had ordered a *Revlarian* pint; an entirely different unit of measurement to the regular pint, and rather like drinking an entire Krilltopian bathtub's worth of dizzying liquid.

The service was excellent, and in a mere two seconds the galactic dictators were grinning aggressively at each other (mainly because they couldn't *quite* remember how a staring contest would work and had decided it had something to do with making your opponent feel incredibly awkward) over their two beverages.

On the other side of the bar, a lilac Manicarian with a body like a half-dog mixed with a half-bull was eagerly jabbering to his two table mates. One was a Xsovzorite named Jath; a grey-faced being constantly scowling at the Manicarian, and dressed in a mixture between a black tartan kilt and a kimono (a popular, if odd, piece of clothing more commonly known as the kimonilt on its home planet of Glasgokyo). The other being was a pale, seemingly serene, hood-wearing figure named Cealth. She waited patiently for a millisecond-long pause in Exath's meaningless monologue, then took her chance to speak, quickly.

"I hope that in our next mission you listen to my advice."

"What d'you mean?!" Exath grinned, practically bouncing up and down in his seat. Jath groaned in melodramatic embarrassment.

"You stole Jath's sunglasses." Cealth replied matter-of-factly.

"I know! They looked better on me anyway!"

"EXATH!" snapped Jath, exploding like a solar volcano. "I needed them to fight the Starswallower! And now, thanks to you, I have a migraine, and for once it's not because I'm hung over! So yeah, *THANKS*. Your fashion sense was *honestly* worth you ruining my one night off!"

"I think what Jath is *trying* to say," Cealth said, in a smoother, more diplomatic voice than the Xsovzorite. "Is that you could have cost *all* of us this one night off."

"How?! By stealing his *sunglasses*?!"

"Everyone knows if you look into a Starswallower's eyes in its home quadrant you develop a migraine- or brain death if you aren't very well evolved! The shades were tinted; they would've stopped THIS," Jath gestured at his face furiously. "From happening! If you'd just stayed on the ship like I said, I wouldn't have been blitzed!"

"An occurrence which lost us time, losing us money and trust with our client, which could have lost us this night out if they'd decided to seriously underpay." Cealth finished quietly.

"Yeah, well done smart-"

"Jath." Cealth said warningly, cutting him off with a significant shift of hood fabric.

"I was going to say guy!"

"Of course you were." Cealth muttered under her breath.

"It didn't affect Cealth." Whined Exath. Cealth said nothing, but for a fraction of a second her two employees felt the air around them grow uncomfortably cold as the hood momentarily failed to cover a sliver of the lower portion of her face.

"Anyway!" Exath swallowed and glanced around the bar, looking for anything to change the subject. "What's our next job?"

"We don't talk about business in public, brain-"

"*Jath.*" Cealth cut him off with a slight shift of her hood. "Don't rise to it."

"Sorry." He scowled, with the air of a teenager being 'unfairly picked on' by his mum.

"You would usually be quite right." Cealth conceded, inclining her head slightly towards Jath. "Ordinarily, we shouldn't discuss our line of work here."

"Ordinarily?" Exath said eagerly, picking up on Cealth's tone. "What's different about tonight?"

"Our target is in here."

"Seriously?" snarled Jath. "You didn't mention anything on the way here!"

"I only received the request as we were landing, so I apologise for the lack of planning time." Cealth paused to swallow a sip of liquid diamond. "Luckily, seeing how this is the planet of the intoxicated, even if Exath *does* give us away, our target can't escape- he has no permit for drink-flying at this time."

"Yeah, but you could've told me before I ordered that forth Skull-scorcher." grumbled the Xsovzorite.

"You can go to the toilet if you need to, Jath." Cealth said, in a slightly exasperated voice. Jath grunted and squeezed out from behind the table, kimonilt rustling past Exath as he edged around the back of the Manicarian's chair and focused on not strangling the sunglasses thief.

"Just don't start without me, alright?"

"So, who is it?" Exath asked eagerly as Jath hurried across the bar, trying and failing to look casual as he scanned the many bathroom doors, urgently searching for the correct symbol of his race.

13

Cealth smiled to herself under the cream-coloured hood, and shifted slightly in her seat, glancing, along with most of the bar patrons with eyes, towards the table where the Supreme Galactic Overlord and cosmic hawk were progressively getting more and more drunk- the two dictators had started consuming some liquids so toxic, that many of the other patrons had begun placing bets on which one would be the first to implode. Drinking in Bar Aquila really was a spectator sport.

Back at the table, the cosmic hawk, scowling furiously at the Supreme Galactic Overlord, downed a thimble full of orange, slightly glowing liquid, similar to honey in consistency, and lent back in his chair, momentarily enjoying the light show that was unfolding only in his eyes. Then he realised he was completely smashed, blinked, and sighed in frustration as the pretty lights vanished.

"...so really, we should have some kinduv way of making planets ninto nuther shapes. I know it would mess up some gravity issuesses for colonists, but seriously, who honestly **CARES** about t' gravity?" The Overlord finished, seemingly talking to no one in particular, but enjoying being able to lecture anyway. The Obligon sitting in the corner looked up, with an interested expression, as his vortex- like face sucked in the information reverberating through the surrounding air, then slumped back into his own depression and inhaled his drink; a thick substance similar to dopamine that glooped away sadly.

The hawk glanced at the Supreme Galactic Overlord for a moment, then realised that if he wanted to escape bankruptcy, he could just leave the Overlord to pay their bill (which by that point would've fuelled the economy of an entire planet), quietly snuck out of his chair and headed for the back door, where all the deluxe spacecraft were parked.

He darted past the silvery, sporty little Starskimmers, the luminous Solarseekers, and one, magnificent, Celestelia; a craft that had clearly been adapted with the best elitist kit money could buy. The hawk paused to appreciate it briefly, noting, with the kind of enthusiasm a ten year-old displays when ogling a supercar, that, with its dynamic yet scientifically practical shape, this model would reach speeds just brushing *slightly* below the speed of light, that it came equipped with a small arsenal of lasers, and, more to the point, that it would've cost its owner the Earth. Literally. A hulking, threatening guard, (likely hired by from Bar Aquila's staff, while the client was inside drinking) bedecked in her own watchful eyes, stood guard over the ship, one hand grasped so tightly on a Cellsplitter, it looked as though they were fused together. Even as the Hawk moved away, having finished admiring the ship, forty of her eyes followed him, registering his every move as he strutted past the exorbitant ship. The other three thousand and thirty-seven eyes were all scanning the other passers-by, many of them glowering warningly at those brave few who came too close, and a couple drooping slightly, taking a quick nap before their shift.

The cosmic hawk strolled behind a long shuttle- which almost certainly belonged to a pack of rich tourists with nothing better to do than drink themselves out of said fortune- that sat right next to the wall marking the end of the parking area. Taking off from here would be best; the numerous ships, besides obscuring Galex's view if he came looking for the hawk while waving an extensive bill, would distract any remotely tech-savvy being, let alone the suave galactic overlord. The hawk yawned widely and stretched his wings, preparing to take off, the feathers at the tips of his wings bushing slightly against the wall on one side and the tourist ship on the other- when suddenly, he caught sight of a solitary hooded figure walking towards him and froze.

Most Starswallowers have no fear of assassination, for the simple reason that they believe, quite justifiably, that almost nobody would be mad enough to try and kill them. The cosmic hawk was not so oblivious. Having been told at a young age that, yes, it was possible to be killed by a lesser life form, he and a few members of his clutch had come up with a list of four individuals just mad enough to pull off a Starswallower assassination. Cealth was currently located firmly at the top of that list.

The cosmic hawk realised he was shaking. He'd barely noticed it at first, but now it was obvious- he was shaking so much one of his feathers had come loose. Behind him, two more figures appeared, cutting off his escape route. There were no witnesses, no exits, and he couldn't even take off because he'd misjudged the size of the gap and was now sandwiched, pinned by his own wings. There was also the gut's worth of alcohol to consider, the effects of which tended to vary from species to species- and the cold adrenaline shaking him violently as it tried to prepare him for a fight or flight response. Needless to say, it wasn't helping.

Cealth stopped a few paces away from him and smiled under her hood.

"Good evening."

The cosmic hawk frowned slightly, but nodded courteously in response. His mother had drummed it into his head a hundred times- manners are more important than almost anything else in life. Except Bar Aquila's Revlarian beer. Or maybe he'd made that last part up- after all, he had just drunk a lake's worth of the stuff.

"I'd like some information from you." Cealth smiled, perfectly composed. Behind the hawk, Exath glanced at Jath in confusion, while Jath kept his eyes firmly fixed on the Cosmic Hawk's back, his Cellsplitter primed and ready in case the Starswallower tried something. He didn't know what Cealth had in mind either, but, unlike Exath, he'd served under Cealth for decades and knew better than to question her decisions.

"In- information?" frowned the Hawk, certain he'd misheard the assassin.

"Yes." Nodded Cealth. "Regarding the exit of the universe."

"No!"

"No?"

The Cosmic Hawk was sweating furiously- his response had practically been instantaneous, and could well result in his death. The exit of the universe was a forbidden place- an area of swirling death where no one, not even the Supreme Galactic Overlord himself, was allowed to go. He remembered the vague, blurry sights and sounds of Sandros 6, and swallowed. After what had occurred on *that* planet... after Neutroby... No. The exit was far too dangerous for any being- let alone an assassin like Cealth- to visit. The chaos that had nearly enveloped the universe thanks to those creatures- even drunk it sent a shiver dancing down his spine.

"What a shame." Cealth said, her tone contradicting her words; not a hint of emotion had entered her voice. "Oh well. Boys, you'd best turn around. **Now.**" She added as Exath hesitated. Jath shrugged and turned around and, a moment later, Exath followed his lead. lowered her hood. A moment later, the hawk's mouth opened, and a flood of information burst out.

Chapter 4

The space pirates whooped with exhilaration, Pho and Nix, the conjoined Gemini, competing for volume, first mate Sam, the time-slipped human, vocally jostling with Captain Tungsten for the most aggressive bellow, and Auren, the only non-remarkable member of her respective species on the ship, surveyed the situation with bland, almost diplomatic disinterest, before adjusting the volume on her four compatriots' universal translators to shut them up. Immediately Pho and Nix winced, collapsing sideways in pain and groaning with one voice as their eardrums reverberated furiously. Sam and Tungsten on the other hand, who had removed the translators before beginning to empty their lungs in anticipation of Auren, continued to roar, oblivious to the attempt to silence them.

Captain Tungsten was a lime-faced Horizor, a species renowned for their inability to feel emotions- although occasional genetic mutations that enabled an offspring to feel *something* did occasionally occur, as in the case of Tungsten, who'd been cast out by her people for having the ability to feel rage (and, so Sam claimed, love). Afterwards, she'd started gathering a crew of the most battle-ready heavy metal enthusiasts she could find, stolen a ship named the Nebula Eater, so called because of the gaseous destruction left in its wake, and successfully founded the Space Pirates.

There were currently just five of them, but every single pirate was ruthless, over-excitable, and had one goal in mind; to play gigs in every sector known to Starswallower, achieve legendary status among bands, and become a more well-known group than the all-Exoangelist pop singers *Just Panic*, who'd been out-performing them in album sales for nearly three years.

"Captain!" barked Auren loudly, grabbing Tungsten's abandoned translator and shoving it firmly into the captain's ear. "We're approaching the Aurelia sector. Should be within range of the Federation headquarters in about two hours."

"THANKS!" barked Tungsten, matching Auren's volume and flinching slightly. "But don't do that! A Horizor's ears are her own private- oh damn!"

"Yes!" yelled Sam. Auren turned away, ignoring Sam' attempt to high-five her; by distracting the captain, she'd essentially handed the human victory in the bellowing contest.

"Note to self," growled Tungsten, adjusting the universal translator in her ear by holding down the volume control firmly. "Hide the translators better next time."

"Plans?" Sam asked, eagerly, glancing out of the ship's window towards the distant galaxies. "You said you'd tell us what they were when we got closer."

"True." yawned Tungsten.

"Well?!"

"Nix, Pho," Tungsten glanced towards the duo. "Go to the bridge and take over from the auto-pilot. Auren, prep the instruments. Sam, shut up and listen."

"Already done!" smiled Sam.

"Not if you're still talking. Right!" Tungsten grinned, showing off all fifty-eight of her razor sharp teeth. "You know how those Melcharian scum-slugs, Just Panic, keep beating us to the best bookings?"

"Yeah." growled Sam, unconsciously cracking her knuckles.

"Well, Auren and I had a little chat, and we've worked something out." The Horizor beamed aggressively, a thrum of adrenaline pulsing through her veins as she anticipated the look on Sam's face. "Turns out, the Federation have been developing a light-speed drive for years. Actually, works too. It's going to be the fastest thing in the universe after the Starswallowers! Their only problem is finding a new fuel source for it- seeing as *we* stole their mega-quartz crystal last solar week, which is the only piece of kit in the entire Federation with enough capacity to run that baby!"

"Hang on!" grinned Sam. "You're saying we'd be able to out-speed the Panickers?"

"Easily. Once we've taken the drive anyway."

"I love the way you think!"

"Is that all you love?" Tungsten raised an eyebrow and, much to her irritation, turned a faint jade- which, in her mind, rather ruined the moment.

"If you two have quite finished flirting, I require your presence in the armoury." Auren's voice abruptly burst through the universal translators, making them both jump.

"Did you turn our translators into communicators?" Tungsten asked, forcing her voice to stay level.

"I might've done. Sam requested it actually- said that having better communication between crewmembers would help in the event of another post-gig Panicker assault."

"And are Nix and Pho listening to this?" continued the Horizor, closing her eyes briefly.

"We are." The cocky, overly smug response of Nix came with utmost clarity less than a moment later. In the background, Pho could just barely be heard yelling at his sibling that it was his turn to use the translator. "We share ears for Galex's sake Pho! Why does it matter?!"

Tungsten rolled her eyes and leapt up, leaving through the sliding doors before Sam could get a closer look at the shade of her face.

"Just for the record, saying you love how somebody thinks doesn't mean you're *in* love with them." Grumbled Sam into her translator- but as soon as the doors had closed behind Tungsten, she grinned.

The armoury was roughly ten cubic metres in length, height and width, the floor coated with an all-consuming shade of black that almost seemed to pull you in as you looked at it, and lit by three, cuboid, white lights embedded into the ceiling.

If anger could be condensed into a single colour, it would have been the exact shade coated on the armoury's four, looming walls- not that the purposefully intimidating crimson was visible from behind the towering stacks of amps, bolted into place to prevent them from drifting away during zero-gravity flights, racks of acoustic guitars, customised basses and a few double or quadruple-necked electric guitars (an advantage of being a Gemini was that it generally granted you the ability to multi-task on a frankly ridiculous scale, having four arms and two brains; and one such talent was the ability to wield the quad-necked axe) which were firmly strapped onto the wall.

Auren was sitting at one of her many drum kits as though it were a throne, glowering at Tungsten and Sam as they approached- Sam had to resist the urge to grab one of her charred basses to defend herself from the fuming Dorian- who leapt up as they stopped a few feet away.

"Rehearsal." She snapped. "Now!"

"That's a bit sudden!" Sam' eyebrows flexed. "Are you sure?"

"Is your translator malfunctioning?" Auren cracked her knuckles aggressively. "Because I'd be all too happy to fix it for you."

Sam' hand flew to cover her right ear, where the ear-bud like translator was lodged, as Tungsten quickly intervened. "She only wondered, why now? We're an hour away from the Federation base, and it would be a better use of time to go over the plan once again-"

"Allow me to reiterate, captain." The Dorian sat down again, waving a drumstick like a baton as she spoke. "The *Panickers* will be in sector Prime tomorrow- the dead centre of the known universe. If they manage to get there before us, (which they most certainly will if we don't acquire the light speed drive) they will be able to host one of the furthest reaching concerts in history- satellites in the Lucia Glassias sector will be able to pick up their signal! Obligons could watch it live! But, when *we* arrive there first, do you honestly want to improvise our set? Surely you can see how unforgivably sloppy that would be, captain."

"I'll go get Nix and Pho." nodded Sam, backing out of the room rapidly, as Tungsten surrendered with a shrug and began hauling reels of cables down from the walls.

"*THE BROKEN KINGDOM CRUMBLES!*" screamed Tungsten, to a massive amalgam of thunderous riffs and Sam' accompanying bellow. The guitars' death screams were drowned out as the heartbeat of Auren's drums rippled through the room, amplified by the metal walls and her own custom built speakers.

It was only after their hearing had returned, that they finally heard the increasingly desperate yelling of the radio upstairs-

"... Repeat, you have entered Federation space! Please slow your engines and prepare to be boarded. Unidentified craft, please respond, over! I repeat, you have entered Federation-"

"Let me handle this." Auren said, swinging herself off her seat and marching smartly towards the lift that spanned the length of the tubular ship.

Nix glanced at Pho and raised an eyebrow. "You were *supposed* to play in sync with me during that last riff. The echo effect? Remember?!"

"What?!" Pho cried, head whipping around to glare at his twin so quickly it caused their conjoined legs to stagger. "That was during *Doomsday Parade*! And what about you and that finger jerking you call music at the end of *Colossus*?"

"That 'finger jerking' was an improv riff!"

"Actually, I thought it made the solo more interesting-" Sam started to cut in, but Pho let out a loud bark of laughter that interrupted her.

"See? You've made *Sam* defend you! Does it fill you with confidence, knowing that a being with tiny ears and the most minimal auditory range this side of Aurdua supports your music?"

"Attention!" Auren barked, slamming her palm onto the radio console to reply, and causing the squawking of the Federation officer to abruptly cease. "This is stealth vessel 0118998827119723. We are under orders to maintain radio silence and cannot comply with your request, over."

"Unidentified vessel-" started the Federation officer, swallowing in alarm. "I cannot comply with your request to maintain radio silence. You have no means of visual identification, over."

"Federation ship," Auren tensed her vocal chords and released a frustrated sigh similar to a Yarflargian (the standard grunts of the Federation). "We have no visual means of identification due to the nature of this vessel, over."

"Stealth vessel," amended the officer. "What is the nature of your assignment and whose jurisdiction do you fall under?"

"We fall under the command of Friea Starre of the 99th corp." said Auren. "We are carrying a highly volatile object of classified nature. Requesting your co-operation in guiding it to headquarters."

"C-commander Starre?" The radio gulped. "S-stealth vessel, uh, your request, yes, it's... granted." stammered the officer. Behind Auren, Pho and Nix were punching the air, while Sam and Tungsten silently high-fived one another. Tungsten slapped Auren on the back, but the Dorian brushed her off, pointing to the sensitive microphone nearby. "P-please use docking bay 10. I... I shall inform command not to disturb your crew."

Ten minutes later, the Federation HQ was in disarray, Yarflargians scrambling to find the source of five, simultaneous explosions, as the space pirates quietly dismantled the light speed drive, carried it back to their ship and proceeded to scramble any and all Federation messages they picked up, delaying the disorganised Federation long enough for Auren to reassemble and activate their new engine, shooting off into space, overtaking the bewildered *Just Panic* members' ship, the Doomsday Comet, and landing in Sector Prime, brandishing instruments and unloading giant amplifiers in time for the concert.

Chapter 5

The Supreme Galactic Overlord, Galex Nallim Cam, woke up with the grandmother of all hangovers, from which all lesser hangovers were descended. Every part of his skull seemed to be trying to murder him definitively, and even the distant beeping of a clock suddenly seemed to be so aggravating, that he wanted to throw the timepiece into a black hole, never to return. What was worse was that he seemed to be floating in space, inside a ship that he couldn't remember ever owning before- and his hands were cuffed. And he appeared to be in a hold. So, all-in-all, he decided, this day was already complete-

"Morning feathers!" yelled a voice. Galex's head imploded with the force of a neutron star.

"I am going to kill every single part of you." He whimpered viciously, squinting around for the owner of the voice with a ferocity rivalled only by the inhabitants of Gorgonia Three. "I am going to find some headache pills, take all of them, then remove your vocal cords, and stuff them back down your throat."

"Delighted to hear it!" Smiled the voice. *How does a voice smile?* Galex thought helplessly. The voice just seemed to audibly beam at him, and with an aggressive cheerfulness to boot. The figure attached to the voice pulled aside a curtain- right as the ship passed a star. The hold was flooded with a glorious light, and the Supreme Galactic Overlord made a noise like a sad kitten and curled up.

"Cheer up Feathers! We're nearly at Castra now, so you enjoy the peace and quiet here because I can really assure you that you won't get a nanosecond of privacy down there!"

"Castra?" croaked Galex, wondering how his throat could possibly be so dry after *so many* Skullsplitters. "Never heard of it. Why am I here?"

"Oh, *you* know!" the voice trilled playfully. "After you demolished most of Revlar, we had to intervene. I mean, you *were* encroaching on our sector of space without a permit, and originally we *were* just going to arrest you for that... but no one really likes to annoy the Aquilans- and Deity knows taking one of their best customers away mid-glass would have done that- so we waited for you to do the annoying for us!"

"Since when did I need a permit for landing on Revlar?" grumbled Galex. And then realising there was a more important issue- "And just who on Cygnus do you think I am? The cosmic chicken? You can't just go around arresting <u>me</u>!"

22

"And you can't just go around destroying Revlar!" The voice suddenly became patronisingly happy. Galex supressed a shudder. "We have laws in this half of space you odd-limbed juggernaut!"

At this point, all cognitive function the overlord had possessed at one point in his long life deserted him, and he uttered the most universally understood four-letter word he could think of. The voice completely ignored this, and chirped on.

"Oh, would you look at that! We're docking soon! If I were you Feathers, which I'm really glad I'm not, sorry to be so brutally honest, I'd lie down pretty sharpish- the gravity can be a little too strong if you're not used to it!" With that, the annoying voice departed, leaving the overlord ten seconds to figure out what it had been talking about, and then a further twenty seconds to pry himself off the floor of the ship under the sudden weight of several tonnes of air.

Galex was eventually dragged out of the ship by two expressionless Yarflargians (large, beige beings known for their complete bluntness) who deposited him on the surface of the planet, and then proceeded to stand guard next to him, seemingly waiting for something.

Galex glanced around Castra with distaste, remembering why he'd tried to erase this lump of a planet from his memory in the first place. It seemed to be doing everything it could to deliberately make itself ugly- the sky was yellow, and not even a nice lemon or exotic Carvaruit worm-gold; just a smoggy, puke-like paste of undiluted, unfiltered yellow. The ground was a gritty sand that lodged itself in your eyelashes with the slightest hint of breath, and concealed hidden shards of solid rock that drilled into the unwary feet of the sand-walkers above. The few creatures that mooched about on the surface were slow, stubby and coated in bristles- the initial Starswallower scouts had visited this lump for a total of two minutes before agreeing it was useless, being so uncomfortable that it wasn't even worth taking over, so they had abandoned it. Now it seemed that some smart-aleck had snuck onto it behind their backs and turned it into a military base. Just *brilliant*.

The two Yarflargians suddenly moved, simultaneously snapping to attention as Galex registered a distant figure moving towards them. Now and then, it seemed to suddenly grow closer, just as a heat haze rippled in front of it, so Galex couldn't be sure if the figure was actually teleporting or just disappearing behind the hazes for a time. The figure finally grew close enough to see, and Galex groaned. His Armageddon headache smacked into his brain for a moment and he swayed slightly before forcing himself to stand bolt upright. One of the guards glanced at him in confusion- since Yarflargians functioned exactly the same no matter which way up they were, they were incapable of losing their balance and therefore had no concept of such an affliction.

The figure stopped in front of Galex and removed the swath of fabric protecting her face from the antagonising grains of sand. Her skin was the kind of blue you'd expect from an O-type star- a mesmerising, blazing blue; so bright that it almost seemed to glow. Her head was completely bald, and her several pairs of eyes, two on the left of her face, two on the right and one in the centre, were all slightly differing shades, two resembling a ghostly jade, two an ethereal gilt, one a silent, opaque amethyst. She had six arms, didn't possess a mouth, nose or ears (at least, not that anyone knew of) but somehow still functioned like most other beings in the galaxy. Galex had met her several times before and had found that he liked her less each time. Today was no different.

"Commander Starre." He growled. Her name was one of those coincidences that occur in a massive universe, and had nothing to do with the Earthian word, despite her glowing appearance.

The Federation commander folded two of her arms, left her lower set hanging smartly by her sides, ready to reach for her Cellsplitters should the need arise, and stretched with her upper set. Her shoulders crunched. "Galex." She nodded, all eyes now trained firmly on him.

"It's pronounced Supreme Galactic Overlord now!" Galex replied, coyly. It might've been cliché, but it was the best thing he could think of with his skull attempting to pulverise his brain.

Starre shrugged with her upper shoulders. "Not in this half of the universe. You're under federation rule here."

Perhaps now is the right time to toss out a bit of expositional information about the way the known universe was divided up; when the first few species ventured into space and started to try to map it, they quickly realised that a big problem with the universe was its movement- planets didn't just stay on the same axis, they moved, and not necessarily in relation to one another, making navigation more similar to predicting the weather than simply driving from point A to point B. Then there were solar systems above and below other planets, suns with no satellites, satellites with no suns, comets and asteroids that whirled through space unpredictably, and in the end, the cartographers realised one thing- space is **_REALLY_**, stupidly, big. Then there was the issue that they didn't know what shape the universe was, so they couldn't decide on a shape for a map. And then people started taking over planets and demanding addresses.

In the end, as governments and dictatorships and administrators and allocators and all manner of other rulers began swarming in and demanding that the universe be divided up like a series of countries, the map writers started to go vaguely insane and formed their own tightly knit group (almost certainly *not* a cult) which, after millennia of solitude and space travel, re-emerged and presented its solution; the universe was, until proven otherwise, a slightly squashed sphere. Five or more neighbouring galaxies ruled over by the same government made up a sector, anything less was a sub-sector or just a collection of galaxies. The sectors would be named after the cartographers who mapped them, and, when a new part of the universe was found, it must immediately be mapped and, where possible, colonised to avoid confusion.

To simplify things even further, half of the sector- ruling governments formed themselves into a coalition called the Federation, while the other half was ruled over by an ancient race known by many different names, but generally referred to as the Starswallowers, who had conquered so many sectors, and therefore owned so many planets, that they eventually decided to elect a leader to order the aristocratic ruling class of cosmic Starswallowers about.

Galex had won the election through a combination of bullying, bribery, drinking contests and insane parties that had lain the competition out until a month after the election was over. Ever since then, he'd been politically arm-wrestling the Federation, both to annoy them, and to constantly remind them that a hybrid essentially ruled half the known universe, infuriating the majority of purists in the Federation, who didn't believe that the Starswallowers (who were constantly augmenting themselves with artificial and biological parts) should even be classed as a species, let alone be allowed to rule half the known universe.

Now, however, the Federation had somehow taken over planet Revlar, which was *supposed* to be the one of only three neutral planets in space due to... alcoholic reasons. Combining the borderline theft of his favourite planet with his grand hangover, the patronising voice and the *methane-breather* that was Commander Starre, and the Supreme Galactic Overlord was getting pretty annoyed by the events of the last 28 Earthian hours.

"And what about the Cosmic Hawk?" Galex scowled, thinking that if he had to put up with this federation rubbish he should at least find out if the hawk had paid for the drinks or not.

"What *about* the Cosmic Hawk?" Commander Starre unfolded her arms, two of her five eyes narrowing.

"Well... where is he?"

"How should I know?"

So, the sneaky avian snuck out while I was being arrested. Galex thought, irritably. *What a jerk! I should never have let him win that starring contest... stupid blinking machine.*

"The point is you're here, on *our* territory. Normally we'd have you hauled up before the Democratic People's Elected Bloke, but-"

"Sorry *what* is he calling himself now?!" Galex spluttered with laughter, shaking so hard one of his guards seriously started to wonder if he'd swallowed a Jellantia.

Commander Starre's jaw tightened, and her five eyes locked onto Galex with the aggression of a Nightcrawler, (a particularly vicious yet undiscriminating creature, in that it doesn't really care what species it eats, just so long as it gets to eviscerate it with one of its five rows of teeth.) and when she spoke, it was in a worryingly polite tone.

"The DPEB," she amended, watching Galex carefully and blinking one set of eyes at a time to ensure that he didn't try anything stupid while they were closed, "Is away on business. Unlike *you*, he actually takes the happiness of his subjects seriously. So, for the time being, we," and here her top eye narrowed, nastily, "are going to put you through your paces."

"Which in universally understood terms means...?" Galex asked, mockingly tapping his universal translator in a manner reminiscent of the Cosmic Woodpecker.

"It means," Commander Starre said, somehow seeming to sneer without a mouth, "That I'm going to put you through the toughest training regimen I have, and if you're somehow still capable of flight by the end of it, you can clear out of my star system and get back to your own sector."

"Sounds like a great deal!" smiled Galex, straightening his back proudly, before being squashed slightly by the intense gravity. "When do we start?"

"You won't be so excitable in two days' time."

"Oh, I'm so scared."

"Do you always have to have the last word?" Starre's central eye darkened.

"Always." Galex affirmed with a madman's grin.

Chapter 6

The cosmic Hawk, ruler of the Laran sector and best friend of the supreme galactic overlord woke up with a nasty headache, presumably descended from some evil grandmother hangover, which drummed on his skull to the beat of his heart. He lay still for a while, feeling the surface pressed into his back for any clues about his surroundings, and racking his brain furiously for any tiny memory of what had happened the previous night. He felt the cushioning of some cool, leafy matter under his spine, the shiest brush of a breeze nudging his feathers, smelt an atmosphere thick with strange, unfamiliar gasses and was momentarily glad that his species could survive in any atmosphere- until he remembered Cealth and decided that his species couldn't survive in some environments after all.

His eyelids lifted, and his beak momentarily fell open. He was sitting, as he'd guessed, on a series of small, leafy plants that carpeted the ground all the way to the horizon, comprised of hills which lay far in the distance, their outlines so misty that they were beginning to blur into the surrounding sky. Here and there, trees with trunks the colour of malachite swerved out of the leaf carpet, ivy-like plants curling all the way up the branches, where they spilled over and out, fist-sized white flowers with five, chunky petals bursting forth like frozen explosions.

The sky- a light violet shade- was almost completely free of clouds, and the tiny star that was the planet's sun glowed faintly, pale and distant. The outlines of the large satellites that orbited the planet, on the other hand, blazed like white floodlights in stark contrast to the dark sky- as did the trillions of stars accompanying them, flickering now and again instead of being their usual still selves. Around the cosmic hawk, chunks of sandstone-like brickwork lay ruined, a few pieces still *just* forming arches, but most crumbling, and covered with plants that flowered in every shade imaginable- somehow blossoming despite the lack of sunlight.

Jath was leaning against one of the columns, a faintly visible, clear blue spacesuit shielding him from the atmosphere like a skin-tight bubble. Exath wasn't wearing one, but was hunched over on all fours, his purple fur bristling slightly, eyes darting around the plain as though expecting a predator to leap from the bushy ground. Cealth was calmly sat on a fallen pillar, the cream hood gone from her face and replaced by a blank white and gold helmet which she wore along with an indistinct, grey atmospheric shield.

"Good evening, cosmic hawk."

The cosmic hawk grunted in response, glancing furtively at the stars, still looking for any familiar patterns or constellations. He saw none.

"I'm afraid I have to apologise for last night. Usually we don't have to take our informant with us, but given the circumstances..." she shrugged, and the cosmic hawk's mind kicked into gear, a stream of thoughts flowing sluggishly past the headache's blockade.

He remembered the impromptu drinking contest between himself and Galex, the brilliant idea he'd had to leave the semi-coherent Supreme Galactic Overlord with the bill and to fly back to his home sector before Galex became sober- only to be ambushed by Cealth. She'd told her men to turn away, she'd lowered her hood, but after that... nothing but a blank void, an annoying vacuum of nothingness in his memory. How strange. Well, at least it narrowed down the number of species she could be. To about a thousand. Mind wiping was becoming worryingly common these days.

"We had to stop for a bit to repair our ship- there's nothing better than blitzing through the cosmos at light speed if you want to eviscerate your engine. I thought you'd probably like to regain consciousness about now, given that we're on solid ground." Cealth stated, her voice a fluid monotone.

"Thanks." He snapped back, putting as much sarcasm as possible into his voice. He just hoped Cealth's species, whatever it was, understood sarcasm.

"You're welcome." Apparently not then.

"Where in the cosmos are we?"

Cealth smiled briefly under her helmet before replying. "On Oonaer."

"Never heard of it." The hawk replied, frowning and looking around again, curiously. For such an obscure rock, the life living on it was quite pleasant. Now, if he could escape and return to the world of Cygnus, perhaps he could bring a few colonies of builders back to it and-

"Don't think of using it for another mansion!" Exath snapped, interrupting the hawk's train of thought.

"What are you, psychic or something?" the hawk blinked in surprise; the little Manicarian's guess had been suspiciously accurate.

"No. I just don't like your kind's annoying habit of colonising every natural-"

"Exath." Cealth cut her lackey off mid-flow, before explaining quietly to the Cosmic Hawk. "I do apologise. He's new."

"I've been working with you for three years!" yelped Exath.

Jath snorted. "Which planet's years, genius?"

"Oonaeran!"

"Well then," smirked Jath. "If we're going by that time frame I've been working with her for- oh let's see... thirty-*seven* Oonaeran years. So, go whine about it to someone who cares, greenhorn."

Exath got to his four legs and stormed over to where Jath was smirking. "Say that again you kimonilt wearing-!"

Cealth stood abruptly and strolled over to the cosmic hawk, casually pulling her Cellsplitter out of its holster and firing a warning shot over her shoulder towards her bickering henchmen as she did so. They shut up quickly and sat down in the leaves.

"I can only apologise for this lack of professionalism. It's been the same ever since I employed Exath."

"Which one's he?" the Hawk asked, casually inching away from the barrel of the Cellsplitter.

"The Manicarian." She replied, equally casual as she motioned for him to stand up and move, repositioning the barrel back towards him. "Let's go somewhere a bit quieter. If you've never been here before it's probably best you learn *why* this planet wouldn't be as good a second home as you think."

"More like second hundred- !" the cosmic hawk began to boast, before registering a Cellsplitter jab and wisely shutting up.

"We'll be back by tomorrow," Cealth called to her henchmen. "Fix the ship by the time we get back, and *don't* waste time bickering!"

The two walked in silence for a while, the tiny sun fading from the sky as they walked, and the stars becoming more distinctive. They were beautiful, those monolithic balls of flaming plasma, and each one probably had a solar system to call its own. The sunset on this planet was strange, the ghostly green clouds curling through the darkening sky giving way to golden wisps, which slowly vanished as the planet turned away from them. The two planetary satellites, those bright, glowing orbs, simply hung there, unmoving from their limited planet side perspective. All in all, it was the most gorgeous sunset the cosmic hawk could have imagined- except he still couldn't recognise the stars. *How far did we travel?* He wondered.

Cealth stopped, quite suddenly. The hawk frowned and stumbled forwards- until he noticed that what they had stopped in front of was not, in reality, a continuation of the leafy hills, but a sudden drop; the edge of a cliff. Below them, he could just make out a series of tree-coated buildings- abandoned, like the ruins Cealth's lackeys had been sitting on before. Gradually, he realised something quite worrying; in the entirety of the time they'd been walking, he'd seen quite the bio-diverse planet- the diversity of a muggy jungle mixed with the natural obscurities of the deep sea. But not once had he seen a single animal, heard their alien, territorial calls or even caught a nasty whiff of droppings.

"...so, who built it all?" he finished the thought aloud, nodding at the buildings below.

"Manicarians and Ribesants." Cealth replied, and for the first time, her voice seemed almost sad. "They were the only two species of animal that ever lived here. They evolved from some common ancestor or other, but it became extinct quickly after evolution. A freak meteorite destroyed a large area of the plants and allowed them to build that city-" she pointed to the collection of plant-smothered ruins, "-in the crater; otherwise everything would have been swallowed by the plants."

"Couldn't they just get rid of them?" frowned the Hawk.

Cealth almost smiled. "You try." The cosmic hawk grabbed the thin leafy stem of one of the plants they'd been walking on and yanked. Nothing happened. The stem simply wouldn't respond to the hawk's efforts- it didn't just ignore them; it was as though the plant was oblivious to the force's mere existence. "If anything stays for too long on this planet," Cealth continued, refusing to let anything break her monologue, even the spectacle of a galactic dictator trying to weed. "The plants will cover it, choke it and then never budge again- and they grow quickly. A colonisation ship found this planet about a year after the meteorite fell, and took them all off-world. Ever since, this planet has been silent."

"Oonaer..." muttered the Hawk, frowning. "That sounds familiar. What does it mean?"

"The lonely planet." Cealth replied. "This is the only planet in the Solar System. The satellites you see up there are just reflections of this planet off its strange atmosphere."

"What on Cygnus is the atmosphere made of then?!"

Cealth shrugged, and the two fell into a momentary silence.

"Why are you telling me this?"

Cealth glanced round to face the galactic dictator, her blank helmet betraying no emotion. "Because you asked. Because I have to tolerate Jath and Exath squabbling all the time. They never see the beauty in the worlds we visit- never show an interest in where they are, just what they're doing there. I think they both hate it here in particular, Jath because it's Exath's home, and Exath for exactly the same reason. His ancestors were glad to leave. You can't fight these plants, but you can die to them. It's humiliating. In any event, I just wanted some partially intelligent conversation for a while."

"So, it's not because you're going to kill me? It won't matter what I know because I'll be dead soon?"

"I can't make any promises." Cealth glanced at him without turning her head, the helmet concealing the direction of her gaze. "If somebody had paid me to kill you, I'd have done it without hesitation if that's what you're asking. I'm an assassin because I'm good at it."

The cosmic hawk shifted uncomfortably for a moment, partly because he could feel the tentative brushes of the plants below him as they attempted to grow onto his claws, partly because the atmosphere between them was becoming... odd. "Between the alcohol and the mind wiping, I can't remember much about last night. But... I do remember that you asked me about... *that* place."

"Yes." The assassin's tone neither encouraged nor discouraged the topic, but her gaze was hard under her helmet as she stared at the horizon, and her Cellsplitter still pointed in his direction like the unwavering needle of a compass.

"Who paid you for them?" he asked, quietly. Cealth didn't respond immediately, and when she did, it was with cutting finality.

"No one." She glanced up one final time, taking in the trillions of stars and the magnificent indigo sky, then turned back to her captive. "We should get back to the ship. Hopefully, Jath and Exath will have finished repairing it by now."

"But-!" the cosmic hawk began- but Cealth's faceless helmet swivelled towards him, and he felt the air grow momentarily colder around him. After that, he shut up, and the two walked in total silence across the lonely planet, back towards the bickering henchmen.

Chapter 7

Forty miles. On land. Every day. Before breakfast.

Sixty miles on a stomach of sludge. A single flask of brittle broth for lunch.

Then a hundred miles back to the camp. You want dinner, you kill it yourself.

You want to sleep; you get rid of your roommates.

"I. Am. BORED!" Galex yelled, glaring at the dusty sky like a Cravasian, a species that had perfected the art of death-staring, and had developed a uniquely nasty look for each individual species in the known universe. Except for the Dorians. *Nobody* upsets a Dorian.

He'd been on that pathetic rock called Castra for nearly thirty Earth rotations, but not once had the burning red sun dipped down even a bit. To make things even more unappealing, he was walking through the desert on a planet with no water. True, Starswallowers like Galex didn't *technically* need water- they'd evolved to survive in the vacuum of Space after all, and after that you pretty much assumed that nothing else could kill you, but he still liked drinking. It was the same reason his species still blinked even though they didn't really need to- just basic habit, a remnant of evolution, like humans having goose-bumps where their non-existent fur tried to puff up to keep them warm, or like Starre's many arms; the leavings of her insectoid ancestors.

In any case, Commander Starre's toughest training regime was taking a lot longer than he'd thought possible when he'd agreed to do it in exchange for slipping off back into the vacuum to look for the Cosmic Hawk. Plus, it was just getting insufferably dull, doing the same things day in, day out, which was why Galex had made a plan. It wasn't a particularly good plan and nor was it complex. It certainly wasn't suspenseful enough for me to omit it until the point where it actually happened, in order to build dramatic tension.

Galex had called the space pirates. A few hundred thousand light years away, several years ago, he'd heard mentions of a crew of ruthless, federation kicking, gear poaching, hard-core space-party goers, and had immediately left for the Aqua-Gravitas sector, a bizarre collection of around 56 galaxies, all of which appeared to be pouring, in slow motion, into the colossal black hole below them. Within the sector, he'd found the space pirates cruising between solar systems in their immensely cool and expensive ship, the Nebula Eater.

There were only five of them, but Galex had fallen so suddenly in love with their lifestyle (and, more to the point, their captain) that he'd instantly taken all of them for a large Revlarian pint in Bar Aquila- quickly slipping away once he discovered that Tungsten wasn't single, Sam giving him a Cravasian worthy death stare when he tried flirting with the Captain, muttering under her breath as she did "Takemygirlimmatakeyourarmyastarswallowingmegalomaniacalplanetexcrement."

Even so, he hoped that the pirates would still feel indebted to him after the Revlarian excursion, and (hopefully) Sam wouldn't stab him. Commander Starre had noticed him making the call from one of her soldier's communicators and had given him washing-up duty for the rest of his time there, as well as an extra twenty mile jog after dinner- "And no flying, or I'll be making you re-do the jog every night too!" She had added, with an aggressive glint in each of her five eyes.

Forty-Eight Earthian hours after he'd sent out the distress call, Galex was starting to regret his choice of rescuers- after all, even if the space pirates had received his message which (given Castra's lack of reception) he doubted, they would still be passing through constellations in the Aqua-Gravitas sector, several hundred galaxies away. Unless they'd upgraded the Nebula Eater since the last time he'd seen them, it would take them several million Earth *years* to get to Castra. He didn't have that kind of time.

A soldier staggered past him, the stupidly heavy rucksack hurling him momentarily off balance, his four, slightly bowed legs straining to take the combined weight of the rucksack, his own body weight, and the several hundred tons of air crushing down from the planet's gassy atmosphere. Galex watched him with a kind of detached nonchalance, which might've looked cockier if the galactic overlord hadn't been doing *exactly* the same amount of stumbling.

Then, from across the vast expanse of space, through the countless asteroid fields and laser battles, past dying stars and time rifts, across all of the weird and incomprehensively gargantuan solar systems, reality broke. It cracked, split wide open, and pulverised the so-called laws of physics, bending distance and matter, then, reluctantly, mending itself as a small yet magnificent ship dropped into the Federation half of space, cruised into the 0-UM (Ultra-Magnus) sector and landed with a sound like the death riff of a sentient electric guitar.

From across the wastelands, through the hazy gritty air, the death riff was the only indicator to Galex that something had landed on the planet. He glanced at the soldier next to him in total confusion, opened his mouth to phrase a question- and inhaled a beach worth of sand. Commander Starre, meanwhile, had received advanced warning regarding the rift's approach, and was already outside in full uniform to 'greet' the ship as it landed. (I use the word 'greet' with a touch of cinicism, because the federation go so stupidly over the top when attempting to be respectful towards *any* Federation authority figure- let alone the ruler of half the universe.)

The door of the ship opened without a sound, falling away from the being exiting the vehicle. The DPEB was a short, unbelievably **average** being, although this was thoroughly intentional. His species, the Wex, weren't taken very seriously by the majority of space-commuters, but this was because the biologists who'd studied them had been well paid to shut up. The reason for this silence was quite sinister; the Wex were shape shifters- of a sort. Every single being that looked at them would see something different, but it was always a reassuring and inoffensive form. In the old days, the Wex had used the ability to become the most ferocious hunters on their planet, but now they just used it to become politicians.

After the first five courses of the lavishly fabricated meal that Commander Starre had ordered for him, he finally got down to business.

"I here you have been holding Galex here." He said, the barest hint of interest detectable in his voice. It might've been thousands of years since his race were considered hunters, but there was still something predatory about the way he spoke about his rival, as though he considered him to be nothing more than a piece of meat to be hunted down and consumed.

"Yes, sir." Replied Starre, careful to keep her gaze averted- the DPEB looked, in her five eyes at least, a little too similar to the infant Nightstalker she'd kept as a pet back when she was a child. It was a form that stirred, amongst other things, a nasty rush of innocent nostalgia.

"Excellent." The DPEB responded, examining the small, gelatinous sweet on his fork with interest as the red sunlight filtered through its refractive interior. "How soon can we transport him to Valtor?"

Commander Starre winced. Valtor was a frozen, hollow moon in the middle of the practically empty Arthur-Vacuous sector, which served as the Federation's most secure prison. Even if somebody managed to escape the deadly, maze-like interior, there were no vehicles or transporters to take them off the moon. And even if, somehow, they managed to get hold of a ship, the secondary satellite of Valtor's planet was fitted with enough weaponry to neutralise an armoured, cosmic-worm mounted Aaaarghan warlord, let alone a tiny prison bus.

Sending someone to Valtor was the Federation equivalent of locking someone up at the bottom of the sea, attaching a remote explosive to them, and linking the detonator up to a mechanism that could ignite the floor. In other words, pretty deadly if you didn't sit tight and try not to think too hard about where your air was coming from.

It was therefore with the professionalism of a well-conditioned soldier that Starre replied, in a total monotone, "Roughly two hours. I sent him off into the Outer Eastern desert with four of my best soldiers."

"Speaking of dessert..." muttered the DPEB, spiking another gelatinous blob with his fork, and examining the tines through the wobbling surface. Starre frowned. It wasn't a joke her universal translator could interpret, so she sat, in total confusion about how they'd gotten onto the subject of pudding, for a considerable time. She'd already eaten her sliced Jellantia and was immensely pleased when the DPEB had finally finished eating, and the ice cream was served. *Say what you like about Earthians,* she thought as she swallowed a delightfully cool mouthful. *But they* definitely *understood puddings.*

(There'd been a heated debate several centuries before, just after the Earth-dwelling creatures had made contact with the rest of the Universe, about whether they should be called, as their hugely popular sci-fi films dictated, 'Earthlings' or, as the Dorians stated, the politically correct 'Earthians'. Eventually everyone decided it was better not to argue with the Dorians.)

"Excellent." Smiled the DPEB with a satisfied sigh. "Destroying one and a half planets within two days," he shook his head, his facial features seeming unsure whether to look smug at Galex's capture or sad at the unfortunate billions of deaths the detonation of Earth and the gargantuan bar fight on Revlar had caused. "I must say, I'll be glad to finally have the other half of the universe under democratic rule."

"Mhm." Commander Starre sliced the top off her scoop of ice cream, turning the rounded ball into a plateau. Somehow she found it difficult to imagine the lazy, idiotic Starswallower being capable of destroying worlds. Then again, she'd seen first-hand the devastation he'd caused on Revlar- it would take the owners at least another week to rebuild Bar Aquila. Still, at least the line had been considerably shortened. If any being deserved to go to Valtor, it was Galex.

Abruptly, the table started shaking furiously. If the DPEB's arrival earlier had sounded like an electric guitar's dying note, this was a violent wave of sound that sounded as though about thirty of the most powerful amps in existence had been smashed together and violently spat out by some crazy rock god. It shattered the legs of the priceless Balogany table, sending splinters flying in all directions like the second big bang, atomic galaxies no doubt being created, civilisations thriving as they hurtled through space, then, as the splinters ripped through the tent fabric, being extinguished forever.

Commander Starre had been trained for many possible events (and a couple of impossible ones too, just in case), and initially felt certain that the source of the devastation had to be some kind of sonic explosive- until her ears stopped ringing from the initial blast and, with the startled awareness of a headphone user turning down their volume and finding out they quite enjoyed the song they were listening to after all, she frowned, recognising the opening chords of *Eye of the Taurus*-amplified to such an extreme volume that they'd started to pull the atomic structure of the room apart.

"Out!" she barked, hustling the **DPEB** out of the tent quickly, only to find herself being buffeted by the aggressive gales of the outside world, sand spraying wildly, and seeming to direct itself with vicious accuracy at her five eyes, four of which squinted, the semi-opaque lashes blocking at least 50% of the overall dust- the final eye watching the **DPEB** carefully, covering itself with a vertical grey membrane. Hastily, she motioned for the two burly Yarflargian guards next to her tent to hurry up and escort the leader of the Federation half of space back to his ship before something else weird happened.

Several miles away, Galex's face split into the beaked equivalent of a grin. He took off with three, powerful strokes of his wings, muscles heaving against the heavy gravity of the planet, and banked sharply to dodge the laser bursts now being fired furiously in his direction. He didn't have the velocity to escape the planet's weighty atmosphere by himself, but the Nebula Eater wouldn't have to worry about such trivial things with **its** mighty engine. *Soon,* Galex promised himself, *you're going to be eating chilli and having some* very *stern words with that little Melcharian, the cosmic hawk.*

Chapter 8

The Federation command centre was located in the exact centre of the Aurelia sector, a few light years away from the heart of an elliptical galaxy known as Dolchis. The location was more for inconvenience than grandeur- the absurd gravity made getting to the democratic headquarters so unnecessarily difficult, that no protestors ever bothered to make the trip. The headquarters were *supposed* to be a symbol for ultra-democracy, so the atmosphere was comprised of the three most-breathed gases in the sector- ethanol, helium and, regrettably, caffinium; a horrible, unreactive, dullish brown mist that just hovered in mid-air, dulling the senses and giving many visitors the panicky delusion that they were back on Melchar.

Ten days after the disaster on Castra the **DPEB** was back in his home sector, and strolling through the thick, atmospheric mix with the detached nonchalance that only a Wex could afford; since he didn't technically breathe, he enjoyed the slightly pained expressions surrounding him as he made the long commute to his office each day- it was one of the few pleasures the democratic people's elected bloke enjoyed; that and the *tiny* privilege of running **half the known universe.**

His routine each day was precise to the nanosecond- he woke up at *exactly* satellite 3452's twelfth orbit of the station, exercised until the familiar orange orb that was satellite 0103 had reached the centre of his room's singular window, then left in his personal tele-sphere, the automated ride taking him half way across the space station, right up to his favourite Delcoid dispensary. He spent two more satellite orbits drinking the thick, glutinous semi-liquid, then commuted directly to his office where he would spend no less than two thousand satellite orbits answering calls from idiots and filling endless forms, files, crossword puzzles and pint glasses, before heading back to his quarters as a silvery, slowly twisting piece of old moon rock drifted past.

Today, however, he was only at the Delcoid phase and already in a foul mood. The space pirates had stolen a Mega-Quartz crystal *and* a cutting edge light-speed engine that had taken thirty years to engineer and had then proceeded to out-perform the Federation-born, all Quavian band '*Just Panic.*' Then Galex had escaped, those damn *space pirates* (disrupting the running of the Federation again!) had helped him- and had then left the sector without taking a single hit from Commander Starre's supposedly 'elite' sharpshooters!

To make matters worse, he was two nanoseconds behind his usually <u>exact</u> routine- and when there are more than twenty thousand satellites orbiting the windows, each one a uniquely recognisable hue, shape and speed, then you would *never* be able to escape your own inadequacy when it came to time keeping.

On top of all that, Bar Aquila had nearly been rebuilt, so his arguments for attacking the Starswallowers were losing weight with every reparatory brick laid. He drummed his fingers aggressively on the drinkosphere, wondering if he could maybe shave two nanoseconds off the length of time it usually took him to finish drinking the liquid- when he became aware of another disruption to his routine, and this time he couldn't move a nanometre to prevent it.

"Is this seat taken?"

Clearly. The DPEB thought, and if he'd possessed sweat glands they would've started working furiously at that moment. *My coat's sitting there.*

The speaker sat- not troubling to move the Wex's coat first, prompting the DPEB to give an internal squeak of outrage.

"I expect you to know why I'm here." The figure stated, irises contracting slightly in response to the vague, neon glow of the coat below it. *" We had a very clear deal. I would give you the evidence you needed to convict the supreme galactic overlord, you would arrest him and watch as the Starswallowers annihilated each other in the ensuing power struggle, then take over. What went wrong?"*

"He-" the DPEB paused, swallowing furiously and flexing his vocal cords to restore their usual pitch. "Galex escaped."

"How?" It wasn't an exclamation. The figure kept its tone level, reasonable, and, even if the DPEB could see its pupils swelling in concentrated rage, the being gave nothing away in its tone.

"Space pirates." Muttered the DPEB, all thoughts of timing relegated to the back of his mind as he mentally scrabbled for excuses. "I didn't know they could travel across the galaxies so quickly. We hadn't tested the light speed drive yet, so-"

"Space Pirates?" Mused the figure, elegantly cutting across the DPEB. *"Interesting. I have to admit, they were a factor I had not considered. How annoying."* It was silent for a time, then nodded its long neck towards him. *" What do you intend to do?"*

"Do?" The DPEB echoed, pathetically. "I can't **do** anything. He'll be back in his home sector by now, and we can't touch him there without prompting an all-out Universal war-"

"How do you know *where he is?"* queried the figure. *"Ask yourself- if you were a human space pirate, and someone as powerful as Galex, with all his money and resources, owed you a favour... what would you do?"*

The DPEB stayed quiet for a time- for all his worries over time keeping, his biggest fear was of failure. He would never give an answer unless he was certain that it was unequivocally correct. "Humans come from Earth..." he said slowly, measuring each word cautiously against his data implant before speaking. "I expect... I'd ask Galex to find out who'd destroyed it."

" Yes."

"So... he's looking for you?"

"I? I did not destroy Earth. I simply... repurposed its population. It is a happy coincidence that the actual culprit is quite easily manipulated, at least where their enemies are concerned."

"So, we use him to kill Galex?"

"Her." Corrected the figure. The DPEB's face fell as he registered that he'd made an incorrect assumption.

"I thought you were talking about Crushianator. He's impulsive, reckless, likes destroying worlds, hates Galex, isn't the brightest..."

"I was talking about Cealth." The figure said, in the sort of tone you'd use when ordering extra breadsticks. "I've ensured that she will meet Galex at a very specific location. He will believe he is in control of the situation and carelessly barrel in to attack unprepared, and she will likely kill him in self-defence. I admit that this isn't as fool-proof as our original plan... but either way, that puffed-up, sector-owning hybrid ends up dead, and you take his half of the universe."

The lilac-streaked Satellite 0080 breezed across the planetary skyline, indicating, quite blatantly, that the DPEB had to leave for his office. Uncharacteristically, he ignored it. "One final question. What do **you** get out of this?"

"You just sweep in and take over Galex's sectors after the dust has settled. The universe will be united, just as you have always wanted. With a plus like that, you hardly need to know any more about my insignificant little desires." The figure paused, then twisted its face into a grin. "Perhaps it's better to say that I will also achieve my life goals."

And with that, the figure stood up and left. The DPEB watched the window for a departing ship, waiting to have some confirmation that the thing with which he had been talking had left. But, as the minutes dragged on, other than the crumpled coat on the chair opposite the DPEB, there was no sign that the figure had ever been there in the first place.

Chapter 9

Waking up in space is a lot less fun than most people think. Certainly, it might appear enjoyable to bob about in mid-air without needing to triple check your jetpack's fuel levels every three minutes or remember when to beat your wings- but being tethered to a pole overnight, then trying to wriggle out of a sleeping bag, or attempting to sit up in bed when there's nothing to sit up **on**... let's just say trying to sleep in space is a highly inconvenient process.

The cosmic hawk was staring at what had (at one point in time he was sure) been the ceiling. Trying to remember which way up was, was infuriating. He wriggled around furiously, trying and failing not to compare himself to a cosmic worm. Inadvertently, he remembered the hunt on Earth and his fury when his existential crisis was resolved, and he realised that Galex had eaten the entire megalodon *by himself.* He finally slipped free of his bonds and landed on what had once been a nice, definite ceiling and was now resolutely, irrevocably, the floor, with a surprised imitation of the cosmic duck.

Cealth, meanwhile, was lying quite comfortably in her gravity supplied cabin, staring up at the view screens above her, displaying real-time views of the universe outside, the stars closest to the ship fading away into the blackness as Cealth's ship, the Celestelia, flew from one galaxy to the next, covering the incomprehensible distances with ludicrous ease, thanks to its 180,000 mile/second top speed, ludicrously efficient design that abused the lack of air resistance in space as effectively as possible, and the constant maintenance that the Celestelia received, thanks to Jath and, when the Xsovzorite was looking the other way, Exath- who despite his whining was extremely proficient at buffing the hull.

Cealth wasn't a romantic- in fact, she cared less about the universe than her Cellsplitter- but she liked to see where they were going, and if the ship passed a stunning nebula on its way across the stars, she sure as hell wasn't going to ignore it.

They were still facing a massive problem in regard to their next stop- Onyx, planet of the hyper-depressed Obligons; a species forced to exist in a cycle of perpetual destruction, thanks to the two black holes that their planet happened to orbit. It was still a huge mystery to all non-Obligoid scientists why the planet hadn't just split in half in response to the ludicrous gravitational pull from the duo of dense, dead stars.

Onyx was the perfect place for Cealth and her crew to hide for a while, until the frantic search for the cosmic hawk died down, and it also happened to be a convenient pit stop about half-way away from the exit to the Universe- on the other hand, it was eight thousand light years away. *Annoyingly*, Cealth thought. *Even with the ship's insanely powerful engine, it would take us eight thousand years to reach that lump of decaying life, work out how to land on it without the Celestelia being torn apart- and then park. I really don't have that sort of time.*

She frowned up at the view screens, watching them through her helmet (which she wore even in private in case some moron (Exath) came bursting in without any warning.) She knew almost every star and constellation above her- even as they shifted, forming new patterns, she could still see the old ones in her mind's eye. It had been one of those quaint, nice little hobbies that the Earthians had brought to the wider Universe- making shapes of animals or objects with the stars- and finding the ancient stories behind the star-creatures was one of the very few activities that Cealth actually enjoyed.

But even as her eyes wandered over the various shapes, she spotted something that made them widen slightly- a tiny, seemingly unremarkable, orange F-type star, part of the Cygnus constellation- that set a long line of neurons sparking as she came up with an excellent new plan. She thought for a moment more, then nodded to herself and programmed in a new set of coordinates, quickly reminding Jath and Exath over their communicators to use the facilities before they hit top speed. She conveniently forgot to warn the cosmic hawk.

The cosmic bird in question sighed with relief as he finally left the sleeping cupboard, then instantly regretted it as the breath joined the thin atmosphere circulating around his body. (Starswallowers survive in space by being able to create a thin layer of atmosphere around themselves. Because of this, they can breathe in any environment by re-cycling gasses that they extracted from nearby planets or stars.)

The corridor was filled with air that seemed to be 70% methane, 20% carbon dioxide, and 10% old socks, which either meant that one member of Cealth's crew needed to learn how to clean clothes in space, or, the more worrying option, that this was the very whiff present on their home planet. *Eugh.* To distract himself from the revolting pong, the hawk took in the surroundings, noting how the mathematically straight corridor was decorated with doors and, more appealingly, how one of these doors had a certain symbol on it.

Finally! The cosmic hawk propelled himself across the corridor, speeding as fast as he could towards the door- when Jath stepped out of a door on the opposite side of the corridor.

Immediately their eyes met, and both beings hurled themselves towards the door- colliding in mid-air, the hawk smashing into Jath's elbow. In response, the

Xsovzorite began spitting out a chain of insults so rapidly that the hawk's translator had to momentarily pause, trying to work out how best to replicate the intensity and passion behind the utterance, then began bellowing a series of syllables so loudly into the cosmic hawk's ear that the Starswallower flinched, momentarily deafened, releasing Jath, who, up until that moment he'd been grappling with while they both tumbled through the air.

Jath reacted instantly, taking advantage of the hawk's distraction, and forced himself through the air towards the door, grabbing it, wrenching it open, then lunging in- the hawk seized his ankle at the last moment, trying to pull him back from the room, but Jath anchored himself by seizing a rivet of metal with his claws, and then planting his foot firmly between the Starswallower's eyes with enough force to make him release the ankle. Jath swept into the room and slammed the door in the cosmic hawk's face.

Damn. He thought. *I really needed that toilet.*

He sighed, turning away from the door, and tried to sit down in mid-air to wait, forcing himself to ignore the sock-like odour that seemed determined to permeate his personal atmosphere- which, until a few moments before he'd entered the corridor, had contained a lovely cocktail of smells that he'd retrieved from several exotic locations- the glassy red landscape of Draconis, Revlar's strawberry-rum atmosphere, the fruity foods of Yaucus, the flowers of the paradise known as Grancia, the dusky pools of the Evelmen colonies, the beaches on Cauch...

The hawk sighed, allowing his eyes to wander down the length of the corridor- then frowned, spotting a small window that he hadn't noticed before, having been too distracted by the toilet door. Hoping to at least get some sort of clue as to where in the universe they were, the hawk pushed himself over to it, and suddenly found his beak falling open. Outside, the cosmos stretched out in all directions- but that was old news. He'd seen more sights than he'd heard words to describe them, but the nebulae here... wow.

Ribbons of purple and blue twisted alongside the Celestelia, as though tracking the ship's progress through the Great Galaxy- further out, he noticed with a start of surprise, the bands of orange and blue expanding out from a singular point in space, blooming suddenly out of the darkness, like the eye of some incomprehensibly huge god abruptly opening, or the eternally frozen explosion of an ancient, long-dead titan of a star.

Looming in the distance, huge cliffs of gaseous rock hovered, without an anchor to hold them in place like the mountains they were- but what had truly caught his attention, forced him to feel the nostalgia of an adult returning to his childhood playground, was the bubble of deep blue and scarlet blossoming in the distance, thin tendrils of deadly vapour waving from deep within as though beckoning.

The Great Egg; a maze of gases within which young Starswallowers would be swooping, twisting, learning how to propel themselves and change direction most effectively in the vacuum, in preparation for a lifetime of flying- free from restrictions or federation rules- within the universe, discovering new planets for their more powerful kin to worry about colonising and conquering; they were the first "Hello!" to any new race they found- the handshake rather than the fist.

We're near Cygnus. The cosmic hawk realised, disbelievingly. *I'm nearly home!*

Chapter 10

"WHAT THE HELL DID YOU DO TO THAT PLANET?!" is not usually the kindest thing to say to someone who's just been rescued from a desert world where they spent the last few months prisoner. However, if this happens to be the same person responsible for destroying your planet, and everything on it, you have my full support to punch them in the face. Unsurprisingly, Sam punched Galex in the face.

"Relax!" he said, completely bemused- and irritatingly unharmed, his personal atmosphere having absorbed the blow. "It's not like it affects you. No offense, but you guys could never afford to get into Bar Aquila in the first-"

"I'm not talking about a *pub*!"

"Neither am I. Bar Aquila is, as the name suggests, a *bar*."

"I'm talking about my planet, Galex!" Sam snarled, her teeth a visible tribute to omnivores everywhere.

"Since when are we on first name terms? And this planet is...?"

"Earth, you moron!" she barked. "The home of my great something nephews and nieces. The planet containing over a trillion sentient life forms! The planet that *you*-," she poked him in the stomach with a nail that, to Galex, seemed far too long for a glorified ape. "-**detonated** just because a few English morons called you lot 'birds' which, let's face it, you basically are anyway!"

"Oh, *that* rock..." he said thoughtfully. "*I* didn't detonate it."

"Well one of your minions then!"

"No. Not to my knowledge. It's a shame too, I was starting to like some aspects of the Earthian culture."

"'Some aspects!' Like what?! The nukes? The weaponry? The wars?"

"Thoth, Horus, Nehkbet... the Ancient Egyptians of your planet knew what they were doing when it came to the worship of... err... winged beings."

"Do you mean birds?"

"Possibly."

"How'd you know all this stuff? Ancient Egypt is kind of obscure." Sam frowned, her anger momentarily dulled by sheer confusion.

The supreme galactic overlord puffed up his chest fiercely. "When I visit a subservient planet, Sam, (particularly one that the Dorians took a personal interest in, during the whole Earthling vs. Earthian debate) I make it a priority to study their culture, even if I appear to be indifferent when I deliver my '**death to all worlds**' speech. I *do* have a 'ruthless star-swallowing dictator' appearance to maintain, after all."

"So... you really *didn't* detonate Earth?"

"No..." he said thoughtfully, ruffling the feathers on his head with a free hand. Then he shrugged. "I wonder who did."

Just then, the door to the lounging area opened with a smooth, yet retro 'chunk', and Captain Tungsten came smiling in.

"Morning, Galex!"

"He didn't blow it up." Sam sighed, sounding almost sulky.

"Guess I win the bet then." Tungsten grinned at her first mate. "You know what you have to do!"

"Yeah, yeah." Sam glanced at Galex "You're probably hungry right? The cuisine on Castra leaves a lot to be desired according to the reviews. I'll get Auren to bring some chicken curry up- uh... that's not cannibalism, is it?"

"Probably is." Galex shrugged. "Honestly I'm so hungry I don't care."

"Hmm." Tungsten smiled at him as Sam left. "We had a bet- if she was right and you *had* destroyed Earth, the Space Pirates would've destroyed you in return."

"And... now that you were right instead of her?" Galex swallowed, reminding himself that, no matter how attractive and friendly Tungsten seemed, she was incapable of feeling happiness, and all too capable of being angry. The second that her expression turned blank and she couldn't be bothered to put up an emotional façade anymore, then things were about to explode. **BIG** things. Could be the next spaceport, could be a sun. Honestly, it didn't really matter.

"Do you care? You're still alive, aren't you?" she grinned. Galex shifted slightly closer to the engine room; it had suddenly become uncomfortably chilly. "But anyway, I came over to ask you where abouts in the Universe you'd like us to drop you now that we've lost the Yarflargians and all."

"There were Yarflargians chasing us? When?!"

Tungsten shrugged. "It was a very quiet chase."

"Must've been." Muttered Galex, shaking his head in disbelief. The Starswallower thought for a few moments, genuinely considering all his options- go back to Revlar and fix the damage, go home and act superior for a few days (days being two Earthian years on Galex's home world) or find out who'd been detonating planets without his knowledge. Actually, thinking about that, he could probably catch the Starswallower responsible for destroying the cosmic worm's favourite migration point (Earth) if he went back to Cygnus anyway. He grinned.

"Alright, I've decided. Can you drop me off by Revlar?"

Over by the galley, floating cautiously next to Auren, the Dorian chef, Sam was scheming.

"I don't know about you, but I *really* don't trust him." She paused, giving Auren the time to respond if she needed to. The Dorian continued to stare at the chicken curry being manufactured in the ship's atomic re-arranger and didn't speak. "I mean, if you'd detonated someone's planet, and you knew there was still at least one member of the species left in Space, you wouldn't exactly tell them the truth, would you? You'd be more worried about keeping your brain in your... wait, do Starswallowers keep their brains in their heads?" Auren shrugged. Sam frowned and continued. "Anyway, the point is that I need to know, for certain, that that feathered freakazoid isn't lying."

Auren turned abruptly, staring **deep** into Sam's eyes. "I expect you would like me to deal with that when I take the curry up?"

"Ideally, yeah."

"Hmm. I have never thought that destroying planets was truly Galex's style. I still stand by the Captain. He did not do it."

"It's *unlikely* he didn't do it, you mean?" Auren corrected, instantly regretting it as the Dorian glared at her.

"Are you implying our universal translators are faulty?"

"Nope! Definitely not! In fact, mine's working better than usual today!"

"Sam."

"Sorry!" she barked, stiffening like a Balogany trunk.

"Don't question my wording, Sam."

"Yes. Sorry!"

"Look me in the eyes, or I will adjust your volume again."

"Sorry for questioning you!" recited Sam worriedly.

"Hmm." The Dorian turned, lifted the curry packet out of the atomic re-arranger and glided out into the corridor. Sam glanced at the sweat beads floating away from her face, cleaned them up before the galley's hygiene alarms started blaring, and hurried away, reminding herself, as she did, of one of the Universe's most important rules; *don't* question a Dorian.

Chapter 11

Many decades ago, a team of slightly deranged scientists decided, after a long drinking party on Revlar, which had stretched through many of the world's pubs, bars, restaurants and portaloos, to try and harness the power of a star. There were trillions of them, they reasoned, so surely no one would miss one. Unfortunately, they had attempted to fly a spaceship while totally smashed and were almost immediately arrested by the space police (whose headquarters, oddly enough, were located on Revlar (probably for... ahem... strategic reasons)) and imprisoned until their hangovers wore off, resulting in an entire university of memory loss being founded alongside to the prison the very next day. (It became very well-known over the years and produced many an amnesiac.)

The plans for the Dyson Sphere, however, weren't lost; one of the maniacs had copied out the plans for the star-harnessing structure onto the back of an Aquilan beer mat, which had changed hands several dozen times, before the wily cosmic owl had paid a notorious bounty hunter a considerable amount to steal it. After that, it was a simple matter of building the immense, colossal structure around a certain F-type star in the *Cygnus* constellation, and **boom**; the Starswallowers had a magnificent and entirely unique star to call home- complete with a superb power source at the core. Nuclear fusion at its best.

Several of the younger Starswallowers had demanded that their epic new home star be given an equally epic name- but nobody was clever or inventive enough to think of one- so, eventually, everyone just started calling the star Cygnus after the constellation it was next to. (The humans from Earth, once discovered, claimed that they'd already named the star 'KIC 8462852'- a name which was instantly rejected and erased from every annul of history that mattered, simply because it didn't translate well.)

Every Starswallower ever laid will emerge onto this monolith a few dozen Cygnus days after birth (a period equivalent to six Earthian years), and immediately be flown, by shuttle (as befits the royal race) to the Great Egg, a nebula where, as the cosmic hawk had recalled, young fledgling Starswallowers will learn to orientate themselves and practise the flight skills needed for a life in Space. The nebula also provided the fledglings with some highly nutritious atmospheric gasses that enabled them to survive indefinitely within the nebula.

Since the artificial Cygnus star-world is the only place in the universe the Starswallowers have been *known* to settle, it's still a mystery to most of the known universe <u>where</u> the anarchist, bird limbed, armed, space-faring beings *truly* originated, and how they came to bear such an oddly striking resemblance to the

Earthian birds- while possessing maintaining arms, a capacity to breathe in the vacuum and survive the harsh extremes both of space, and on the Cygnus home star.

Cealth was lying down, firmly secured to her memory-foam mattress as the Celestelia sped towards the gargantuan power source- and, even though she'd seen the images emblazoned onto the propaganda that had been distributed (read: scattered randomly) throughout the Starswallowers' half of the universe, the sight still made her gasp in surprise when the Dyson Sphere finally came into view on her ceiling screens.

The first thing you noticed was the scale; the monumental **size** of a ball of fire and plasma which blazed, as it had done for billions of years, in space- a symbol of permanence and unchanging *power*; traits which somehow seemed to be magnified by the gargantuan structure reaching across the seething surface.

It's really hard to explain how **big** stars are- someone once had the clever idea of comparing Earth's size, in relation to its sun, to a pea in Westminster cathedral. Other people were more blatant; **IT'S ONE HUNDRED AND NINE TIMES BIGGER THAN EARTH**. To which people responded by rushing out, buying their shopping and firmly watching several sit-coms, humming any random tune they could think of to distract themselves from this fact- which is why most people have no clue how big their own star is. In other words, I blame the sit-coms.

The structure was made from a diamond alloy (which might seem ridiculous to an Earthian, who originates from a planet where such a material is irritatingly rare) straight from the Lucia Glassias sector, which contains 6 galaxies with over 9,000 planets made, almost exclusively, from diamond. The Starswallowers' choice of material actually made sense- it could withstand the searing 6000 kelvins of heat once alloyed with several other stupidly expensive and strong minerals- and it looked unbelievably cool, providing a smooth surface to Cygnus while still containing the impurities needed to weaken the clarity of the diamonds *just* enough to shade the eyes of a casual onlooker from the orange glow of the star locked deep within the blue-ish orb.

It was covered with buildings- if such magnificent structures could really be classed only as 'buildings'- made from materials imported from every over-expensive corner of the 2,304 sectors currently ruled over by the Starswallowers. The many towering dwellings (which resembled castles dipped in liquid spires of crystalline magma, then left to cool) were furnished with balogany and sof-twing hammocks^{tm} that swayed in an artificial breeze.

The atmosphere of Cygnus had been created with the combined efforts of several gastronomes, the largest poll ever created (which contained several billion suggestions), no less than four hundred trips to Draconis and the Megalith Cubed bar respectively, twenty resignations, four billion deliveries and, after two-hundred years of planning and atmospheric collection, an atmosphere thick with the smells and wisps of distant, complex cultures and pungent yet valuable plants.

Cealth examined it closely. If the rumours were true, and the creature she was looking for really did exist on this Dyson Sphere, then it would be almost impossible to find. From a distance, the star looked like a fly trapped in amber- a perfect, orange sphere surrounded by a giant crust of diamond several hundred-thousand meters thick, with a series of powerful, heat-resistant pieces of advanced machinery syphoning the energy of the star at the core. The atmosphere was visible, from space, as a hazy red that Cealth knew perfectly well she wouldn't be able to survive in without an atmospheric shield.

The ship slowed slightly as it approached the star- but that was what Jath had programmed it to do. The moment they entered the star's gravity, they would be yanked to the ground, so they *really* needed to control their speed, mainly because Cealth really liked her ship in one piece (probably due to the extensive and expensive investments she'd had to make for Jath to modify the speed and responsiveness of the Celestelia.)

The ship slowed down enough for Cealth to stop lying down, and for Jath to regain consciousness. The bounty hunter glanced over her shoulder briefly, then momentarily removed her helmet, swapping it for one more suited to the Dyson Sphere's thick atmosphere. The air cooled momentarily around her exposed head, then began to warm once the new helmet was in place. She retrieved one of the atmospheric shields next to her bed, then turned it on and strolled out into the corridor.

Each of the rooms of the Celestelia had a different atmosphere- naturally, each crew member came from a different planet, so it was necessary for each to have their own room, complete with a gaseous mixture identical to that of their planet of origin- with the corridor being the only exception. It contained Jath's preferred atmosphere currently, but, after he'd either left Cealth's service or been killed, it would be changed to Exath's preference. Not only was it an incentive for Jath not to die, but it was also a reward for his years of service and a reminder to Exath that he was still inferior to Jath. Eventually, Cealth hoped, this would stop them from bickering with each other constantly.

Exath's room was, weirdly, a botanical paradise. The plants all seemed a bit tame to Cealth, especially compared to the wild diversity of the Manicarian's own planet-but perhaps that was why he liked it- he knew that he would never be killed by any of them. Jath's room was plastered with beermats from every corner of the cosmos- walls, ceiling, floor, table, chair... you name it, it was coated with them, from the retro, glow-in-the-dark coasters from S'rou' (the planet shrouded, almost constantly, in darkness, except for one hour each year, when the thick clouds part to reveal a singular beam of light shining down on one lucky individual, who will henceforth be known as 'the glowy one') to the hyper-intelligent, 100% digital techno-mats from TL-IF-H, (the planet which, while incapable of understanding anything not written in straight lines, produces almost all of the technology used in its galaxy). The beermat could tell you the time on 5,000 or more planets, survive being dropped in most liquids and, supposedly, withstand time-travel. It was an interesting feature to include.

Cealth frowned, glancing down the corridor and genuinely trying to understand why there were two morons floating around her spaceship. Exath hovered upside-down, drooling slightly and the cosmic hawk was slowly revolving near the toilet. Both were unconscious and looked like they'd just been blasted halfway across the galaxy at a speed approaching light and had then lost a fight with said toilet. Jath swam out of his compartment, atmospheric-bubble already in place, and blinked.

"How?" He said glancing up and down the corridor, checking that there wasn't some other, more serious reason for the unconscious battlers. "I gave them both enough time to get to the toilet before accelerating!"

"Apparently you didn't." She frowned, glancing over to check if Exath was still breathing- a tell-tale bubble of air was starting to form around his head, so she assumed he was. "How long do you think it'll take them to regain consciousness?"

Jath shrugged. "Depends how soon you'd like us down there," he nodded towards the Dyson Sphere. "I can probably get both of these morons awake now if you'd like."

Cealth nodded. "Do it. I'm going to go and find some maps." Then she paused. "Oh, and Jath? You can probably drop the cosmic hawk into space now. We're far enough away from Revlar that they won't be looking for him."

"Right." Jath agreed, experimentally flicking the Manicarian's head. "By the way, boss, um... if I were you, I'd be really careful down there. The galactic overlord's apparently starting to suspect something was behind... that one planet's destruction, so he's on the warpath."

Cealth scowled slightly, but her blank helmet gave nothing away to her subordinate. "I <u>had</u> thought of that, Jath. Thank you. Now if you would...?"

The Xsovzorite nodded obediently, and scooped up Exath, hurling him unceremoniously into the toilet and locking the door. Then he lifted the cosmic hawk up and forced the Starswallower's eyes open, closing his own at the same time. Cealth removed her helmet. The hawk was thrown out into space, his memory of the last two weeks completely gone. He would wake up later, recognise his surroundings and land on Cygnus, totally bemused once the press started demanding to know his whereabouts for the last two weeks.

Then he'd have to pay Galex back.

Chapter 12

The space pirates hadn't dropped him off at Revlar- it was honestly quite annoying- but had instead insisted that he find out who in the cosmos was responsible for Earth's untimely detonation. So, just because he apparently owned them a favour for their rescue and skilful evasion of the pursuing Yarflargians, he'd instead been dropped off at the core of his empire; his capital star of Cygnus. He'd flown the last few light years himself, rejoicing in the sheer jolt of adrenaline that had pulsed through him as he took off, his impulses steering him firmly towards the magnificent hunk of diamond alloy stretching out in front of him, filling every corner of his vision as he swooped closer and closer towards it.

He felt the pull of the star's gravity almost immediately- the sheer wrenching sensation was exhilarating- and he didn't *immediately* fight it, instead using it to boost his speed until he was streaming along so fast that the stars on either side faded from sight, becoming mere collective pools of glowing white gradients.

He could see individual buildings now, along with streets and the occasional space port (complete with vehicles parked with atomic precision between carefully engraved lines). Galex angled his wings carefully, using the power of the star's gravity to sweep him along over its surface. Finally, his destination came into view and he grinned, his feathers rippling away from his face as he did so. Before him loomed his palace; a coiling, rippling structure that seemed to be either growing from the crystalline surface of the Dyson Sphere, or collapsing back into it.

It looked as though some futuristic architect had witnessed a gigantic solar flare, frozen it, somehow melded a Victorian mansion, a space station and a Grancian Hydro-Liz Tree into it, then smoothed the walls of the entire hybridised structure and, in some, bizarre, ludicrous feat of immeasurable skill, had actually made it look **really** cool. Galex adored it and had originally ordered that the structure be replicated across over fifty worlds- before realising that this would take away from the uniquely random aesthetic that the building had perfected and had instead taken out an incredibly aggressive patent on the design to prevent anyone else from even attempting to replicate it.

The only, tiny, detail he didn't like about his home were the crowds of 'prattling mortals' (his words, not mine) outside the gates, whining about everything from the economy to referendums to cheese to his most recent law which prevented anyone from making a gin and tonic on Cygnus (a very long story involving dodgy spelling, coincidences and a restaurant that would, one day, be built worryingly close to Onyx.). In other words, he could never get a seconds' peace without soundproofing his entire home- which he hadn't done, not because he couldn't afford it, but because he was simply far too lazy.

The second he landed, with a **boom** that shook the nearby streets, two Starswallowers came hurrying up to him. One was his secretary, Starthur, the other, irritatingly, his psychiatrist, who'd learned everything about his career from as pair of cosmic worms, *that he hadn't eaten afterwards*! Every Starswallower with a fully functioning frontal lobe knew enough to stay away from the weirdo- which was, in fact, part of the reason why Galex had hired him- the moment the crowds saw the psychiatrist coming, they turned and manically dispersed while he politely offered helpful (if irrelevant or deeply personal) life advice.

Unfortunately, Galex had been unable to hire the idiot as a bodyguard and had been forced to employ him as a psychiatrist- meaning that he had to actually receive 'helpful' evaluations every few Cygnus hours, or the psychiatrist would leave his employ. It was thanks to these sessions he'd had to install the auto-blinking machine to control his nervous twitches.

"Overlord Galex!" his secretary cried.

"No need to sound so enthusiastic." Galex snorted, already irritated. "What's been going on?"

"Well, sir, you're completely behind schedule -"

"So, update me." He snapped, walking in long strides towards his house, so the two others had to practically scuttle to keep up with him. "What's been happening *in my empire,* not with my schedule? Come on, keep up, you're meant to be on top of all this stuff!"

"Right, well... uh, yes!" blustered Starthur, fumbling with a small data implant under one of his feathers. "Uh... the Cravasians started another rebellion-"

"Typical. Get rid of it."

"Sorry?"

"Get rid of the rebellion; the meaning of that statement should have been obvious, even to you. Use a Dorian."

"A Dorian?"

"For my sake... Yes! Yes, a Dorian, by my own feathers, how do you get up in the morning?!"

"Sometimes I really don't know." Mumbled Starthur, gloomily.

"Anything else?!"

"Cheese mines."

"Again?!"

"Unfortunately. Should we stop raiding them?"

"Yes! Obviously! Holy me, it's fairly obvious why you're not in charge, isn't it? Anything else?"

"The Revlarians... uh... well, sir, you aren't going to like this but the Federation-"

"I know, the Federation of hypocrites broke the three-planet treaty. Retaliate by seizing Pangol."

"But... sir, Pangol's neutral!"

"So was Revlar." Galex scowled, darkly.

"Right... well in other news, the Cosmic Hawk has disappeared."

"What?!" snapped Galex, wheeling round to stare at the secretary. At his unblinking, *really* unnerving stare, the smaller Starswallower flinched and averted his gaze. "Why didn't you start with that?! Explain!"

"Right! Well sir, it seems he vanished a few moments before the destruction on Revlar and hasn't been seen since."

"So why does everyone assume *I'm* the one who blew Bar Aquila up?"

"Well... sir... you *do* have a reputation if you don't mind me saying..."

"Yes, I *do* mind. Oh yeah... actually that reminds me..." They'd nearly reached the mansion, having strolled (or in the case of the other two Starswallowers, bustled) across Galex's perfectly kept garden, which was divided up into sixteenths by a criss-crossing network of paths, rivers and bridges- each of the sections having its own small bubble of atmosphere and collection of plants, (the selections of which had come from a series of planets sharing hugely differing atmospheres) varying from the bulbous fruits of Yaucus to the ever-changing hues of Polychroma 12. Galex glanced around for any spies lurking in the bushes, then leant towards his secretary and whispered, "If anyone wanted to blow up a planet without my authority or help, what would they need?"

"Sir?" the secretary frowned, confused.

"Starthur, just answer the question." Muttered Galex.

"Well... it would be extremely difficult to do without attracting any attention... but I suppose if they had a small enough univore..."

"A what, sorry?"

"Something which, unlike you sir, does not destroy planets in the natural way; you simply remove the core of the planet and the rest quickly takes care of itself. What we're talking about, however is the only way a non-Starswallower could possibly remove the core and get away from the planet quickly enough to avoid being blown up along with it. A univore, to put it bluntly, is a creature capable of literally eating planets."

"... What?"

"They send this creature down to the planet's core in its container, it eventually breaks free- possibly the container is time locked- and proceeds to burrow to the planet's core and consume it." The secretary shrugged. "After that, it's a simple matter of returning to the scene of the crime and erasing any evidence."

Galex paused, staring at his secretary thoughtfully. "Why don't we talk more inside? It's starting to get a bit chilly out here."

"In the great scheme of things, this probably won't matter, sir, but I couldn't recommend this, as it would, for the time being at least, infringe on *our* session." Hummed the psychiatrist. "I am under the impression that the evening air is, metaphorically speaking, fuel for the senses, so-"

"Nimboris." Snapped Galex, glaring at his psychiatrist. "I think, 'in the grand scheme of things' those lovely *infuriating* protestors outside would like your help **far** more than I do right now. Go chas- I mean *evaluate* them- away."

"For the greater good, the universe must one day forego all these mortal complaints," lamented Nimboris the psychiatrist. "But ok."

"What is *wrong* with that guy?" Starthur muttered, glancing at his boss cautiously as Nimboris drifted away towards the already retreating protestors.

Galex shook his head. "This is why you *eat* cosmic worms, rather than letting them babble at you all week. Stupid nihilistic morons. Oh, any other developments before we go inside?"

"Nothing major..." Starthur checked his implant one last time. "47 new Starswallowers were hatched this week, one of the last members of the Glitchis species has been rescued and transferred to the major zoo- oh and there's a festival tomorrow."

Galex grunted, having spaced out after the first word, and opened the door to his house in a grand, sweeping gesture. If any other being had attempted this, Nimboris would somehow appear two seconds later to give them a full psychiatric evaluation.

It was a physically harmless, but incredibly unsettling experience that would likely leave the befuddled interloper with a serious case of fatalism or paranoia that meant they'd need a real, preferably *not crazy*, psychiatrist. The eight- foot high door towered over every other Starswallower, but Galex strolled through the opening quite comfortably, pausing only a moment to allow his secretary time to tremble through and quietly heave both doors closed.

The entrance hall was located at the hollowed-out base of the Liz-tree, and, as such, was an interestingly smooth shape, panelled on three of the four walls with a sumptuously tasteless and expensive square pattern that was repeated over and over, with small squares inside smaller squares that in turn contained their own squares, with each quadrilateral fading to a slightly lighter shade of wood than the previous until the last, atom wide square glowed pure white.

The fourth wall had a magnificent, sweeping staircase curling over it, extending upwards, then across the upper levels in a tasteful combination of balogany, balcony and plush red river; the luxurious crimson carpet pooling downwards, over the individual stairs, then spilling out in a perfect rectangle onto the floor below. Behind the staircase was a magnificent mural- it rippled every now and then, changing according to the arrogance and self-importance felt by the Supreme Galactic Overlord standing imperiously below.

Currently, the image depicted was reminiscent of an Egyptian carving; Galex, the commanding, bird-like being standing proudly in the centre- the clear god figure in that scenario. Surrounding him, (the metaphor about him being the centre of his own universe being blatantly shoved into the face of any who glanced at the hologram) were the various galaxies he ruled over- entire sectors tiny in comparison to his gargantuan form. Just below his outstretched wings, seeming as though they were being birthed from his very feathers, the other members of his race soared out, each <u>Cosmic</u> Starswallower swooping back to its sector, a glowing halo-like outline of purple and red blatantly distinguishing them from the other, less important, Starswallowers who followed in their wake.

Galex ignored it and immediately took off, disregarding the stairs and powering through the atmosphere towards the fourth floor. Starthur sighed, glanced at the tiny speck that was his only appearance in the painting, then spread his wings wide and swept up after Galex, amazed at the effortless speed his ruler was able to achieve, even flying vertically away from the intense gravity of the star below. The supreme galactic overlord landed, opened a door and, by the time Starthur had reached him, was reclining in a suddenly futuristic living room. The walls were metallic white, the windows bevelled, tinted blue glass- and every piece of furniture in the room had *corners.*

"Stop gaping and sit down." Commanded Galex, the door sliding smoothly shut behind his secretary; appearance aside, practically every aspect of the house had been deceptively modernised. Starthur sat, nervously. He'd never actually been further into Galex's house than the entrance, and this cold, space station-esque room was no more inviting than the intimidating holo-mosaic below. He sat on one of the swivel chairs, hoping that at least now he could be the same height as Galex if he wanted to. The chair immediately sank two inches.

"We need to talk," Galex continued, frowning slightly as he lifted a cube of fizzing purple liquid to his mouth and sipped from a corner, thoughtfully. The glorified 3d square sloshed grimly as it was reduced to a large wedge, before shrinking to restructure itself. "You seem to know a worrying amount about planet destroyers."

Starthur shifted uncomfortably, fumbling for the seat's height control, and hoping Galex would offer him a drink soon. Life on the star was pleasant, but incredibly thirst inducing. "It's... well... just a hobby..."

"Hmm." Galex made the entirely non-committal sound without opening his beak even an atom. It was an incredibly time consuming skill to develop, so he used it whenever the opportunity arose.

"I mean..." rambled the secretary. "Well... I did study some... things... at university..."

"I don't like people destroying things behind my back, Starthur." Galex said, calmly. "I *really* don't like it." Starthur felt a bead of sweat build up under his feathers but didn't move a muscle to wipe it away. "You see," continued the Supreme Galactic Overlord. "Someone recently destroyed one of my friend's home worlds- a planet which, unfortunately for whoever blew it up, also happened to be an excellent place for hunting cosmic worms. You wouldn't happen to know which planet I'm talking about, *would you?*"

Starthur felt every synapse of his brain screaming at him not to answer, but he swallowed and mumbled "Earth." anyway. *I'm going to die*, He thought, panicking and mentally arm wrestling himself to calm down. *I'm going to die and it's not even my fault this time.*

Galex stood, strolled behind Starthur's field of view, and the smaller Starswallower suddenly regretted choosing the swivel chair- if he turned now, he would be in danger of paralysis. Any being could tell you that, once in a Starswallower's personal sector, any organism who met their eyes would be either killed or paralysed (a skill that explained how they'd taken over so many galaxies), and Galex's eyes could now be in any position.

"Tell me the truth, Starthur." Scowled Galex. "Who destroyed that rock?" Starthur opened his mouth, terrified of saying too much... of revealing his connection to them... and then he simply wasn't there anymore.

Chapter 13

Cealth had never tried to break into a zoo before- *And,* she thought to herself *I'm not especially eager to do so now.* If the rumours were true that a Glitchis had been transferred to Cygnus's main zoo however, there was simply no other alternative. Jath was with her, silent and stealthy in bovarus leather, a Laserifle cradled under his arm- it was the cheaper, if more inaccurate and obscure version of a Cellsplitter- but the Xsovzorite loved the gun for the simple reason that it was completely silent and supposedly untraceable.

Both assassins were wearing shades- of a sort. Cealth's one-way helmet had been tinted, which, while restricting her already limited vision, meant that it would now be impossible for a Starswallower to neutralise either of them. Jath, on the other hand, could've passed for a space pirate with the combination of sunglasses and full-leather. Still, Xsovzorites were known for their bizarreness- after all, the very name of their species had been chosen with the express purpose of being almost impossible to pronounce- and so no one looked at them twice as they left the ship and went their separate ways.

Cealth was the distraction, Exath the getaway driver, so it was up to Jath himself to retrieve the Glitchis. They'd landed in an already crowded visitor's parking bay, fought to get a space- Jath had practically torn the steering controls out when a Cravasian family's warship had chugged into the space they'd been *just* about to park in- and watched Exath join the long line of species attempting to gain access to Cygnus's capital city; the line moved so slowly that he would be ready to slip out and help them make their getaway at a moment's notice.

Meanwhile, Cealth and Jath had used the single feather which Jath had pried from the Cosmic Hawk's wing (shortly before the Starswallower had been hurled into space) to gain access to the VIP entrance- it wasn't particularly subtle, but it was far quicker than the alternative; the line they would've had to otherwise wait in was longer than the queue outside Bar Aquila during the Swelter months.

The two assassins had slipped past milling groups of tourists clustered around life-size Starswallower statues, magnificent, intricately carved fountains bedecked in gemstones and trailing a thick, shimmering substance half-way between solid and liquid, and crept through the long, perfectly laid out streets, between stalagmites which *looked* as though they had been made from frosted, molten glass- in reality they were made from impure, sculpted diamond, the same material as the dyson sphere below them. Within these spires, several Starswallowers dwelt, their giant, hazy outlines barely visible through the opaque material.

After an hour of walking, hitchhiking and one, barely, averted argument as a taxi driver tried to charge Jath twice the cost of the ten minute trip simply because he was a fan of *Just Panic*, and remained convinced, until Cealth stepped in, that Jath was a 'filthy pirate' who frequently 'stole' *Just Panic* albums, they arrived at the central zoo. The menagerie was filled with some of the rarest, most unique animals found in any solar system, thanks to a law instated a couple of centuries before; once any species' population fell to a low enough point, the surviving members would be transferred to the menagerie. It seemed altruistic enough; until the members of several small worlds found themselves being hauled into the artificial environments provided. A tiny but significant loophole meant that, regardless of the species' intelligence, if the Starswallowers could exploit the biology of an animal, then they would 'save' it and have it transferred into the central zoo to await DNA extraction.

The gates hung wide open; a metallic hug to any rich tourists who desired to stream through them. Cealth narrowed her eyes below her helmet, glancing beyond the façade of welcome to the tight security beneath. The place was bristling with cameras, disguised lasers and, interestingly, physical security. *Odd.* Cealth thought, examining the two, seemingly relaxed, Starswallowers reclining by the entrance. The Starswallowers usually liked to encourage the idea that they personally were above being guards- supposedly relying on Yarflargians or Argoshians as hired muscle- but evidently this was not always the case.

Despite having a wind-blown appearance to their feathers, and somehow exuding a 'cool guy' presence (Cealth blamed the light blue atmosphere of Awesomnia Nine that must have been circulating around the duo) the two Starswallowers were concealing the suspect shapes of Cellsplitters beneath their down, and were scanning each member of the crowd with a scrutiny unrivalled by even the most hard headed Cravasian, slightly yellow eyes taking in every aspect of the tourist's appearances and, undoubtedly, comparing them against their data implants to check for any *unwanted* visitors. Cealth memorised her surroundings, then casually stepped into a side street alongside Jath.

"What do you think?" she murmured.

"Two Starswallowers, eight cameras, numerous Wex circulating in that conglomeration of flesh by the entrance..." he shook his head, knowing full well that his boss would already know all this. Even after thirty-seven Oonaeran years of service, she still never stopped testing his powers of observation.

"Twelve cameras. The Starswallowers have special contact lenses, hence the overly frequent blinking. The security is *very* tight. Perhaps you could sneak through unnoticed, but if they see me, they may recognise my helmet. The cosmic hawk's reaction on Revlar proved they have **that** aspect of my appearance recorded."

"`But you haven't been noticed so far."

"You know as well as I do that the Starswallowers by the entrance have data implants as well as DNA scanners. The moment they see me, they're going to ask me to hold my breath and remove my helmet. Perhaps it's time for subtlety to end."

Jath swallowed, hard. "That's risky... I mean- boss, is that *really* necessary? If one person isn't affected..."

Cealth's blank helmet turned to him but, even before she spoke, he knew that she'd already made up her mind. "I'll give you ten minutes. Disable the cameras, find the Glitchis and return here. With any luck, what I'm about to do will be overlooked until they notice that the Glitchis is missing."

The Xsovzorite glanced at his boss nervously. He'd known Cealth for decades, had followed her across the galaxies, killed whoever she'd asked him to without a second thought and tolerated the moronic Manicarian when he had to. He kept the Celestelia constantly prepared to run at her top speed of 180,000 miles per second in careful anticipation of when Cealth would require its speed, updated her technology and made certain to secure the kitchen whenever they were about to lurch through the galaxy **just** under light speed. But never, not once in all his years of service, had he asked her what actually lay below her helmet. She wore a helmet because she had to, and when she removed it, bad things would happen. That was it. That was all he needed to know. But Exath's incessant badgering... the little moron had never stopped asking, and his unceasing badgering had unfortunately revived the burning curiosity Jath himself had extinguished, years before.

"Turn around." Cealth muttered, unclasping her helmet. Jath felt a sudden cold wind rippling past his back and fought the urge to turn back towards Cealth. She walked away, towards the zoo, and he heard the sudden silence that unfolded behind him, as though someone had pressed 'mute' on their universal remote. The silence unfolded, expanded, and, once it started to pound inside his head, almost deafening him, he stepped out of the alley, glanced for a moment at the unconscious figures now piled in front of the gate, then leapt over them, entering the depths of the zoo, pausing now and then to glance into one of the gargantuan enclosures, the bizarre, extravagant creatures below neither noticing, nor caring about the one-way glass above them as he searched for the Glitchis.

For such a powerful creature, Jath almost felt outraged at the quality of the Glitchis' enclosure when he finally found it. The ground was a sparse, static grey and the walls, simulating an infinite, boundless sky, were the colour of scorched toffee. The Glitchis itself prowled cautiously around the edges of its enclosure, and, unlike the innocent, happy creatures Jath had seen earlier, it seemed all too aware of the one-way glass above, pausing now and then to bare rounded, violet teeth at it. It wasn't exactly ugly, but there was something deeply unsettling about the way it strolled around on the six strange appendages extending, parallel, from it's torso, that were somewhere between arms and hooves, and which moved with hypnotising fluidity- almost as if the creature was drumming its limbs in place of fingers.

Its body was coated in a thick, grey-green fur, its limbs ended in slightly curled reddish-purple claws and its head, which loomed at the end of a long, graceful neck, swayed from side to side, like a branch locked in a tussle with the wind. The head was elongated, its pointed ears stuck straight up from the crown of its face, its eyes (a dark, intriguing blue-ish green) narrow and intimidating. It didn't seem to have a nose, which caused the face to slope downwards like a sheer cliff, but, even lacking so base a sense as smell, Jath got the unsettling feeling that it not only knew he was there, staring at it, but also was completely aware of his disconcerted state.

Shaking off this feeling, he stepped boldly up to the glass and elbowed it. His elbow bounced off and he frowned, legitimately confused. He tore with his claws, head-butted and even tried, at one point, biting the glass with his meat-shredding teeth- but it remained resolutely intact. Frowning, the Xsovzorite examined the material more closely, pausing to wipe his finger prints away, then stepped back, took a running jump, and landed with his full weight on the sheet. The glass paused momentarily, as if considering whether it was worth the trouble of dissembling, just to allow this bitey-scratchy thing through... then gave up and crumbled, sending Jath hurtling through to the floor where the Glitchis was waiting.

The creature watched him fall to the floor with surprising nonchalance, then strolled (as much any six-legged being could stroll) towards him, regarding him with its weird, lake-like eyes. Now that he looked closer, Jath thought there were almost too many irises, overlapping slightly to give the appearance of an infinite spiral staircase. He sighed slightly, then pushed himself up into a sitting position and extended a hand to the creature.

"How'd you do? I'm Jath."

"Eeeeraaaaaaaaeheheheh." For a moment, Jath had to check that his universal translator was working, then remembered that the creature wouldn't have one. Even if he had been able to understand what the Glitchis was saying- which, oddly he couldn't- *it* still wouldn't understand him. His eyes quickly ran over the misshapen lump of creature before him, then he removed his universal translator and plugged it into an orifice which he assumed was the Glitchis' ear.

"Hi. I'm Jath," he repeated. The creature's eyes seemed to pulsate as the muscular irises individually contracted, suddenly comprehending his words. "I can't understand you at the moment, but I'm here to break you out. In return, my boss wants your help getting to a planet called Onyx. Uh... blink if you want in on the deal. Grin if you don't."

It blinked. Then, suddenly, it bit into his arm... and they were outside.

It can teleport. Jath realised, massaging his arm as the nerve endings finally realised what had just happened and simultaneously bellowed at his brain.

Cealth strolled up to them, her helmet back in place, casual as a wanted assassin could be. Jath had taken a universal translator from one of the drooling sightseers beside the gate to the zoo and plugged it back into his ear just in time to hear Cealth say "They'll be waking up soon," as she nodded over at the heaps of unconscious tourists. "We should go."

That was it- no 'well done', no 'you didn't get yourself killed'... just back to business, instantly and without question. Jath would've liked to say that he worked for Cealth for the money- which was *nothing* to sneeze at- or for the notoriety- which, despite the fact that few 'regular people' even knew of Cealth's existence, (let alone her accomplices) was surprisingly high among the politicians of the universe. But no, honestly it was something else. Something he couldn't quite explain.

Back on Xvzodghor, his home planet, everyone was constantly competing, each person always attempting to find the next 'impossible word'- something so convoluted and lacking in vowels that no other being would be able to read or pronounce it- all to prove that the Dorians had made a mistake in inventing universal translators. Every Xsovzorite had devoted their life to coming up with one of these words; to do so was the ultimate achievement and warranted a life of respect and praise.

Jath had disagreed. He'd shunned his birth name of "Cxqvrr", instead using the easily pronounceable, monosyllabic 'Jath'. He'd ignored the incomprehensible lessons at school, disregarded the dire penalties regarding the use of universal translators- which the other Xsovzorite claimed was an insult to both their language and culture- and had left Xvzodghor the literal second he was able. He'd met Cealth entirely by accident on the dwarf planet 'Feh!" one Xvzodghorian year later.

She'd been working at the time, and he'd happened to notice her leaving the offices of the linguistics baroness whom he'd hoped to meet, in order to get all

Xvzodghorian words transferred into the dictionary, essentially rendering all 'unspellable' words not only spellable, but widely available to the universe as a whole. It was almost every Xsovzorite's worst nightmare (with Jath being the obvious exception). Hoping to get an idea of what the baroness was like before he was interviewed, he'd followed Cealth with the intention of grilling her on what questions the baroness had asked. Five Feh-en minutes later, he'd noticed her still steaming Cellsplitter.

Cealth had noticed him following her almost from the moment she'd left the offices and had quietly led him away from any witnesses before turning and removing her helmet. Whatever he'd said, in that blank space in his memory, it had obviously made some kind of impact- the next thing he knew, she was interviewing him for a position on the Celestelia. The murder didn't really bother him- finally, another living being was treating him like... well, another sentient life form. She'd never once given him any indication that she disliked him, unlike almost every other person Jath had ever spoken to, and, in return, he'd asked no questions, demanded no explanations for her helmet, and never once disobeyed an order. Even so... a little praise was never unwelcome.

"Glitchis." Cealth said glancing over at it. The creature's head loomed, on a level with her helmet. "Teleport us back to our ship, then to the planet Onyx and you can go." The Glitchis made another screeching sound, and Cealth tilted her head slightly. "Ok. Don't take too long though."

The Glitchis grunted, then vanished.

"What did it say?" frowned Jath, tapping his new universal translator.

"It wanted to get one of its... well, it said minions, but I assume it meant allies."

"If a thing like that has allies, why hadn't it broken out before?" frowned Jath, still baffled as to how Cealth had understood the creature.

The helmeted assassin shrugged. "I assume the 'ally', whoever they are, didn't have the means to do so."

"It wasn't too hard for me."

"No, but I *had* knocked everyone unconscious and temporarily disabled all of the security by the time you found it. How did you break the glass by the way?"

"I jumped at it."

"Ahh."

There was a pause while the two assassins watched the crowds slowly waking up. Half of them stood almost immediately, brushing imaginary dust off their immaculate holiday spacesuits, while the others rolled over, attempting to remain asleep while their acquaintances glared distastefully at them.

"Is something wrong with that?" Cealth asked as Jath pawed at his translator again.

"I think so." The Xsovzorite tipped his head to the side and removed it briefly, twisting one of the external knobs. "I couldn't understand that Glitchis back there. But I can still hear you, so it can't be calibrated completely wrong."

"It was probably just the accent." Cealth said, shaking her head slightly. "You know those things can't properly compensate for the stronger ones."

"Maybe," Jath said doubtfully, twisting the external knob again and listening to the individual clicks it made within the shallow pit of his ear. "But- that doesn't explain how you could understand-"

He was interrupted by the reappearance of the Glitchis and its ally, whose species Jath recognised instantly, and with a horrible lurch of fear in the pit of his stomach. It had brought a Starswallower with it.

Chapter 14

The megalith cubed bar held the prestigious title of the 're-inventor of gravity', for good reason. As mentioned many chapters ago, their customised gravity allowed for the absence of glasses, while still enabling its patrons to stroll or squirm over the pristine floor rather than drifting off into the void outside in a happy, drunken bubble of glorified ethanol. True, it was no Bar Aquila, but, given the Revlarian bar's current slightly-destroyed state, business had been booming. The owner (a Jardek by the name of Urma) had wondered why he hadn't thought of literally destroying his competition before- until he remembered the ferocity of space lawyers. Brr.

At any rate, the bar had recently become a hotspot for the superrich hyper-drunks of the universe, and Urma had been capitalising on the profits his wealthy clientele brought him, investing in several new wings of the building, so that, from the outside, it looked even weirder than the phosphorescent quintrupeds of Celop Two.

The bar had been sturdily built on a generously sized asteroid, its slightly greenish corridors looping under and over the space rock, so, from the outside, it looked like an octopus trying to touch its face with all eight tentacles, while attempting to remain upright and not fall over. (The humanoid equivalent would be uncomfortable in the extreme, so, for the safety of overeager readers, it is not described here.) The main body of the bar was a large white dome half-sunken into the dusty iron surface of the asteroid, and below this was a hive of activity, with furious physicists and air-sculptors working feverishly to churn out every requested drink shape that the smug patrons above demanded.

Galex examined the perfect, if miniaturized, replica of his body sloshing in front of him with something approaching confusion. The cosmic swan inclined her head to the waiter as he passed her an intricate Celtic knot, the three interwoven drinks that comprised it pooling together gently in the very centre, to create her cocktail. Across the table, the cosmic hawk gazed furiously at his drink, annoyed that the boffins below had actually managed to create the cup-shaped Skullsplitter he'd ordered. It was even filled with ice. He was just contemplating requesting a perfect replica of the labyrinthine surface of Bowie 34, a comet colonized years ago by a group of insane cartographers, when he was abruptly startled back to reality as Galex snapped out a question with surprising aggression.

"Just answer the question, Vedrfolnir." Galex barked as the hawk gazed at him in confusion. His heartbeat noticeably sped up as Galex used his full name- something he rarely did, for the simple reason he found 'Vedrfolnir' unbelievably annoying to pronounce. Whatever the question he'd just missed was, it had to be important.

"Uh... I don't know..." he said, slowly, pretending to think.

"I'm not too sure either, to be fair." Galex shook his head. "I mean, it just shouldn't... work, you know?"

"Uh... I think there are some... aspects that do add up..."

"Yes, but the overall picture's just a bit weird."

"I know, but I think it could be true."

"What do you mean 'it could be true'?! You said you weren't sure!" Galex cried, and for a moment, the hawk thought he'd heard the supreme galactic overlord's voice break.

"I mean..." Vedrfolnir stuttered, backpedalling as quickly as he could. "I wasn't agreeing with... whatever you said..."

"Not cool." The cosmic swan sighed, admonishing the cosmic hawk with a superior glare. "Galex, don't listen to him, you're magnificent."

"Thank you!" he barked, glaring at the hawk. "This is why people don't notice when you're sucked off into space, hawky boy!"

"I'm paying for Aquila, alright?! And please, for the love of Cygnus, do **not** call me 'hawky boy'!"

"It's not alright!" snapped Galex, his beak clacking aggressively. "And when I ask one of my friends 'do I really look like a chicken?' the answer should *not* be 'it could be true'!"

 "To be honest, I didn't hear you-" started the hawk.

"Do I look like a chicken to you?!"

"I don't know what that is."

"Doesn't matter. Do I look like one?!"

"No...?"

"NO!"

"Now shut up and drink your skullsplitter." Ordered the cosmic swan, fed up with the bickering.

The three Starswallowers paused to drain their various liquids, the spacial fish tank (a giant bubble of water floating in mid-air, containing around forty different kinds of sea life from three of the most peaceful galaxies in the Snowant sector) glowing a soft blue in the corner opposite.

"So, what *is* a chicken?" asked the hawk. If Galex had been holding a glass, he would've smashed it against the table, then proceeded to dance furiously with the hawk until he apologised for bringing up the issue of Galex's appearance again.

"You know that planet some moron destroyed without my orders?" Galex growled. The other two nodded wearily- he'd talked about nothing else for the last week. "Well, *it* lived there." He nodded, ominously.

"Did you just bring this up so you could complain again?" sighed the cosmic swan.

"Yes!" snapped Galex, aggressively prodding a large bubble of alcohol floating in front of him, then swallowing the liquid as it floated into his gullet. "I still suspect Starthur."

"Don't we all?" Growled the hawk, stirring his ice with a finger. "Guy always was creepily nice. D'you know, he tried to groom my feathers once?"

"So, Vedrfolnir!" smiled the Cosmic Swan tightly, a little too eager to change the topic. "Remembered anything yet?"

"No."

"Anything?"

"No."

"Come on, give me something here," she muttered out of the corner of her beak, her volume just low enough to hide her words from Galex. "Otherwise he'll start whining about Earthian curry again."

"I've told you," yawned the hawk. "I remember leaving Revlar-"

"And dumping the bill on me," Galex grinned aggressively.

"- and then the next thing I knew, I was waking up near the Egg Nebula with 'la grande hangover'."

"You have *no* idea what a grand hangover feels like!" snarled Galex. "When I woke up on Castra-"

"But I did remember something else last night!" yelped the hawk, desperately.

"Oh really?" the swan said, loudly, over Galex's desperate attempts to reminisce.

"Yes! I remembered that I saw a Xsovzorite in Bar Aquila!"

"What?" Galex frowned, stopped mid anecdote. "Wow. That place *has* gone downhill if they're letting that sort of culture destroying scum in."

"Hmm." Muttered the cosmic swan, trying and failing not to think about the irony in Galex's statement- as a planet breaker, he'd destroyed at *least* as many cultures as the Xsovzorites.

"Yeah, I know right? And what was weirder was, he was chatting up this Manicarian-looking guy."

"Nothing weird with that." The cosmic swan said, a little too haughtily. "Inter-species relationships are *fine*, thank you very much! This is a *modern* society!"

"I think what he meant was 'a typically hard-working purple quadruped and a bipedal word-smasher were... *consorting*'." Galex cut in, ever the budget translator, slightly too smug that he'd remembered a more sophisticated synonym for plotting.

"Consorting? Galex, have you been using a thesaurus again?" grimaced the swan.

"Unequivocally!" Barked Galex, proudly.

"Anyway, I was just trying to say was it's weird. Why would a *Xsovzorite* of all things be talking to one of the most hardworking peasan- I mean species- out there?" exhaled the hawk.

"Money?" suggested the cosmic swan, frowning slightly. "The real question is, how did a disreputable linguistics butcher and a member of a famously poor species manage to get into Bar Aquila?"

"Another reason for those builders to hurry up and repair it so we can complain." Growled Galex. "And then grab fifty skullsplitters."

The barkeeper shot all three Starswallowers a nasty glare. He valued customer loyalty- and knew perfectly well that the second Aquila was up and running, every one of his new, planet-owning, giga-rich patrons would run back over there- and the fact that they were going to complain was little consolation. For all he knew, the Aquilan barkeeper could simply apologise, and his wealth of customers would be back in those overpriced balogany seats, drinking *Aquila*'s skullsplitters instead of Megalith Cubed's, and ordering those weird, beryl-spewing volcanoes... *Sorry Cealth.* He thought, aggressively striding over to the trio. *But three Starswallowers will pay a heck of a lot more than your bribe in the long run.*

"I know," He growled. The trio of galaxy owners glanced at him, casually- it's a little known fact that, somehow, all Starswallowers have the ability to look equally as relaxed as each other. "How those vortex-feeders slipped in, I mean."

"Ah, a waiter," Galex said, lazily. "About time. I'll have a Citric Circe in the shape of an inside- out Quavian egg."

"I...?"

"Omniscient mouth-grenadine." The cosmic hawk drawled, his feathers shifting into a slightly more comfortable position for his back. "Shape of an erupting volcano."

"Sirs, I meant..."

"Liquidised red-beryl." The cosmic swan said, snippily. "In the exact shape of the Sandros 4 mega-crystal. I want to see its *faucets.*"

"Right away," growled the barkeeper. "But I *was* going to give you the information you wanted."

The hawk frowned. "One- why? Two- how? Three- who?"

"Fourth, what?" Galex added, having lost the thread of conversation a while ago.

"I think he's telling us why there was a Xsovzorite in bar Aquila," the swan muttered in Galex's ear.

"Yes," Agreed the barkeeper. "And one- because I want business and you're immeasurably rich, two, because I'm usually spying on the competition and only got shifted to bar-duty because of the huge influx of customers recently and lastly, I'm Death, nice to meet you."

"Likewise," nodded the hawk. "So, you want us to pay you to fuel our conversation?"

"Well... when you put it like that-"

"Here's an idea," grinned Galex. "Give us the information now, and we'll see if it's worth a refill."

"I was watching Bar Aquila's side entrance for any *coverts*- customers that've bribed their way past the eon-long line- when I saw these three figures. Looked fairly normal until I saw their species. A Xsovzorite, a Manicarian and a suspicious hooded figure aren't exactly your usual coverts- you get Neoniths, Gothorrides, nerds... but never Xsovzorites. I overheard the Xsovzorite's name- he and the Manicarian were squabbling over something- and did some research while I was waiting for them to come back out. Uncovered some pretty juicy gossip too; the Xsovzorite's got a rare genetic defect- doesn't care about grammar butchering."

"That *is* juicy." Frowned the swan. "Is that even possible?"

"Apparently." Shrugged Death. "Anyway, the Manicarian's called Exath, and, according to his colony, he's been missing for nearly two of their years. No contact with any of them- which is unusual for such a social bunch. But it's the hooded one that I was most interested in- she wasn't wearing a shield, so she could breathe in Aquila's atmosphere- and, thanks to the mess of unique gases in Aquila's atmosphere, this means only one of two things- she either came from Revlar-"

"Or she's an Obligon." Frowned Galex, having silently searching the snippet of information up on his mental holopad a few moments before. "But that's not unusual- Obligons can afford to get in. Me and hawky-"

"*Never* call me that again, Galex."

"-Even saw one the last time we were there. They aren't exactly poor- if they'd actually get off that death trap of a planet more often and stop crying, they'd actually be really useful to the rest of the universe."

"She was wearing a hood," repeated Death. "That, in itself, is unusual. Obligons don't need to hide their faces- they aren't self-conscious in the slightest, since they're too depressed to worry about their appearances."

"So then-" There was a pause, during which the cosmic hawk and the cosmic swan watched Galex's expression cautiously, as though waiting for the detonation of a time bomb which they had failed to defuse.

"I thought we agreed to eradicate them!" snapped Galex, with a ferocity so sudden it made the other three jump.

"I thought we had!" the hawk yelped, only aware of how immature he sounded after he'd finished speaking.

"Genocide means 'kill *every* member of the species!'" raged Galex. "I told you... I TOLD you...!"

"A being like her shouldn't exist." Snapped the cosmic swan, siding with Galex's rage. "Not anymore! Well, I suppose now we know how you lost your memory for two weeks, Vedrfolnir!"

"Who is she?" Galex shouted, with animalistic ferocity- although comparing his level of anger to *any* animal would've been a gargantuan injustice by that point. "I need a name!"

"C-Cealth." Stammered Death, sincerely regretting everything in his life that had led him to that point. The Starswallowers' eyes were hard and cold, smouldering with the energy of twelve neutron stars.

Galex sank back into his chair and smacked his face with a free hand. "Cealth... of course." He muttered, so quietly, even his fellow Starswallowers had to strain to hear him. "OF COURSE!" He leapt up, turned and charged towards the exit, pausing only to yell "You're paying this time!" to the hawk before launching himself off the asteroid, wings powering him through the cosmos, stars merging into blurred gradients as his speed increased exponentially... a theory burning through his mind.

Chapter 15

"So... what was he talking about?" Death swallowed. He was off duty now and had quickly taken advantage of Galex's vacated seat, leaning in towards the remaining two Starswallowers to continue the conversation.

"We had no choice." The swan sighed, bitterly, glancing towards the hawk for some indication of how best to start explaining the topic to an outsider.

"We'd never seen the Obligons as a threat- nobody had- after all, they were just these depressed nobodies from a corner of the Universe that nobody really cared about." The hawk shrugged.

"And then the genetic mutations began to occur. Thousands of these creatures just suddenly... evolved. Normal Obligons absorb emotions in the air- but they're always so swamped in their own misery that the few positive feelings they absorb are cancelled out. It's why they're always so miserable. Reverse Obligons on the other hand..." the cosmic swan trailed off.

"They could extract their emotions and break free of their misery." The hawk continued. "And the second they were free of the negativity they... changed. Suddenly they weren't just able to absorb emotion anymore. They could eat memories, personalities... the whole shebang."

"We went to see them, expecting to meet a new strain of Obligons- a species that would actually be some fun to be around, and some use to the universe."

"We didn't expect to arrive on a planet devoid of free will."

"They asked to meet us on Sandros 6." Recalled the cosmic swan.

"There is no Sandros 6." Frowned Death. "There are only five planets in that solar system."

"Exactly." muttered the cosmic hawk. "There are *now*."

"By the time we arrived, every emotion in the air was gone, every species had been de-personified. All except for the reverse Obligons."

"And they were just standing there, with those... faces." The hawk shuddered. "Have you ever seen an Obligon's face?"

"Unfortunately." Nodded Death. "Used to keep flocking here like pilgrims before we upped the prices. Their money- I mean attitudes- were honestly the only good things about them; they were always quiet. Never caused trouble." He paused to tap his drinkosphere, and a puff of slightly lilac smoke drifted out of it with a distinctive whiff of robberry ethanol. "Starry faces." He hesitated, trying to recall the vague, Obligon-shaped memories. "Totally flat. Spherical. Looked like a vaguely attractive black hole. With eyes."

"Yeah," agreed the hawk. "Well these guys had the same basic face shape, but the whole black hole dealy? Not so much."

"Ever heard of a white hole?" asked the cosmic swan, dipping her neck slightly to sip her liquidised red beryl. "It's an idea which a very tiny number of theoretical physicists have been playing around with for years. Supposedly, it's the exact opposite of a black hole- spews **out** stars and planets... completely fictional of course. But if it *was* real, it could have been located on the reverse Obligons' faces."

"We didn't work out what was going on until they attacked Neutroby." The cosmic hawk prodded his volcano-shaped Omniscient mouth-grenadine gingerly. It muttered something in Galaxian- the native tongue of the Starswallowers- and then spewed out a few small drops of hypnotizingly red liquid which he promptly swallowed.

"Neutroby?" inquired Death.

"The cosmic owl," the cosmic swan glanced distractedly at the spacial fish tank as a huge, silvery kelp-like squid flicked past in a trail of fist sized bubbles. "He wanted to find out more about the mutation that'd created these new Obligons. Got a bit too close for their liking and the next thing we knew..."

"They'd drunk him." The cosmic hawk said, bluntly. "It's the only way to describe it. He was just standing there, then he swayed and fell over... and all this stuff was drifting into one's face."

"Then they started attacking the rest of us. We eradicated them all- at least... we thought we had."

"Sandros 6 was obliterated to hide the evidence. Last thing we needed was the universe knowing how to kill us. The Federation would've leapt at the chance to take out Galex- probably still would, now I think about it."

"No one but the Starswallowers can remember the event now, because their memories were erased. A universe wide memory wipe- all occurrences of Sandros 6 or the reverse-Obligons deleted in a giant cover-up."

"How?" Death blinked, staring at the Starswallowers with the single, pure green optical sphere that rested in place of his eye. "That's impossible, even for the Psi-gorgons!"

The hawk shrugged. "We used the last reverse Obligon. We thought she'd been killed immediately afterwards. Now, it looks like she escaped after all." He shook his head. "I don't know how to feel about that. We killed her entire species, but the number of beings she must've killed on Sandros 6... it doesn't bear thinking about." He paused. Then, in a forcibly upbeat voice added "At least now I know what caused my memory loss."

"It did seem a little too fishy that you'd managed to drift from Aquila to the Great Egg in the space of a mere two weeks." Agreed the cosmic swan.

"But... I don't get why she didn't just kill me if that was the case." The hawk said, oblivious to the swan momentarily. "She *definitely* has a grudge against the Starswallowers- who wouldn't, after what we did?"

Death glanced between the two Starswallowers, who had become sombre in the face of their guilt. "How many reverse Obligons did you kill?"

"About three thousand." Replied the cosmic swan. "But before you forget, they'd killed an entire world themselves. There were about **twelve billion** intelligent life forms living on Sandros 6 before *they* came."

Death whistled, drumming his fingers on the table thoughtfully. "Genocide is still genocide though."

"You're right." Nodded the hawk, a little sleepily. "Genocide *is* genocide."

"Come on. It's past your nap time." The swan stood, hoicked the hawk up by the arm and tossed a single, bright pink diamond onto the table. "Keep the change, Death. Consider it a bribe to never repeat this tale. If the Federation got wind of this and decided to send Cealth to attack Galex... well. I'm assuming you don't exactly want a socialist environment." She raised an eyebrow at the gilded carpet pointedly.

"Oh Galex, no!" Death swore, scooping the bright gem up. "It'd kill business. Well... have a safe flight, your swiftness-ses."

"Thanks." Nodded the hawk, starting to wonder why the ground was waving at him. "Oh, and by the way-" he leant over to Death and hissed into his universal translator. "*Never* upset a Dorian."

"Auren, can you hear me?" Galex muttered into his universal translator. "I thought you'd bugged this thing back on the Nebula, and I really hope I'm right. If I am, then listen- Cealth- the assassin- she's a reverse Obligon. She's probably the one who detonated Earth- most likely she thought it'd cause trouble for the Starswallowers with the Federation. If any one person held a grudge... well. I'm heading to Onyx now- hoping I'll at least get some leads on her- it *is* her home world after all. Bring some *big* guns. And lasers. Lasers are **always** good."

"Lasers inbound." Auren replied, softly. And with that, the Nebula Eater looped round in mid-flight and burned aggressively through the solar systems towards Onyx, planet of the depressed.

Chapter 16

As a planet, Onyx was, for want of a better word, horrible. The entire atmosphere of the world was cold, Obligons now the only species that could bear walking its dismal streets. The species in question slumped from one job to the next, hopelessness and long stretches of blank depression resonating through their heads. If you were late to work, you would be the only one to notice. If you were fired, it would be expected. But they forced themselves on, suicide never being seen as an option for the simple reason that it would do nothing. Death would be sadder than life, at least for their families. At least while they were still breathing they could exchange their levels of emptiness with one another.

Cealth *hated* the planet. Her rare mutation had forced her to hide from her own parents before the Starswallowers could find her- her need to live overpowering the desire to extract their emotional pain. Jath understood being forcibly parted from his species due to a trait he couldn't help- it was partly why she'd decided to ally with him instead of killing him back on 'Feh!' Onyx represented everything *wrong* with the universe- the inequality, the people forced to suffer in silence at the edge of the creation because the thick-headed, rich 'Galactic overlords' who wouldn't help them, too scared of creating another set of reverse Obligors to improve the Obligons' lives. Instead, they choose to parade around, preening, acting superior and inconveniencing *everyone* else, and all the while acting like they were better than the Federation.

"Let's just fill up the Celestelia and get the hell off this rock." Scowled Jath, rubbing his arms slightly through his atmospheric bubble to maintain his body heat.

"For once, I agree with you," Exath grunted. "Boss, was there really nowhere else the Glitchis could've dropped us off to refuel?"

"The exit to the Universe is a mere sixty thousand light years away," Cealth sighed quietly. "You should probably stop complaining and start refuelling if you really want to leave."

She left them to it and walked away before they could begin bickering.

Her hood was covering her face again, and the helmet was gone. She breathed freely, and, despite the sheer, empty, emotionless void she could feel raging against the vortex that was her face, determined to break through and nullify her the same way her fellow Obligons were depressed on a daily basis, her biology protected her, an atom thin layer of iron resolve shielding her from the dismal gale. A cold waft of air shifted the cloth over her face slightly, and one of the passing Obligons straightened slightly as she passed him. She glanced at him through the one-way fabric, silently wondering, as he slumped away, if she would recognise him if he turned around.

She paused to let a lone, pale humanoid figure pass, and then whipped suddenly around, blinking in alarm as the human raised a laser and scowled at her in aggressive triumph.

"Hands in the air, you planet destroying-!"

"Excuse *me*?" Cealth interrupted, taking in the appearance of the alien and identifying her species with a raised eyebrow. "That's slightly hypocritical."

"Shut up. I'm from the past and humans haven't destroyed any planets back then. Hands *up*." Repeated Sam.

"Why?"

"I don't know!" The human huffed exasperatedly. "It's just something people said back on Earth when they were about to shoot someone."

"What if their victims don't *have* hands?"

"Then we generalise massively. I'm going to ask you one question-"

"Is it 'are you going to raise your hands?'?"

"What?" Sam frowned, momentarily thrown off guard. "No! It's 'Did you destroy my planet?' and WHY?"

"Technically," Cealth smiled pleasantly. "That's two questions."

"Don't be a smart-alec! I've got a laser, I don't have to think about grammar. And answer the question!"

Cealth sighed, fighting the urge to say "*You should never start a sentence with 'and'.*" And instead responded "Your planet- Earth?"

"Yeah." Snapped Sam, hand tightening on the laser.

"I was not the one who destroyed its inhabitants."

"Liar." Snarled Sam, firing. Cealth's hood fell, and the blast from the laser was abruptly consumed- pulled into the vortex of Cealth's face. Sam, unfazed by the blatant ineffectiveness of her weapon and, like all righteously angry people, ignoring basic logic, kept firing while she shouted. "**You** set up Galex- you wanted the universe to think he'd blown up an inhabited world and get the Federation to use that as an excuse to start a war! But you didn't count on the Dorians being able to hack his universal translator, did you, ya freak?! He worked out what you were, and the space pirates heard every word!"

"Interesting theory." Cealth's voice became slightly distorted as she sucked laser after laser into her face, as easily as an eye receiving light. "But almost entirely incorrect."

"Quit *lying*!" snapped Sam. "And can you at least take one laser blast? This is unfair!"

"Stop aiming for my head then. If you did that, then I wouldn't be able to absorb your shots."

"*That's where your vitals are!* If I shot you anywhere else, it wouldn't *do* anything!"

"You *have* done your research, haven't you?" Cealth calmly strolled up to Sam through the dotted line of laser blasts and, somehow, twisted the weapon out of the human's hands. "But think- what would be my motivation for destroying an entire planet? Revenge on the Starswallowers? Please. There's only so much vital juice you can spill before you start to realise you're simply encouraging people to kill you back."

"Oh REALLY!" Sam barked, backing away from the laser now being pointed squarely between her eyes. "You're the only person that fits! You destroyed Earth, abducted the hawk and wiped his memory- probably got him to do something else to antagonise the Federation, like blowing up Bar Aquila- and then returned to your home world to wait for the results."

"Your **theory** is moronic." Cealth said, bluntly. "If I'm lying, then why haven't I already shot you?"

"Because- that's a point actually. Why haven't you?" frowned Sam, stopping dead in her tracks.

"Because I'm no liar, and I don't really want to upset the Dorian in your crew. It would be... inconvenient."

"How d'you know-"

"Give me *some* credit. Even assassins listen to music- besides, the bounty placed on the space pirates was actually starting to piqué my interest. Three billion Signa is nothing to sneeze at, even if I would have to collect it from the Federation."

"But then, if you didn't destroy my planet, who the hell did?!"

Cealth's eyes locked onto Sam's face like the targeting system of a missile. "The last thing I wanted was another planetary genocide. When I heard about Earth, I began tracking down the one- or *ones*- responsible. I'm trying to find them right now."

"'The last thing **you** wanted?'" echoed Sam. "You stupid reverse Obligons destroyed every sentient being on Sandros 6!"

"Do you really believe that Starswallower nonsense?" Cealth frowned. "They've been spreading that lie for years- but only to other Starswallowers. I wasn't aware that anybody else remembered the planet."

Sam grinned. "Like I say, I'm from the past. I remembered Sandros 6 from *my* time, and I was really surprised when no one else did- so I did some digging, and I uncovered the whole mess!"

"Not the **whole** mess. We never destroyed that planet- that was the Starswallowers."

"You *drank* the minds of every creature on the planet!"

"And we were about to return them when the Starswallowers started attacking us!" Cealth snapped, feeling anger for the first time in around thirty years. *It must be the human's emotions affecting me.* She told herself. *I ordered myself not to lose control again.*

"They only started attacking because you guys killed the cosmic owl!"

"No! We explained our abilities to store the minds of life forms within our own bodies, and he asked to experience it. Then we started getting shot at!"

Sam swallowed. "Well. This is awkward."

"Agreed."

The two life forms looked at each other silently for a few moments. Eventually, Sam smiled uneasily. "Starswallowers *really* need to chill."

"Agreed." Cealth pulled her hood back over her face, turned and began walking back to her ship.

"Oh, err... Obligon?"

"Yes?" She slowed her pace slightly but didn't stop walking.

"Galex's on his way here now. I'll try and explain what's going on, but if he ignores me..."

"He will." Cealth finished. "But trust me, my ship will be difficult to catch, even for a Starswallower."

"Cool."

At that moment, a Dorian strolled over to the two of them. Her expression was blank, unreadable, but, from the way she stared at Cealth, it was perfectly clear that she wanted nothing more than to inconvenience the reverse Obligon for as long as possible.

"Stand down!" Sam barked. "She's okay."

"Mm." Auren muttered, continuing to glare at Cealth, steadily. "You allegedly devoured the entire universe's recollections of Sandros 6. Frankly, I find that hard to believe."

"I have... unusual abilities."

"Apparently so."

There was a pause, then, almost simultaneously, both beings removed their universal translators. They stared at each other, and Sam felt the air momentarily shift around her- they were communicating inaudibly, Auren's grasp of languages coming to her aid as she spoke in Obligoid tones. Sam's universal translator was just about to begin interpreting the languages when the duo abruptly replaced their own and spoke over the attempted translation.

"Farewell."

"Good luck."

Cealth returned to her ship, ignored the bickering outside and stepped into the spare cabin, currently serving as the Glitchis' bedroom.

"Are you ready?"

The Glitchis turned its neck towards her, then leapt off the bunk it had been squatting on beside its minion. Cealth nodded in response and left, closely followed by the five-legged being. Back in the cabin, Starthur hesitated, watching the retreating backs of both beings, then slipped out after them. The Starswallower had work to do before they arrived at the exit to the Universe.

Chapter 17

The universe is weird. It seems infinite- but infinity is an impossible concept in everything but numbers. Everything must have a beginning and end- that's the law of *all* things. Therefore, it only makes sense that the universe *must* have an edge- even if this edge is inconceivably distant from everything else.

Cealth stood next to the exit to the universe, on the lone rock embedded into the huge, rippling surface in front of her. She could feel the rush as the wall was pushed backwards, travelling hundreds of miles outwards even as she paused to blink, but the rock kept her grounded. Somehow, several billion years ago, this piece of detritus had been flung into the exterior of the universe and had been stuck there ever since, like the bung of the universal plug hole. The wall itself was neither solid, liquid nor gas. It was like fire in texture, except temperature was completely absent from its surface. It was the same colour as a black hole- you'd say it was a transparent blackness if you couldn't see the light pulsing through from whatever was on the other side. If pure chaos had a physical form, then the wall would come pretty close to mimicking it.

Jath and Exath had remained on the ship with Starthur- even now they were powering away to another galaxy to serve as a Galex distraction. Only the Glitchis remained beside her. There was a pause as she examined the edges of the rock she was standing on- then she breathed a sigh like the final calm wind before the storm. She glanced back at the Glitchis and smiled bitterly.

"I suppose this is the moment where you betray me?"

"*And why would I do that?*" Its voice was a hissing rasp, odd for a creature of such absurd proportions- and held a controlled note, an emotional dam preventing any hint of sensitivity from dripping into its tone.

"Please, don't insult my intelligence." Cealth shook her head, heavily. "I worked it out a while ago. You've been playing myself and the Starswallowers for a long time- did you honestly believe that neither side would notice?"

The Glitchis grinned, revealing its suspiciously sharp teeth. "*I haven't the faintest idea what you mean.*"

"Yes, you do." Cealth paused to compose herself, finding any hindering aggression in her system and quelling it before it could interfere with her actions, checking that the Glitchis was facing towards her- towards the wall of emptiness. "I'd been trying to find you *things* for a very long time. But I didn't realise you would be stupid enough to gather in one place." Cealth drew her Cellsplitter and examined a long scratch running down the barrel. "Did you honestly believe that your kind would be safe if you just sat on Earth for long enough? If so, then you **really** miscalculated, Reath."

Even as Cealth spoke, she had primed her Cellsplitter. On the very last syllable she brought it up towards the Glitchis, firing before she had properly aimed- knowing that one second could cost her the opportunity she'd been waiting for. Cealth waited for the usual hiss as her blast dispersed the cells of the creature before her- but this time it didn't happen.

Instead her eyes widened with surprise at the empty space where the Glitchis had stood not a moment before.

"Did you honestly believe I wouldn't take advantage of your advance warning?" It hissed from behind her. Cealth whipped round to face the voice, but the creature was already gone, having teleporting away before she could do anything more than blink. *"If anyone miscalculated, it was you."* The Glitchis launched itself at Cealth and sunk its teeth deeply into the arm holding the Cellsplitter. She shouted in pain and tossed the weapon to her other hand, catching it with undeniable deftness and firing in almost the same moment. The Glitchis released its grip and span away from the oncoming blast.

"If you suspected, if you knew, what I was, then why hesitate to kill me when you were surrounded by allies?" Every 's' that the Glitchis uttered was rasped through its teeth until it was almost unrecognisable, and Cealth's universal translator had to pause for a precious moment to catch up with the conversation. Disregarding the currently unintelligible question, Cealth darted past the Glitchis to reposition herself, her back to the rippling wall of nothingness, her eyes fixed firmly on the creature pacing about in front of her, its rolling pairs of legs moving with hypnotic fluidity. *"What's the matter?"* It cackled. *"Scared to turn your back?"*

Cealth ignored it, choosing to focus on the Glitchis' movements rather than its words. The wall was essential to this assassination; the Glitchis couldn't teleport to something it couldn't see- and the wall was virtually invisible. If she could predict where it would teleport next, all it would take was a single blast from her Cellsplitter to end its miserable life. *Stay calm, stay focused and always stay three steps ahead of your opponent.* She thought, firmly.

"Very clever of you, choosing this place as our battleground," the Glitchis nodded, its head swaying with the motion of its legs. *"Plenty of distance from the rest of the universe, and no physical way for me to get behind you, yes? I can't do any damage here, yes?"*

"Something like that." Cealth murmured, eyes locked onto the Glitchis, observing those rolling irises to get some kind of a hint as to where the thing would teleport- she'd noticed it glancing towards its next position before it moved, scouting the terrain before it teleported there.

"Very clever!" taunted the Glitchis, almost seeming to bounce about on those strangely stubby legs- it reminded Cealth, bizarrely, of the Nightcrawler she'd defeated in unarmed combat during an unwanted excursion on Yaucus- that tribal

tangle of civilised chaos- the same prowling, unnaturally short legs, that caused the Nightcrawler's belly to hover only slightly above the forest floor, made it capable of moving so quietly, that even the hyper-sensitive sonorous-bird (one of the many bizarre beings occupying the same jungle as the Nightcrawler) couldn't detect its presence even in the months of darkest sleep, where half the planet fell silent as Yaucus's sunlight vanished into the deep purple clouds.

Cealth reacted the instant that the Glitchis sprang- firing once at the creature as it leapt through the air to reach her, and then again as it teleported to avoid her blast- its eyes giving away its next position- and then staring in disbelief as the creature teleported for a *third* time, unable to react as...

"*Checkmate, 'Cell'.*" hissed the Glitchis, kicking Cealth's helmet with such force that it split, the air contained within whistling out past her disbelieving face and into the void. "*You shouldn't have started a fight you could never win.*"

The reverse Obligon collapsed backwards onto the rock, already starting to feel ice collecting on her eyes, the moisture working against her in the freezing vacuum of space. The Glitchis shot her one, last, contemptuous glance, then teleported away, ready to return to the Celestelia with the 'terrible' news that Cealth wouldn't be coming back.

On the asteroid, staring up at the galaxies swirling away in the far, far distance, Cealth felt a stab of fury so intense that she could almost believe the ice forming on her eyes would melt. Forty-five seconds left to live. It was a small mercy: if she'd been human, it would've been far less.

Chapter 18

Beneath Cygnus, away from the billions of prying, extra-terrestrial eyes, was a second layer- a sub-terrain city that wrapped around the interior of the dyson sphere- if the world above was the blanket covering Cygnus, then this level was the pyjamas. This was where the elite of the elite lived; the cosmic ruling class of the Starswallowers. It also happened to be where the Starswallower gene-splicing facility was located.

Over a million years ago a technologically advanced species (descended from basic Earthian pigeons that had been shuttled into space, to test the capability organisms had to survive in extra-terrestrial conditions) had decided to start artificially modifying themselves after noticing how slowly they evolved. They'd begun by harvesting the organic material of the peaceful Melcharians with whom they shared the planet they'd crashed on, mainly because the Melcharians could regenerate limbs and felt no pain, and then started progressing onto gathering the cells of more advanced species as their technology advanced. Finally, gloriously, they one day gained the ability to travel in space without the need for specialised suits.

The 'cosmic' class of Starswallowers had since progressed to having technological implants alongside their biological ones, enabling them to cruise between their sectors, which their inferior regular Starswallower counterparts had been leisurely conquering, and integrating the most useful DNA they found into both themselves and their offspring. It was really quite efficient.

After leaving Onyx, furious that he'd missed Cealth, Galex had charged past the Nebula Eater as it wheeled to face him and Sam started waving at him furiously from the cockpit, mouthing something he couldn't be bothered to translate, and charged straight back towards Cygnus- not due to any Cealth-related incident, but simply because there was an irritating, flashing notification in his eye implant that he couldn't get rid of until he'd been 'upgraded' back at the bio-engineering lab. It was infuriating- these notifications only ever popped up when he was right in the middle of something, took about forty minutes to be completed and there were hardly ever any noticeable differences before and after he upgraded. Even on the rare occasions when there *was* a perceptible change, no instructions were provided telling him how to use it, so it usually went to waste until he accidentally activated it twelve Cygnus months later.

He broke through the ruby atmosphere at half the speed of light, luxuriated in the combination of exhilaration and adrenaline for a little over a minute as the crystalline ground loomed ever closer, the distant, maze-like houses and streets that crisscrossed the dyson sphere gradually becoming ever more detailed as he angled his wings instinctively, sensing the air currents roaring around him and adjusting himself to stay on top of them, still accelerating. He revelled in his own speed for a moment longer than he should've done, missed his landing strip and wrenched himself round in a feat of manoeuvrability that any watching adolescent Starswallowers would immediately attempt to imitate, with dire glares from their mothers and silent promises of reprisal.

Galex landed with barely a feather out of place, stalked past Nimboris and the fleeing protestors with his fingers plugged firmly in his ears, then entered his luxurious palace and strolled into the lift, which connected to the mental circuit implanted in his frontal lobe and responded instantly; smoothly boosting down the spherical shoot to the floor Galex had thought of, like a vertical light-cruiser bullet train.

The cosmic heron loomed over him as he left the lift, and he raised an eyebrow at her as he made his way to the laboratory.

"I thought *I* was the tallest Starswallower, Cosmarie," he grumbled.

"Not anymore!" she replied, a gracious indifference infecting her tone. "After all, we haven't seen one another in eight Cygnus days! I *have* grown considerably since then."

"Four Earthian years," Galex muttered, under his breath. "I *will* standardise our time one day... or... year... Damn it, this is exactly the problem with living on a star!"

"So, how *have* you been?" the cosmic heron drawled- then glanced over her shoulder as soon as Galex started talking. "I'm sorry, I missed my turning. We *will* have to catch up at some point though! You should come around to my spire at some point! We could invite mother too!" Ignoring Galex's indignant spluttering at being denied a chance to complain, the cosmic heron turned and strolled away- with three strides of her ludicrous legs she had vanished off into the distance.

"Sisters," growled Galex. "They look alright when they're hatchlings, and then they grow up and become taller than you..."

By the time he'd arrived at the bio-lab, Galex had thought of fourteen different ways he could've handled the conversation better, each scenario ending with him sweeping off imperiously, having just delivered a severe comeback to any possible noise his sister could have uttered.

The facility had originally been run by the cosmic owl- but, ever since the genius' untimely death, it had instead been managed by a team primarily led by the cosmic dove. It was hardly an equal trade for Neutroby- the loss of the cosmic owl had been a severe blow to Cygnus, and the pangs of loss felt by each Starswallower still seemed to echo through the hollow interior of the dyson sphere- but the dove was dedicated, and regular genetic upgrades found their way to the cosmic Starswallower elites one way or another.

From the outside, the facility looked like a giant ball-bearing that'd been pushed halfway through the (8-mile thick) diamond layer surrounding the star inside Cygnus- but on closer inspection by a geometric genius, it was revealed to be a henahectagon- a hundred-sided polygon- made from a mixture of metal and glass in such an absurd, methodically random tangle of swirls that it could only have flolloped out of the cosmic owl's imagination.

Galex strolled up to one of the henahectagon's many panels and rapped on it. Behind the panel, a series of complex biometric procedures engaged, each one intent on examining every identifiable trait Galex possessed- from his eye colour to his feather arrangements, even taking a sample from the distinct mixture of gasses swirling through his personal atmosphere, each gas informing the computer exactly where the Starswallower had been, so it could compare the data with the extensive flight plan stored inside the atomic computer the entire system operated on. Finally, the door (on the opposite side of the building to Galex) slid open- its position not a design flaw, but rather a final test; each Starswallower entering the facility took a different amount of time to reach the door, and the computer had taken this data and timed how long the door should stay open for before closing on the tail feathers of the tardy Starswallower attempting to enter.

Attempting to ignore the process, Galex took off with a snap as his wings opened, the atmosphere surrounding them momentarily struggling to compensate for the rapidity of the motion, then blasted through the air to the other side of the building, looping at the last moment and gliding through the panel slightly upside-down as it slid closed, clipping a couple of atoms off his claws as they swept through. The supreme galactic overlord landed with an indignant squawk, straightened up, ruffling his feathers, then turned politely to the cosmic dove as the pale Starswallower hurried over to him.

"One day," Galex growled through gritted teeth. "You'll fix that door."

"Are you giving me a recommendation or a threat, Galex?" The cosmic dove sighed, glancing at his data implant as he spoke, and hurriedly writing something down. Without waiting for a response, he turned towards the large pair of doors at the far end of the room, nodded at the automated reception desk, which had already logged Galex's arrival and had been waiting for the signal to open the doors, before continuing. "It's been far too long-"

"Tell me about it!"

"-Since your last check-up." Finished the cosmic dove, glancing at Galex cautiously. 'I hope you weren't about to suggest we go out partying again. I actually have a job now, which is more than I can say for you."

"I'm the ruler of half the known universe!" Galex yelped. "You can't exactly get a better job than me without being a democratic, manipulative-"

"Well that's beside the point, isn't it?" the cosmic dove cut Galex off mid-flow and narrowed his eyes at a retinal scanner set into the wall next to one of the operating rooms. It bleeped, and a red light suddenly came on in the wall next to it. "Oh, for Galex's sake..." muttered the cosmic dove, under his breath. "I *told* her I wanted this room free this afternoon, and does she listen? *This* is what happens when you get apprentices..."

"Problem?" Galex asked, smugly leaning on the wall next to the cosmic dove. "Well, if we can't do this now, I suppose I'd better come back later..."

"No, you don't!" the cosmic dove seized Galex's arm before he could escape and glowered into his eyes. "You are *not* 'escaping' another appointment that easily! A cosmic overlord should have the most recent, expensive upgrades- and here you are, even when the upgrades are *free*, ignoring them blatantly and becoming ever more outdated! I have your best interests at heart, Galex- I really do- so stop whining, come into this operating theatre and wait for *five seconds* of your life!"

He hauled Galex into a second operating room, pushed him onto the pale memory foam table in the centre, and raised a plug, threateningly.

"Is this *really* necessary?" Galex sighed, melodramatically. "What're you honestly going to change?"

"I'll be upgrading your personal atmosphere so that it maintains its integrity under even the severest of conditions, improving your firewall so we don't have another digital accident- the last thing we need is another hacker- and altering your genetics."

"So, when you said five seconds-"

"I meant five *Cygnus* seconds. Look on the bright side, you'll be even faster after this upgrade, and you *do* like bragging about your speed."

"That's a point." Frowned Galex. "But are you going to get rid of all my preferences? It took me about three Earthian weeks to set them up last time!"

"I might have to momentarily siphon off your personal atmosphere..."

"*Why?!*"

"Just relax, Galex, it'll shave some time off this operation and ensure you actually have something to do after it's been completed."

"I have *plenty* to do without going around retrieving my gasses, thank you very much!"

"Please. You're a figurehead Galex, and you know it. When was the last time *you*, as a Starswallower, actually had to do something other than deliver a speech or detonate a planet? We both know you have no **real** political power."

As the cosmic dove spoke, he was tapping furiously on a monitor- either setting up Galex's upgrades or playing solitaire, it was impossible to tell. Galex relaxed slightly as a small tube began to siphon off his personal atmosphere, giving the cosmic dove the opportunity to plug a few more cables into him. Having extracted the mess of gasses, the tube administered a small quantity of powerful sedative and Galex grinned sleepily as it entered his bloodstream.

"Wassup with the lights?" Galex examined the suddenly rainbow-y lights in the ceiling above him, surprised to find he couldn't move. "Errything's gone a bit melty." He said, happily.

The cosmic dove ignored him and injected something else into the bloodstream- this time, a set of miniscule nanobots carrying tiny programs designed to re-write Galex's DNA, while ensuring his white blood cells didn't attack them. They were swept along in the current created by the beating of Galex's heart, rushed around a tight, veiny corner, then found themselves travelling alongside a monolithic red cell which they quickly pushed themselves into- receiving a small signal as they did so, instructing them quite clearly to being editing the DNA within.

A long, twisting double helix drifted towards the nanobots and they reacted instantly, removing a few sections from the centre and replacing them with something new, then dividing- one half of the nanobots remaining inside the cell, the new half leaving it to look for a new one. All around Galex's body, in almost every single red blood cell, his DNA was being altered carefully, the new genes beginning to appear on a cellular level while the nanobots replicated themselves.

After their job was done, every nanobot would be remotely deactivated by Galex's cyber implants, and then pass harmlessly out of his system- along with any other detritus in his body. At the same time as all of this was occurring in the organic parts of his body, Galex's cyber implants were receiving updates and gradually modifying themselves accordingly to aid their owner's biological functions, augmenting his sight, hearing, reflexes, immune and pulmonary systems, as well as compensating for the new additions to his genetics.

The cosmic dove leant back in his chair and calmly watched the progress bar rolling from one side of the screen to the other, a convenient percentage of completion next to it and an ever changing, flickering list of upgrades present just below it. He really *had* been lucky to have taken a sample of DNA from the teleporting Glitchis just before it had been stolen.

Chapter 19

The reverse Obligons were one of the universe's great mysteries; few beings outside the Starswallowers could remember them, and even those that did had no idea how they had come to be, or what had become of them. Those strange beings had become an unknown, a momentary anomaly in an otherwise ordered universe. As with most broken civilizations, it had started quite well.

Several decades ago, a detachment of around three thousand Obligons had been standing on the exit to the universe, (having been hired to study it by a wealthy Krilltopian) when they had inadvertently moved the boulder which formed the bung of the universe. A wave of something bright had passed over them, and those standing closest to the exit had yelled in pain, collapsing unconscious onto the rocky surface, and leaving the few Obligons who'd been submerged in less light to restore the rock to its original position, quickly, before anything happened to them too.

Whatever had hit them, whatever substance it was that had managed to impact them from beyond the wall of their universe, didn't appear to be negative- at least, not at first. Certainly, it had changed them; the 3,000 Obligons from the rock had slowly found ways of removing their negative emotions and breaking free of the misery that had drowned their species for millennia. Filled with an exhilarating spectrum of previously unfelt emotions, the bright faced beings had returned to Onyx, their home planet, eager to assist the other members of their race- and eventually similarly affected species- in breaking free as well, and it was with this desire in mind that they had contacted the cosmic Starswallowers.

On a now dead planet, known as Sandros 6, that dream had been exterminated. The venue itself had been chosen at the request of the reverse Obligons, who had adored the planet's rich ecosystem; several million species called the planet home, and every single one benefited at least two other species in a life-supporting way.

Each day, the reverse-Obligons had been discovering new abilities and refining them to perfection, exhilarated both with their progress and the rainbow-like spectrum of emotions they could now feel. They could move memories around, delete them- even transfer them to another being, and could store the emotions of other beings within themselves and examine them at will. They could feel happiness, joy, excitement, hope, love, compassion- they knew when something was supposed to be funny, and when they should show consideration and understanding; notions that the Obligons as a species simply couldn't feel- or even comprehend- for millennia.

Cealth, and her brother, Soulth, had been experimenting with their abilities alone, away from the rest of the reverse Obligons, when they heard a distant explosion that sent birds scattering and trees writhing, their leaves blown back from something huge. The pair had run towards it, expecting to see the Starswallowers landing- and not the combination of both exhilarated and terrified reverse Obligons standing frozen in a clearing.

In the centre of the circle, Cealth's uncle, Reath, lay slumped on the ground, as though unconscious. Cealth's heart contracted slightly, as she wondered, (optimistically in hindsight) if her uncle had been in a fight with one of the many creatures on the planet. Her assumption was backed up as she pushed right to the front of the crowd and saw a huge nightstalker, maybe twenty feet in length and nearly half that in height, standing over Reath and baring its three rows of teeth madly. Even as Soulth joined his sister in attempting to push through the crowd to help, however, the nightstalker suddenly became rigid and keeled over, a sliver of shadow unspooling from its eyes, before disappearing into Reath's mouth.

A moment later, Reath stood up, to cheers and whoops from the surrounding reverse-Obligons, noticing his niece and nephew a moment later and waving them over cheerfully.

"What just happened?" Cealth glanced at the nightstalker cautiously, but it remained unconscious.

"Was that another new ability?" Soulth's usually subdued voice was tinged with curiosity, which was quickly reflected on his face as his uncle grinned again, nodding madly in response.

"Isn't it amazing? We can transfer our minds into the bodies of other creatures!" He grabbed Soulth's hand before either sibling could respond. "Here! You try. You always said you wanted to be a nightstalker, didn't you?"

"When I was six." Soulth frowned. "The nightstalker- is it okay?"

"It'll be fine," Reath said dismissively, waving a hand loosely. "I didn't touch its mind. At least... I pushed it temporarily aside, so that I could control its body."

"It *is* breathing." Cealth confirmed, gingerly placing her hand a few centimetres away from the nightstalker's maw. "I think it's only asleep."

"Well there you go then!" Reath beamed. "With this new ability, the possibilities for what we can achieve are endless! We can cure aging by moving from body to body! We can help the Dorians with translations through inhabiting new species! We can even aid in the capture of wanted criminals!"

Soulth's previously uncertain expression lightened slightly, as his concern for the nightstalker was dwarfed by his uncle's rapid-fire list of the ability's potential. The crowd murmured excitedly, whispered communications shooting between them as a rosy haze of optimism filled the air.

"It's only useful if the possessed species recovers." Cealth stepped forwards, nodding to the nightstalker, her sharp realism catching the other Obligons off guard. They fell silent abruptly as they picked up on her caution. "It's asleep, but how long will it stay like that?"

"I agree with the small one." Outh, the second tallest reverse-Obligon in the group edged through the throng, his words blunt, being uncomfortable about addressing the huge crowd, but determined to speak. "We should wait to identify the side effects before doing it again. Study this nightstalker."

"We should test the ability more." Soulth argued, eyes darting to his sister questioningly, surprised by her attitude. "We could show it to the Starswallowers when they arrive. Think of the good they could do with it! Besides, we don't even know if every animal would react the same way so what's the point in only studying the nightstalker?"

"So you would jeopardise more animals?"

"The boy wants to help others! Don't condemn him for that!"

"But if we waste lives developing this ability, then we would be doing more harm than good!"

The reverse Obligons stirred uncomfortably; conflict was a new experience, and not a pleasant one. To look at your neighbour, to even sense the air they breathed, and you could tell that you disagreed, and that you thought less of the other for it. The debate began to spark as aggression billowed like shredded forest leaves, Obligon shouting at Obligon, until, finally, they were interrupted by the nightstalker. It bellowed furiously, shaking the ground with the force of its hostility, and lunged at Cealth, who twisted, mind flashing with panicked thoughts which she would never have been able to react to quickly enough, frozen by terror and by the wild, dancing light of it's many-irised purple eyes... before being shoved aside by her uncle, whose shadow seemed to fall from his eyes and dart to the crazed animal's, as Reath froze the nightstalker in its tracks, his control over the animal so absolute that he'd sent it sprinting back into the jungle and out of sight in mere seconds.

There was a moment of stunned silence, a slice of calm before the storm, and then the excited whispers began to spring up, delight, excitement, shock and wariness all colouring the atmosphere as the reverse Obligons quickly absorbed the facts; the nightstalker had recovered, Reath's new ability had saved Cealth's life, proving that the ability was incredibly useful; and since the nightstalker hadn't been harmed, there now seemed to be no drawbacks to it whatsoever! The only worry was if the nightstalker would come back any time soon- but now they would be ready for it.

"I owe you an apology." Cealth swallowed and pulled herself to her feet, nodding at her uncle as the Obligons around them began likewise apologising to one another. "I just thought... when I felt the air around the nightstalker, I couldn't feel anything. It must've been asleep."

"Hey, we all make mistakes, Cell." Reath smiled gently.

"Well, now we can show the Starswallowers what we're capable of." Cealth glanced up at the sky in anticipation, before a thought occurred to her. "Hey, uncle, where's Soulth?"

With an abrupt cry of excitement, several reverse Obligons began pointing upwards, gesturing towards several faint black specks, flying in formation, and whooping as the first few cosmic feathers fell to the ground before them. The Starswallowers were coming.

"Uncle Reath?" Cealth repeated, glancing around. "Did you see where he went?"

"Mhm." Reath's eyes were fixed firmly on the sky- but the air surrounding him had turned a sour, shamefaced shade which Cealth alone, unfixated on the sky like the others, seemed to detect.

"Uncle," she growled. "Whatever you're hiding, you'd better tell me quick." Reath glanced at her sideways, guilt colouring his face. A moment later, Cealth spotted Soulth, lying unconscious a few feet away.

"Oh, you didn't."

Reath opened his mouth to reply- but the Starswallowers were already landing in the giant clearing, huge feathered heads casting great shadows over the reverse Obligons, eyes blazing with life and energy which seemed to both terrify and awe. Standing there, surrounded by their uniquely coloured atmospheres, they glowed in every shade perceivable to the Obligons' eyes.

Galex stepped forwards, the flock of cosmic birds parting for him politely. Eight feet tall, with feathers a retina-destroying white, and eyes like the detonating core of a red dwarf star, the towering Starswallower would have easily cut an imposing figure without the aid of the glittering bio-mechanical implants caressing the undersides of his wings (at this point in time, it was more fashionable to show-off your enhancements rather than conceal them beneath your feathers as in later years). As it was, every reverse Obligon sank into an instinctual bow, silently awed by the creature's overt might, and the stuffy confidence which filled the air around him.

"*What did you do?*" hissed Cealth again, barely moving her mouth as she narrowed her eyes at her uncle.

"*It was his idea.*" Reath glanced up at the Starswallowers, but they didn't seem to have noticed the exchange- more focused on laughing as Outh accidentally bent too far over and performed a truly spectacular forward roll; with his glowing face, he looked like a Catherine wheel.

"*What was?!*"

"*He wanted us to stop fighting, so he took possession of the nightstalker.*" Reath paused, then backtracked hastily as his niece's icy gaze momentarily stopped him in his tracks. "*We wanted everyone to work together again! The nightstalker probably would've recovered naturally anyway. I needed everyone on board, so we could show the Starswallowers the ability! Do you know how rich we could be? My brother and his wife- your parents- they'd never feel depressed again...!*"

"We need to tell them." Cealth made to straighten up, but Outh, still in his uncontrollable spin, bowled her over. She gritted her teeth in a forced smile as the attention of the Starswallowers turned on her. Reath seized his chance.

"Your highness-es, I don't mean to intrude on the fun, but I think it's time to show you what we can do."

"I thought you already were." Galex's comment, however weak it may have been, drew a gale of slightly forced laughter from the Starswallowers before he raised a hand to silence it. "Alright then...?"

"Reath."

"Reath." Nodded Galex. "Show us 'what you can do' as you put it."

"Wait!" Barked Cealth, glaring furiously at Reath and scrambling to her feet. "I don't want to interrupt, but-!"

"Then don't." Galex's tone became dangerous, each syllable fired from his mouth with the intention of puncturing the eardrums of both groups with severity.

"I have to."

The reverse Obligons stared at Cealth in shock; not only was she ignoring the leader of their half of the Universe's warning, but she was radiating an aura of golden-red determination and anger on a level with Galex's mounting indignation. Whatever she was going to say was deadly serious. For the Starswallowers' part, they screeched insults, in both parts shocked and appropriately outraged.

"Sit down child!"

"Go wash your mouth out with Melchar water before you speak again!"

"You need a dictionary installing into your brain, so you can remind yourself who the Supreme Galactic Overlord is? Because I'd be happy to do that for you! With a hammer."

"Melchar-crawler!"

"Carvaruit worm!"

"Xsovzorite!"

"Cealth." Outh glanced at her and shook his head sharply, speaking quickly and softly. "You should shut up, and fast. They don't like-"

"The mind-switching has a side effect!" She practically bellowed above the collective jabbering of the Starswallowers. Silence fell within seconds, as all eyes fixed on her. All except Reath's, whose gaze remained fixed on the ground, as he considered his next move.

"Mind-switching?" the cosmic owl stepped forward, his pop-eyed gaze made even stranger by the silver wires that shone, barely visible, through his irises, crisscrossing like the threads in a spider web, under the bronze lenses of his orb-like eyes. "The ability you were going to show us was mind switching?" He stampeded past Cealth in his eagerness and grabbed Reath's hand. "Show me!"

"Of course." Reath nodded, his eyes sparkling with eagerness- and, Cealth recognised with disgust, greed.

"BUT-!" She tried again.

"Don't worry about my niece," Reath cut Cealth off sharply, then nodded to indicate her to the Starswallowers. She stared at him, disbelieving, hardly able to comprehend how or why he said what he did next. How he doomed their race with such a base dismissal. "She's just a child. Thinks that the recovery time for the possessed being is too long. She means well."

"How sweet." Nodded the cosmic owl, clearly not paying any attention. "Now then, shall we get started? We **have** to see a demonstration!"

If she had been clearer, if she hadn't been so stunned by her uncle's harshness, or her brother's betrayal, if things had moved slower that day, allowing her to process it all...

"Of course, your highness." Reath's self-satisfied eyes glowed, and there was a moment where, as the dark shadows slithered from his eyes towards the cosmic owl's, Cealth realised what would happen before it did, as though she had flashed forwards in time.

If she could have stopped him- maybe tripped him up so he couldn't see the cosmic owl, the being whose body he would steal- if she could've appealed to one of the other reverse Obligons for a bit of common sense... maybe if she could've tried harder- if some way, somehow, she could have known then what she knew now- how the Starswallowers would unleash their full fury onto the reverse Obligons in retaliation for the perceived murder of the cosmic owl... of Neutroby...

Reath's body slumped to the ground, and he flexed the cosmic owl's fingers, stared around through eyes that were not his own- yet which now clearly showed his presence, the irises having multiplied and turned a bitter purple- and then spoke, with Neutroby's voice, his combined avarice and awe twisting its sound.

"This is amazing." He beamed at the reverse Obligons, childish excitement tinging the sophisticated tones of the Starswallower's tongue. "This is amazing! I'm so tall now!" He stared at the Starswallowers in eagerness- all but Galex had moved rapidly backwards, and the cosmic swan was staring at Neutroby's body in undisguised horror. This was creepy; plain and simple.

Galex, perhaps to show the others that there was nothing to be afraid of- just a lesser being in a glorified suit- strolled over to Reath, still looming a foot above him, and poked him firmly in the feathered chest.

"Ow!"

"Well, you haven't activated the defences." Galex raised an eyebrow at Reath almost admiringly. "He would've done that in a heartbeat when he saw me coming, so you certainly don't have the same guts. Congratulations are in order; this new ability... what did you call it again?"

"Mind switching."

"Mind switching!" nodded Galex. "I can think of around five different applications for it right off the bat. The cosmic owl will need to study your biology, of course, before we can use it... uh, would you mind giving him his body back?"

"Hmm?"

"His body."

"Oh, right!" Reath smiled nervously, his mind finally catching up with the reality of the situation. "Of course! Right away!"

If she could've warned the Starswallowers beforehand, somehow- if Reath had discovered the ability sooner, maybe the cosmic owl would have been able to make some kind of backup system for the Starswallowers' minds...

"What's the problem?"

"No problem! Just need to catch my breath. I'm not used to having such large lungs..."

The crowd laughed- but it was levity disguising tension. The cosmic swan was now staring at him with undisguised revulsion.

But she hadn't done, had she? What had happened could never be fixed. Ever. No matter how much she learnt, regardless of what she tried... she had been the only one, besides Reath, who had known that the mental transfer was one-way, that minds don't just come back... who else would've been able to stop him? Who would've tried? Who would have known?

"I'm waiting, Obligon." Galex's tone had turned cold and menacing. He could no longer pretend to be civil.

The laughter had stopped. The jubilation was petering out.

Soulth had known. If the realisation had come to her sooner, then she would have been able to sneak away and find him before anyone had been hurt. As it was, the menacing advance of the Starswallowers on Reath, and the sickening crunch that followed as his attempt to flee was prevented, served as a good enough distraction for her to run toward the jungle, through the foliage, searching desperately for the nightstalker that had 'attacked' her.

"Soulth." She whispered his name at first, terrified that her voice would be picked up by the Starswallowers' super hearing (they had that, right?) and only increasing her volume when she realised that the jungle was still thundering away normally, drowning her out with ease, the wildlife screeching, cawing, bellowing, and bawling, hammering away like the chorus to some unperceivable song. "Soulth!"

A glance to her left and the light scraping of claws leaving stone, the flashing of a pair of specially adapted eyes, boring into her own with the practised ferocity of a hunter ready to combat a million and one different threats, the snarling jaws a millimetre from her face, and suddenly the nightstalker was flung away, tackled by a second hunter, whose purple irises bounced as they hit the edges of his eyes...

Cealth scrambled to her feet and stared at the two grappling beasts, their dark, almost violet fur bristling in agitation as they slashed, bit, tore and let loose rumbling growls that caused the dirt to shake. Finally, with a roar of triumph, the second nightstalker sent the first sprinting back into the jungle, the ground thudding in time with its retreat. No... hold on... The ground continued to shake even after the nightstalker vanished, and a horrible feeling rose in Cealth's stomach and throat as she realised what it was.

"Did you see that?" Soulth laughed, somehow twisting the words out of the nightstalker's elongated gullet forcefully. "I'm a wild animal!"

"Soulth." Cealth glared at him furiously. *Traitor. Enabler.*

"Okay, okay, I'm sorry." He lent down so his massive head was on a level with hers. "I'm sorry that I lied. Even so... I'm the top of the food chain!"

"Reath's in trouble."

"What?" He choked, the syllables getting caught in his throat as he bristled with alarm.

"You possessed this thing and tricked the others into believing that animals could recover from possession, and now-"

"They can!"

"They can't."

"But uncle said... he told me he'd tested it before-"

"It doesn't matter what he said. He possessed a Starswallower, and now he's refusing to return to his own body! If he was telling the truth, why would he be acting like that?" Cealth raised her arms in exasperation, and the ground trembled again. "Look, can you even feel the nightstalker's mind in there?"

"I don't..." Soulth gulped, his eyes wide in terror as the realisation hit him. "If the Starswallowers get to Reath, they'll..."

"They already have done." Cealth snapped, gritting her teeth. "He's put this entire planet in danger, which is why **you** are going to try and impersonate the owl before they do anything. It's our only option."

An explosion rocked the world, undeniably loud at this point. Without another word, the duo ran back towards the clearing, Soulth's paws slamming into the ground with methodical rapidity, Cealth scrambling over every root, through every knotted shortcut, ducking under mulchy vines and stumbling along to the beating of the planet beneath them. The emotions riding the wind towards them were bitter, and before they had even reached the clearing, both already had a good idea of what they would find. That didn't make it any easier to see. The Starswallowers were gone- the only reminders of their presence the blue-ish feathers sprinkled before the slumped bodies of three thousand Obligons.

Soulth stopped dead, and Cealth let out a choked noise, stumbling like a sleepwalker to her Uncle's side. Suddenly she straightened up, pupils contracting as primal instincts took over from the overwhelmed emotional ones.

"Do you... feel something-?"

A cloud of swirling black mist sped out of the jungle, comprised of hundreds- no, thousands- of twisting, writhing strands of smoke, and both reverse Obligons yelled as they registered the anger and sheer malevolence radiating from each one. These... things, whatever they were, were very much alive, and deadly.

They passed Cealth as though she wasn't there, and she half-registered how as each one brushed against her, her face glowed, a powerful lightness which seemed to invigorate her whole body and repelled the smoky creatures, who gave her a wide berth as they streamed towards...

"Soulth!" Cealth let out a panicked shout, and the light shielding her flickered momentarily, responding poorly to her negativity. The things passing her stirred, excitedly.

"Cealth!" A panicked yell cut through the air towards her. "Cealth! They're not-" Soulth was temporarily obscured from her by a hail of the things, but they soon parted just as abruptly, and the nightstalker stood before her, smiling with a savage delight which she knew Soulth would never have displayed.

Chapter 20

"Hello, niece." The nightstalker had said, its eyes pulsing with a savage delight that only increased when it opened its mouth and spat out another of the creatures- a shadow radiating confusion, panic and defensive fury, that she recognised with a surge of dread.

Soulth...

She had run. Torn across the planet towards their shuttle, entering in the co-ordinates for the farthest flung place she could think of, leaving Sandros 6 mere minutes before Galex's tunnel, bored right through the planet's core, triggered that world's destruction.

The Starswallowers had caught her, of course. Hovering above the planet's atmosphere, watching to see if any of the body-swapping reverse Obligons would come after them- they had seen what the reverse Obligons became once their bodies were destroyed. Those twisting, twining creatures had simply been too dangerous to allow off that planet. Cealth wasn't deemed as threatening, still being in possession of her body, but was seized nonetheless, and within hours of Sandros 6's destruction, all mention of the planet and the life that had thrived there had been erased by her, on Galex's personal orders.

The creatures survived. Lurking in the shattered remains of Sandros 6, and eventually beginning to roam free across the universe once the Starswallowers had left, possessing whoever they wished and passing undetected through the many worlds they inhabited. Outh possessed a lesser Starswallower known as Starthur, Reath the Glitchis that Cealth had encountered. All across the universe, the Distorted Obligons, as Cealth now called them, began infecting creatures of authority, always staying out of sight, never **quite** arousing suspicion, never allowing word of their continued existence to leak out. But Cealth knew. It seemed just a bit too convenient that the leaders of the Federation half of the universe were suddenly able to compete with Galex's empire- almost as though half a dozen people with more of an agenda had abruptly taken their place.

It had been easy for 'Starthur' to visit her cell- as Galex's secretary everyone assumed that he had some kind of reason for being there, and so didn't question him- wary of his lectures on correct protocol, the shortest of which had been known to last for three Cygnus hours, and of his usual proximity to the cosmic worm hugger, Nimboris.

Quietly, so as not to alert the guards, Outh had offered her an escape. *"Join us,"* he had said. *"Your uncle and brother miss you. We're planning an attack on the very heart of the Starswallower empire as you and I speak- revenge, for what they did to Sandros 6. Not to mention, to us."*

Cealth looked at him silently for a moment- his eyes, purple and with those strange split irises, were hidden, and his eyes looked very much like those of Starthur (it seemed that the Distorted had learned to do that much), except for the hatred and discomfort which now lived there, twisting his gaze into something virtually unrecognisable.

Then Cealth asked, in as much of an undertone as Outh had- "Why only come for me now, after all this time?"

"It has been... difficult to acquire the correct body." Outh tilted his head slightly. "The Starswallowers built new defences after encountering us. It's harder to keep control now- and it was never very comfortable to stay in a body for too long to begin with."

Cealth nodded, hardly aware that she didn't care about the deletion of the Starswallower's mind, and that a coldness sat where her remorse for the loss of the creature's life should have been.

"Do you have a plan for getting revenge?"

"Of course we do." He scowled, anger at the Starswallowers taking over his tone. "Those megalomaniacs stole our bodies from us! Forced us to live like... like beggars! Vagabonds that have no true home, but have to squat anywhere they can- that's how Reath put it, and we all agree with him! It's been nightmarish having to live like this- but now we're going to give the Starswallowers a taste of their own medicine. Do you still blame us for this? Or will you help us this time, Cealth?"

"Of course I will." Cealth had been brought up short by this, suddenly compelled by an almost patriotic urge to aid her species in spite of a slight nagging feeling telling her, in no uncertain terms, that this was wrong. But she had been young. Bitter. Angry that her life- her family, her future, even her freedom- had been stolen from her. She had needed somebody to blame; and who better than the beings who had destroyed the bodies of her friends and forced them into stolen shells?

She had easily left the base with Outh by her side, the guards not quite grasping just how dangerous a prisoner she was- Galex could not, after all, have admitted even to his own species that there were beings capable of annihilating Starswallowers with a simple blink- which allowed them to leave that sector unchallenged.

Cealth's reunion with her uncle, however, had altered her temporary sense of righteousness. It had begun much the way she had expected- on their temporary home base, an abandoned moon littered with the ruins of a species which had long since left in pursuit of a more desirable world, her species had been waiting to welcome her back, she had reencountered him.

"Cealth!" Her uncle had smiled warmly, now in the body of a highly generic-looking Vex, his fur parting in a motion similar to a greeting wave. "I'm sorry we couldn't have come for you sooner. Soulth- and I- have missed you."

"Uncle." Cealth had paused, unsure, given their last encounter, whether or not to hug him. He made the decision easier a few seconds later.

"Now that we have your shell- that is, a reverse Obligoid body- we can finally speed up our plans."

"Excuse me?" Cealth gave him a look, and he froze momentarily before seeming to realise that what he had said required further explanation. And quickly.

"Our forms require rest after a certain amount of time possessing a body." He gestured over at Outh, whose smoky form had just left Starthur with a huge sigh of relief. *"Regrettably, we aren't exactly in the most... controlled mindset after we leave our shells. We become little more than instinct fuelled by whatever emotion we were feeling when last in a body."*

"So where do I fit in here?" Cealth asked, silently connecting the fury, rage and regret she had felt from the Distorted when she had first met them with Reath's explanation of their lingering emotions.

"We don't need to rest while in a reverse Obligon body." Reath smiled at her warmly- and she could practically feel his smugness at having been the one to work this out oozing from every pore in his new face. *"If we use this shell, we can better control ourselves between assignments."*

"'Shell'." Cealth retained her prior expression of cynicism, now mixed with slight distain. "That would be **me** then. **My** body."

"Ah. Well yes. But you couldn't be in there while we were using it- so it is better to think of it as... a... shell..." He trailed off as he registered Cealth's glower.

"And what would happen to me? Would I become like you? A ghost? That was one thing I was never able to figure out- how did our minds- **your** minds- survive after your bodies were destroyed? The cosmic owl didn't-"

"The cosmic owl!" Reath's smiled widened to an almost scary degree. Cealth, unfortunately, recognised the expression- it meant her uncle was about to be immensely smug about something. *"His mind still exists! I found it!"*

"You...?"

"I didn't delete it. Not back then! Back then, we- as reverse Obligons- instinctively stole minds, but didn't erase them."

"'Back then.' So... now-"

"Sadly," Reath interrupted, cutting across her before she could utter much more. *"Now it is a different story. It's impossible to store minds in our current states."*

"So you destroy them?" Cealth's face slackened in horror. "This is exactly what caused all of this!"

"And if I had found Neutroby's mind sooner, it would have been an entirely different story, I am sure." Reath's face became deliberately blank. *"But I didn't- the mind is far too large for you to search thoroughly, especially under pressure. Besides, he was tucked away. You can have him if you want."*

"What?" Confusion, raw and simple, filled Cealth's voice. Reath could have been speaking about an unwanted pet. An Earthian hamster for his whining niece, to quiet her down.

In response, Reath's eyes glowed, and a ball of light shot into Cealth's pupils. She leapt backwards reflexively, rubbing her eyes furiously, trying to clear the greenish shadow of light moving steadily across her retinas with every blink.

I've had enough...

Cealth stiffened as the voice moaned through her head like the wind in a derelict house.

Please... This isn't what I want... I never wanted this...

"You see?" Reath crowed. *"It was a simple mistake. Now, I am going to need to borrow your body. Koath will have to rest as soon as she returns from her mission."*

"I..." Cealth glanced at her hand, which was shaking. In her mind, the cosmic owl continued to whisper, in such a state that he seemed not to notice Cealth's presence. It was as though he were wrapped up in his own, nightmarish existence. A second glance at her uncle was all she needed to convince her- something was terribly wrong, even if, with her loathing and confusion mounting, she couldn't quite place exactly what this 'thing' was. Reath raised an eyebrow at her hesitation. "I need to think about this."

"You can't." Reath's tone became hard, and it was as though a façade had finally lifted. With a surge of dread, Cealth recognised the same anger-imbued creature that she had first seen back on Sandros 6, lurking behind his stolen eyes. This creature was not her uncle, whatever it might call itself. Reath may have been selfish, but this... *"You will leave that shell immediately. We will use it to recover, and we will overpower the Starswallowers with its help. Galex's memories, his experiences, his raw power, will enable us to colonise the entire universe, piece by piece, species by species."*

"Why?" Cealth stared, shocked by Reath's abrupt paradigm shift. "The universe- Reath, we only want revenge on the Starswallowers! Why on Onyx would you attack everything else?"

"Because I cannot feel, Cealth!" The screech must have been held in for years, so laced by venom and jealousy it was. Cealth shifted backwards, nervously. *"I want to know happiness again! Sadness, hope, delight, regret- ANYTHING BUT THIS!"* He covered the distance Cealth had been steadily putting between them in two

short strides. *"Do you realise what it has been like, locked in this state? Because the last thing Reath felt was unadulterated fury! We had only just learned to feel, for Sol's sake, when emotion was stolen from us again! I won't exist like this. I **refuse!** But if we absorb enough minds, enough memories, then we will be able to restore our emotions from the collages of a quintillion minds!"*

He's mad.

Cealth's back stiffened in alarm. The owl sounded as though he had finally woken up- aware of the goings on of the real world again.

I know the feeling.

"I need an answer now, Cealth! I won't be impeded by you!"

You need to get away from him. You live here- not him. You can take this away from him. He needs your body for him in do this. You want to stop him, right?

"I need to think, uncle." Cealth snapped, so sharply that at first Reath seemed too surprised to respond. Then, as his expression began to harden again, Cealth continued, quickly. "This is a lot to take in. I need time to prepare myself for... becoming like you." This, at least, he seemed to understand. Some past version of himself, reminding him of the agony *he* had gone through, momentarily took the place of the loathsome creature.

"I... understand." His face twisted into another smile- it looked as synthetic as the last. *"Take a few minutes. The ruins on the southern side of the moon are especially elaborate. I think you'd like them."*

He keeps the ships on the northern side.

Why do you trust me? Cealth thought. *I'm a reverse Obligon too. Why would you help the species which imprisoned you?*

Neither of us has another choice. I, at least, am privy to your memories. I spent a lot of time in that... thief's head, so I know how to locate them. And I know you tried to do what was right on Sandros 6. Once a liar, always a liar- and you are not.

Cealth strolled behind one of the nearby columns and ducked out of her uncle's sight, changing direction almost immediately and hurrying around towards the orange glow that illuminated the distant sky and indicated the runway for several dozen ships. She was just about to sneak into a beautiful cream and gold Celestelia, when a figure stopped her in her tracks.

Soulth. It had to be. The same over-large eyes, the smooth, flowing head which crested ever so slightly differently on every Obligon, which he had managed to level out through years of muscle building... the same person who, when asked what job he would take after becoming a reverse Obligon, answered that he would love to either become an opera singer- or, more seriously, just to do what he loved...

But it couldn't be him. The line of his eyebrows was wrong. Twisted. Almost... cruel. No... sadistic.

Cealth ducked behind another chunk of ruin, this one having been shoved into place as a temporary retaining wall for the spaceport, and watched her brother silently. A moment later, however, he stopped, glancing casually up at the sky before speaking in a husky monotone.

"You know, I can feel your panic through that wall." He turned towards her, a disgusted look crawling up his face as she stood up, revealing herself. *"You always were a coward. Curled up into a little ball like that. How pathetic."*

"You're one to talk." Cealth's voice shook, making the insult sound more like a question. Soulth sneered.

"It looks like you've gained a yellow streak since I last saw you."

"And what about you? What on Onyx did they do to **you**?"

Soulth shook his head mockingly. *"'They'? The others had nothing to do with my... altered mindset."*

"They turned you into a Distorted, didn't they?"

"Oh, no." Soulth smiled at Cealth's questioning gaze. *"No. That was you. All you."*

"But-!" A surge of panic whipped through the air, and Cealth's head began to throb as her heartrate began to thrum faster.

"Abandoning me on Sandros 6, like the coward you are, to be detonated along with the rest of our family, starting the argument on that day which meant our uncle couldn't test the side effects of mind switching, and leaving me to be ambushed by the Distorted, when they tore me from my body!"

"That wasn't my fault!" Cealth shouted desperately. "I couldn't have done anything! We were children..."

"And don't get me started on how you ran away when the Starswallowers attacked instead of doing something!"

"I went to fetch you!" she said, staring at him desperately, willing him to understand. They could both feel the guilt oozing through the air with every word she spoke. "They would have only believed me if they saw you! They saw me as a child-!"

"That's an excuse that we can both see through, Cealth! You were the only one in a position to stop our uncle!" With some effort, Soulth forced the scowl from his face and replaced it with an ugly smile. *"Well, it doesn't matter now anyway. You aren't leaving this moon. You will help us to destroy the Starswallowers, and then you'll help me to kill uncle."*

"What?" Cealth was taken off guard. "But... I thought you were working with him."

"So does he. But in reality, we all want a piece of Reath for putting us in this mess. Besides, with him gone, there'll be no one left to tell us what to do. We'll spread through this galaxy freely. We'll tear every thought from the heads of those around us! And then, once we have learned about everything this universe has to offer, we'll just go looking for the next! I always did wonder what the light we saw outside this universe was."

"That's exactly what Reath was going to do!" Cealth said. "Have you truly lost your minds? You must be able to see why this is wrong!"

"I see why it's wrong!" Soulth said, angrily. *"I just don't particularly care. Morality is a concept for creatures that give a crap. And I don't! Not after what you did."*

She had punched him. It had made sense at the time- but apparently hitting someone full in the face with your knuckles is incredibly painful for both parties. She flinched backwards, cradling her fingers and massaging them furiously, even as Soulth howled- his eyes, unlike those of a humans, weren't protected from Cealth's punch by the bridge of a nose.

"WHAT is going on here?!" Reath bellowed, striding towards the swearing siblings.

"She punched me!" Soulth howled, still cradling his face.

"Is this true?" snapped Reath, rounding on Cealth.

"After he told me about his plan to overthrow you!" Her voice shook slightly as she reached the end of her sentence. If she was lucky... If Reath took the bait...

"She's lying!" Yelled Soulth. *" You can hear her voice shaking!"*

"Then why are you getting emotional?" Reath's lip curled.

"You wouldn't be the same if you were accused?!"

Cealth quietly walked away from the two squabbling Distorted, and stepped into the parked Celestelia, sealing the doors against their hostility, and activating the internal lights. She stopped as she reached the cockpit, staring blankly at the controls. She had never flown before. She could drive perfectly well- she had learnt back when she was an Obligon- but flying?

They had gone too far. Reath, with his jealous, greedy nature, she could believe that, if it suited his needs, **he** would steal the minds and memories of every creature in the universe, but Soulth?

A flick of a switch and the headlights, so blinding that they would easily illuminate the blackness of space, came on. Cealth's blood ran cold. There was no conceivable way that they could overlook this. She started panting, frantically searching for the switch, or button-

Cealth.

-or lever, or dial-

Cealth!

-or WHATEVER the stupid thing which would let her take off was!

Perhaps you could stop panicking for two minutes and start listening to me.

You! Cealth audibly huffed with relief.

Yes, me! For Galex's sake child, stop panicking and listen to me! I built this ship!

You- what?

I designed it! A bunch of Manicarians built it. Hit the red button!

But isn't that normally-

-The one you aren't supposed to press, I know! But if you built a ship, you'd probably do exactly the same thing and make the most exciting one the launch!

Cealth punched the button furiously, and she heard a quiet moan from the cosmic owl, remarkably similar to the noise Soulth had made when she had punched him.

Do you mind not destroying my pride and joy? You barely needed to brush it...

Cealth opened her mouth to respond, only to be silenced by the immense acceleration of the vehicle, which pressed her into the seat as it tore past the gravity of the moon, the engines humming with a quiet, almost self-satisfied, tone, which told the driver quite clearly that any being who thought they could build something better was a puffed up, Melcharian-loving, Federation idiot.

The last reverse-Obligon slipped out across the stars, searching for every last one of the distorted, who had scattered after she had left their moon, predicting, quite correctly, that she would inform the Starswallowers of their location. With the detached emotional efficiency of a being who knows what they must do is right, if monstrous, she began eliminating each and every single distorted she found and, as a by-product, gaining an unwanted reputation as the universe's deadliest assassin. Forty high profile targets were eliminated, each secretly a possessing, genocidal distorted-Obligon. Under the cosmic owl's guidance, and with initial reluctance, she collected the bounties on them, using the money to upgrade her ship and to hide her face from the Starswallowers who she inadvertently ended up working for several times as they rewarded her Federation kills.

The two strategized together often, planning how Cealth would destroy the Distorted, working out which politicians were suspiciously efficient and destroying the distorted within, and, finally, finding a way for the cosmic owl to return to a body- his own having been eliminated a decade before in the detonation of Sandros 6. It took decades, but she had eventually succeeded. Starthur's shell, as the body of a Starswallower, was the perfect home after she had eliminated Outh.

By this point, Jath and Exath were both working for her, obeying her every command- even if they did have to bicker about it with one another first. Starthur, the Starswallower turned distorted, was been sighted in his home quadrant- a situation made dangerous when Exath seemingly 'stole' Jath's sunglasses during the assassination, due to the Starswallower's ability to induce migraines in anyone who looked directly into their eyes in their quadrant. In actuality, Cealth had dropped a casual hint to Exath about stealing the Xsovzorite's sunglasses so that, after she'd eliminated the distorted, she could return the cosmic owl to a body without raising any eyebrows- Jath being partially blinded by his migraine, Exath a little too dense to realise what was truly happening.

Decades ago... this had been **decades** ago... it was a unit of time that lost significance after travelling to so many worlds. On some planets, they had such a slow orbit that a decade could last for two thousand Earthian years- while on a swift-spinning asteroid, a day could last mere minutes.

Earth. That had been a success too. Over two thousand of the distorted had decided to congregate on the blue ball of controversy; they'd heard that Galex would be visiting the planet with several hundred dignitaries and had leapt at the chance to possess him. Cealth had been there too- with a small univore that would destroy the core of Earth and detonate the planet. It would have taken too long to search every single one of the trillions of beings on the planet in the hopes of finding the two thousand distorted, and nobody would have listened to her warnings; after all, she *was* supposedly the most dangerous assassin in the universe. Why would anyone trust a wanted mass murderer?

She didn't relish saving Galex from them, but she blamed the deaths of her siblings on the actions of Reath- not on the Starswallowers. Besides, the consequences of Galex being possessed would be nightmarish- countless trillions of billions of minds erased in the blink of an eye.

Cealth's eyes opened sluggishly and she silently cursed. She had briefly gone into shock, losing who knew how many precious seconds that she could use to remain alive. One quick glance at the digital clock in the top left hand corner of the sparking helmet display remedied this, and she began a silent countdown.

Forty seconds. Cealth forced herself out of the reverie and made herself blink. It hurt. Good, her nerves were still working.

Thirty-five seconds. She struggled to her feet cautiously- too much exhilaration and she'd lose her last, precious breath- too little and she'd waste the tiny amount of time she had left.

Thirty seconds. She had to find a way to patch up her helmet- all the air was rushing out of the crack that the Glitchis had made when it kicked her.

Twenty-five seconds. Another ten seconds and she'd black out. Cealth removed the helmet, ignoring the sucking sensation of the vacuum around her face and examined the crack, cautiously.

Twenty seconds. She could feel her vital fluids boiling agonizingly inside her veins, but ignored the sensation, glaring at the split as she pushed the two sides of the crack together- it looked like a street after a planet-quake.

Nineteen seconds. Cealth's conscious mind started to float away, but her body kept squeezing the two sides of the split together.

Eighteen seconds. Cealth drew inwards with her face, forcing the particles of the split together. Her hands started to feel detached, as though they didn't belong to her- whether from cold or impending unconsciousness she couldn't tell.

Seventeen seconds. The pull she'd created with her face formed a vortex, the sides of the helmet being draw together by the pull. Another blink, her nerves too dead to protest this time.

Sixteen seconds. The helmet finally sealed itself- a tiny slit, about a hairs width in diameter, was still present, but that didn't as much matter.

Fifteen seconds. Cealth pulled the helmet on and felt herself losing consciousness even as the blast of Onyxian air hit her, pumped into the helmet by her suit.

Fourteen seconds. Cealth felt her body land softly on the meteor- or maybe she'd impacted it at terminal velocity; at this point her nerves couldn't really tell her.

Thirteen seconds. The whistling of the few particles of air her face didn't absorb fell on deaf ears- she'd passed out by this point, her body conserving energy. She'd use less air up this way.

Twelve seconds. If she'd been human, her biology would've let her down by now- her blood would've reached boiling point, the moisture on her tongue would've evaporated and her lungs, starved of air, would've collapsed inwards.

Eleven seconds. As if it was any consolation, the vacuum of space was an excellent preserver; no being's body could be destroyed by the ravages of time, and it would still exist thousands of years later.

Ten seconds. Her brain had now begun to shut itself down alongside her conscious mind, to save as much air as it could, her other systems trying to continue with their normal functions despite the dwindling supplies.

Nine seconds. Few beings realise how hungry a machine the multicellular body is- it eats through over six billion breaths in a lifetime, thirty thousand gallons of water and well over seventy thousand kilograms of food- and that's just for a human.

Eight seconds. But the body is intelligent- it knows that the brain controls the supplies it needs to function, so it sends it signals that *cannot* be ignored, and the brain responds.

Seven seconds. Every cell in the body has a designated function- all culminating in their attempts to keep the being they make up alive.

Six seconds. If the body is intelligent, then the brain is stupid; it forces the body into dangerous situations and then expects the body to get them out- which it *usually* does through pure instinct.

Five seconds. The body will always try to obey the brain- because without the brain, it cannot do anything; it would simply become an empty shell that would lose power and die.

Four seconds. It took billions of years for multicellular organisms to evolve- but then the brains started to appear and take control.

Three seconds. Before long, the body was beholden to the brain; but after a while, the brain realised that *it* didn't necessarily need its body.

Two seconds. The brains started to think- and as they thought, they realised how to live without their own bodies, and of ways to build and engineer better ones.

One second. But, you may question, if you can simply shed your body and move onto a new one, are you truly *yourself* anymore?

Chapter 21

"Starthur, you planet-crunching, species-betraying, Melcharian scum-slug! Get out here and face me with what little dignity you have left!" bellowed the cosmic overlord, feathers rippling aggressively as he spread his wings wide.

"I'm guessing you *don't* want to deal with that?" Jath asked the cosmic owl, casually hovering his foot over the light-speed accelerator.

"No- not now anyway." Sighed the cosmic owl, glancing at his old friend through Starthur's eyes.

"Right, well- EXATH, GET YOUR SEATBELT ON!" Jath turned to roar at his colleague.

"ALRIGHT, ALRIGHT!" Exath yelled back, hurrying into the cockpit. "I was just... taking a leak."

"Thanks for that." Jath nodded sardonically.

"Brace yourselves!" The cosmic owl cut in, firing the Celestelia's twin jet engines and watching Galex swoop out of the way of the pure white flames with admirable agility. "Have you prepped the engine for light speed?"

"Yes!" Jath snapped, exasperated. "I *have* done this before, funnily enough. Brace yourselves!" He pushed the accelerator down a centimetre, and the ship almost seemed to blur into its surroundings as it burst past the speed limitations of physics, exploding past the slightly stunned Galex, still trying to right himself after the twirling manoeuvre that'd sent him into a zero gravity spin.

"Nice ship!" the cosmic owl forced himself not to grin, knowing he'd be twice as likely to bite his tongue if he did.

"Thanks!" Jath shouted back. "Cost a ruddy fortune, especially after all the modifications!"

"Yes, I *was* wondering how it's capable of going so fast without shaking itself apart! Now, we should reach the next galaxy in- oh." The cosmic owl cut himself off, staring at the navigation instruments in alarm.

"What?"

"He's still following us." The cosmic owl said disbelievingly, twisting around in his seat to stare at Galex from out of one of the specially tinted one-way windows.

"Perfect!" Jath snarled, twisting the controls so the ship lurched terrifyingly, barely avoiding an oncoming comet. "Right, go make some friendship bracelets together."

"What?!"

111

"Have a picnic?! Go mad! Just get him away from my ship, I don't want droppings on the roof!"

"Whose ship?!" The cosmic owl squawked, deeply insulted. "*I* designed it!"

"And I improved it!" Jath growled back. "Now go distract him before I have to pull us out of light speed! I do *not* wanna do that until we've at least reached the democratic half of space!"

"Why?" Exath bellowed over the incensed howl of the engine.

"Galex can't touch us there!" The cosmic owl called back, then paused, thinking for a few moments. "Well, unless he's had a few skullsplitters..."

"GET YOUR ANATOMICALLY CORRECT HEAD OUT HERE!" the trio winced as the voice was remotely transmitted through their universal translators.

"Well... okay he *can* touch us there then." The cosmic owl sighed. Then, in response to Exath's eyebrow raise- "Federation law doesn't apply to the intoxicated. Little known loophole Galex and I found years ago. They used to ban alcohol, so the law still assumes that all drunk beings are from the Starswallower half of space, and therefore don't fall under democratic jurisdiction."

"Excellent time for a history lesson!" Jath barked, lifting his foot off the accelerator a fraction. The ship slowed drastically- now it was only cruising at 335 million miles per hour- and Jath braked slightly before turning to the cosmic owl. "Right, get out."

"Sorry?!" The Starswallower blinked.

"You heard me! Go distract him!" Jath jerked his head towards the airlock.

"Why me?!"

"I'm the pilot- and also the only one with reflexes sharp enough to pilot this space bus, so don't try to take my place- Exath wouldn't last two seconds against Galex- oh, and you're the only one of us **who can breathe in space**."

"Oh."

"Yeah!"

"I hate it when my superior genes work against me."

"Get moving, or I'll eject you!" Barked Jath. The cosmic owl scowled at him, then his expression relaxed, his face becoming totally blank. Inside his head- or rather, Starthur's head- he was utilising a small animalistic gene he still possessed from the days when his pigeon ancestors had waddled around on Earth; their inability to feel fear, even when confronted with something large and toothsome, finally becoming useful.

The cosmic owl strolled to the airlock with worrying nonchalance, swept open the door, loped into the small chamber, and then took off the second that the exterior door opened, falling out into the vacuum of space and feeling the weird, all-encompassing silence of the void sweep over him.

"HI! WHAT'S UP?!" Galex roared with surprising aggression at the cosmic owl, who'd sped up to fly alongside his former friend.

"Oh, not much." The cosmic owl replied casually.

"DETONATED ANY GIANT ROCKS IN *MY* SECTOR RECENTLY?!"

"As a matter of fact, no."

"THEN WHY HAVE YOU BEEN RUNNING LIKE A SPRINTER SINCE I ASKED THE FIRST TIME?!"

"Cardio."

"..." Galex's brain stopped working. His mouth opened obediently, but no golden comeback fell out of it. "Uh?"

"It's good for you," the cosmic owl said, casually. "You ought to try it at some point."

"What am I doing right now?!"

"Flying under the speed of light?"

"Yeah!"

"And you're already out of breath, aren't you?"

"My breath is literally circulating around me Starthur! How can I be out of it?!"

"You're unfit."

"Sorry?!" Galex spluttered, staring at the cosmic owl, who was casually flying sideways next to him.

"You've been augmented, yes, but your biological half is shamefully under-equipped." Nodded the cosmic owl sadly. *Very nice job on the mechanical augmentations though. Whoever they put in charge of that isn't doing half bad.*

"I- what... since when did *you* talk to *me* like that?!"

Should I tell him? I am *supposed to be distracting him, so why not?* The cosmic owl swallowed, cautiously, then replied. "Ever since I transferred my mind into Starthur's body."

"You're a parasite!" Galex cried enthusiastically, taking advantage of the lack of gravity and flipping over onto his back, his wings beating in slow motion, accelerating him smoothly. "I *knew* the brain parasites would come for me one day! *They* didn't believe me!"

"What?" Frowned the cosmic owl. Then he shook his head, glaring at Galex. "No, you moron, I'm Neutroby."

Galex blinked. "Aren't you dead?"

"Yes- no- kind of. It's a long story. I was absorbed on Sandros 6 by Cealth, my original body was destroyed in the explosion of the planet, and as such I couldn't return to it, so, far more recently, Cealth absorbed a distorted-Obligon out of Starthur's body and inserted my mind into it."

The supreme galactic overlord grinned aggressively. "So you *are* dead, you old so and so! How've you been?"

"Did you even listen to a word I just said? How much have you drunk?" Neutroby asked, genuinely concerned.

Galex grinned manically. "Let me put it this way- I just had some upgrades, my atmos' got siphoned off and the only way to get it back without wasting a ton of time re-visiting those planets-"

"-Was to essentially breathe it in as soon as your doctor left the room." The cosmic owl finished, disapprovingly. "Why did I ever think it was a good idea to tell you about that?"

"There was a LOT of ethanol in that cloud."

"I need you sober!" snapped the cosmic owl. "I'm trying to have a serious conversation with you!"

"What's death like?" Galex asked, casually.

"I'm not dead, you idiot!"

"How am I an idiot?" Galex blinked in surprise. "I thought that was quite a reasonable question."

"It's a term of endearment."

"News to me."

"Look- I can't talk to you while you're drunk."

"Is this a ghost-y thing?"

"Apparently it's a Galex-y thing. Just... follow me."

"I can't right now," Galex smiled dreamily. "I kind of have to do this thing- I'm chasing some assassins who're probably going to try and destroy the Galaxian dynasty, hope you understand."

"Good Galex..." muttered the cosmic owl. "'The Galaxian dynasty', is that really what we're calling ourselves now?"

"Yes!" smiled Galex, glancing at the cosmic owl. "Actually, I think it was your idea, Starthur."

"I'm not Starthur."

"You look like a Starthur."

"As I told you not ten seconds ago," The cosmic owl scowled, rapidly losing patience. "I. Am. Not. Starthur! I'm Neutroby!"

"Neutron Toby..." drawled Galex, examining the smaller Starswallower with one lazy eye. "I remember when we hatched, and you wanted to be called Stormageddon. Or was that Vedr... vedrfln..."

"Vedrfolnir?"

"That's the one. Such a stupid name, his mother always was weird..."

"Galaxy Alex, are you going sentimental?"

"I blame Revlar." Nodded Galex. "Why've they gotta have a planet in the middle of an ethanol cloud? It's just WEIRD!"

"Says the essentially immortal, cyborg bird-hybrid covered in atmosphere."

"Touché." Nodded Galex, sleepily. "I've always wanted to say that. Never understood what it meant though, the Dorians refuse to translate it."

"Does that matter?"

"No." Galex yawned. Then he frowned, looking around and spinning momentarily on the spot as a result. "Where's that ship gone?"

"Away." The cosmic owl frowned. "And they were meant to wait for me."

"For Galex sake!" Barked the supreme galactic overlord, causing the cosmic owl's muscles to twitch instinctively. "Well what's the point in pretending to be drunk if my targets just slipped away?!"

"You... were pretending?"

"Never crossed your mind, did it?!"

"No." Admitted the cosmic owl, truthfully.

"Now what's all this rubbish about being Neutroby? And more to the point... where's Cealth?"

"I *am* Neutroby, Galex."

"And I'm the cosmic swan." Snapped Galex. "Let's talk this out down there," he nodded towards a small asteroid rocketing towards them. "My wings are getting tired."

"I told you." Muttered the cosmic owl. "Cardio."

"Shut up."

Chapter 22

For centuries, Doria had been a neutral planet- one of only three in the entire universe protected by a treaty preventing their seizure, either by the Federation or the Starswallowers- although this trio's number had been reduced to one by the recent seizure of Revlar by the Federation and Pangol by the Starswallowers.

The Dorian's home planet remained unclaimed by both sides of the political spectrum; an entirely necessary measure, as its inhabitants, the unnervingly intelligent Dorians, were more than capable of bringing down whichever faction upset them. Centuries ago, the Dorians had been 'discovered' by a ship of Yarflargian Federation soldiers- who'd initially mistaken the (then incomprehensible) Dorians as some kind of cattle, due to their slightly bovine appearances.

Decades had passed, with each generation of Dorians being told the same tales of butchery that had been visited on their species, until, one fateful day, the extra-terrestrial settlers who'd feasted on the Dorians for so long had simply vanished. Of course, the Federation had swiftly retaliated, sending wave after wave of troops to attack the dwarf planet- all of whom had vanished, the same way the initial Yarflargian settlers had.

Finally, the Federation were forced to sign a peace treaty with the defensive little world- and, to aid negotiations, the first universal translator was constructed by the Dorians. Stunned at the intelligence of a species previously only valued for the flavour of their meat, the Federation agreed to leave the Dorians alone. News of the treaty had reached the Starswallowers, who decided that, if the Federation didn't want the planet, they'd better have it instead. The first assault was a massacre. So were the second, third, optimistic fourth and desperate fifth attempts. No one, not even the hatchling cosmic owl, could quite understand how a species from such a far-flung galaxy could be so dangerous.

Eventually the Starswallowers were also forced into signing a treaty, realising the benefits of the universal translator as they did so. Gradually, every species in the universe began to wear universal translators- any creature seen without one wedged firmly into a hearing orifice would be laughed out of every social group- not that the translator lacking individual would recognise the alien sounds as laughter.

At the push of a button, the Dorians had the power to bring any species to its metaphorical knees; turning off their universal translators would force them to learn the languages of the trillions of other species in their respective half of the universe in order to communicate. In fact, the universe as a whole had become so dependent on the universal translators that the Dorians had swiftly become one of the richest races in the cosmos- and many considered them the unofficial third group of rulers in the universe, alongside the Starswallowers and Federation in terms of power and influence.

The last time that a race had upset the Dorians, they'd been isolated, ostracised and had mysteriously faded from history, until even the name of their race had been forgotten to time- leading to the well-known, universally understood piece of advice, ceremonially spoken before any deals were brokered, any treaties signed, anywhere in the Universe; never upset a Dorian.

The Nebula Eater hovered inconspicuously in orbit above the marble-purple surface of Doria, drawing no attention from the criss-crossing lines of space traffic pouring into and out of the planet's atmosphere- although the luxurious model parked with mathematical precision right next to it likely had more to do with this than the overall incognito appearance of the ramshackle Nebula. The conspicuous model in question was the Celestelia- and, as any casual passer-by could notice, the vessel had been magnificently upgraded, with speed, quality and elegance prioritised over the sheer cost of the vessel.

Jath and Exath had left the Celestelia two hours before, in response to a hail from the Nebula, when a highly intense Dorian had demanded that the two of them came aboard the ship, first assuring them that the space pirate's vessel had complete diplomatic immunity while in orbit around the planet below them. Jath had been suspicious at first, believing the arrival of the space pirates to be too good to be true, but the promise of diplomatic immunity, and essential protection from both maniacal sides of the universe for a few hours was too good an opportunity to pass up.

Ten minutes after the hail had ended, the Xsovzorite and the Manicarian had donned atmospheric bubbles, concealed Cellsplitters below their clothing and entered the Nebula through the ship's airlock, Jath preparing for any negative outcome of the meeting, Exath simply planning to use the Xsovzorite as a shield if the need arose. The door to the airlock had been opened by a slightly scowling human, who'd ushered the duo into a rounded common room, where a lime-skinned Horizor had risen to great them.

"I'm Captain Tungsten of the space pirates." She stated, shaking Jath's hand so firmly he'd winced. "Welcome aboard my ship."

"Thanks," Jath said, awkwardly. "But before your hail, I was under the impression that we'd got here... um... unnoticed."

'In *that* ship?" Sam raised an eyebrow quizzically.

Exath snorted- he'd told Jath on numerous occasions that the Celestelia, with its glowing white and gold colouration, was far too obvious to be the vessel for a legendary assassin.

"It *was* a relatively stealthy entrance." Tungsten said soothingly, once the snickering coming from Exath's direction had died down. "But we've been looking for your vessel for the last ten Dorian days, so we weren't about to allow you to simply get past us."

"Ten *days*?!" Jath yelped. "But... Ce- I mean, the *boss*- only told us where we were going yesterday! How in the name of Galex did you know where we were going before we did?"

"Simple." Tungsten shrugged. "Auren- the Dorian who hailed you just now- met with Cealth a few days ago on Onyx and arranged that you'd meet us here after Cealth had discovered who was behind the detonation of Earth. I thought she would've told you. She said you'd have a Starswallower with you who'd explain everything?"

"Uh..." Jath suddenly felt very uncomfortable, despite the luxurious memory foam sofa that he'd been reclining on.

"Jath kind of ejected-" started Exath before being cut off by a tactical coughing fit from the Xsovzorite in question.

"He's out hunting!" blurted Jath.

"Really?" Sam snorted again, with undisguised distain. "I've come up with better excuses in my cryostasis!"

"Sam, they can't understand sarcasm. Their respective species are physically incapable of using it. It's tragic, I know."

"I can." Jath said weakly. Everybody ignored him.

"Shame." Yawned the human. "Oh, by the way, Nix needs you up at the bridge. Something about an asteroid." She shrugged. "Dunno if it's the 'world destroying' kind or just the 'move a few inches out of the way' type, though."

"Fun," said Tungsten, getting to her feet slowly. "I'll go and see. Oh, and Sam? Can you find out what their *actual* excuses are?" she gestured at Jath and Exath.

"Yeah," nodded Sam eagerly. "Permission to throw them out the airlock if their lies aren't good enough?"

"Yeah, sure." said Tungsten, her expression completely passive- at least as far as everyone but Sam (who could see the slight change in her captain's pigmentation indicating the Horizor was feeling particularly smug) could tell.

"Right!" Barked Sam, causing both men to jump, slamming both hands onto the table as Tungsten left the room. "Where on Earth did you two leave that Starswallower?!"

"Well... not on Earth," Frowned Exath.

"I know that!" She snapped. "It's a saying! God... why does nothing *ever* translate correctly?"

"Would you like me to account for the individual sayings of around four trillion species as *well* as providing simultaneous, accent-less translations?" Auren said, walking silently into the room behind Sam, whose previously slouched posture suddenly became erect. "What are you doing in here with these... *people?*"

"Interrogating them! Tung- err- the Captain said I could!"

"Really?" Auren said, frowning. "Have they told you anything so far?"

"Well I'd only just started to question them, so-"

"Sam," said Auren. "How many times must I remind you- communication and interrogations are *my* department, not yours."

"I still don't get that," Sam muttered, pulling the Dorian aside. "You're the *chef!* How can you be the interrogator too?"

"Because I am a Dorian, and unlike your... species... we can have more than one speciality."

"What's that pause supposed to mean?!"

"You know just as well as I how violent humans are. That pause means that you need to stop arguing with me, return to your cabin and do so before you make us look unprofessional."

"I *am* professional! I just... know how to relax."

'Which proves my point that *I* am the only person aboard this vessel qualified to perform this task. Not you. Now go away." And with that, the Dorian turned (smiling a little too self-contentedly as Sam left the cabin) back to her 'guests'.

'I apologise for my... colleague. She becomes improper when she gets excited."

'Mm." Muttered Jath, uncomfortably aware that this was his social nightmare-isolated from his boss and stuck in a room with *Exath* and a Dorian. The

120

Manicarian himself remained uncharacteristically quiet- he could feel the tension in the air weighing down on them like a quintillion-ton atmosphere.

"Now then," Auren said, voice now placid but totally devoid of emotion. "I believe that I know what happened out in space. *Don't* correct me if I'm wrong, because this course of action would be remarkably bad for your health." She paused to adjust a tiny control disk implanted in her universal translator, effectively rendering Jath and Exath incomprehensible to each other, while not restricting flawless communication between the individuals and herself.

"Approximately ten days ago, having been pursued by the Supreme Galactic Overlord across several galaxies, you engaged a light-speed drive. When this too failed to outrun Galex, you employed the Starswallower, whom you were transporting, as a decoy- and all to reach this world without pursuit," She paused again, this time using a small inbuilt touchscreen in the arm of the sofa she was reclining on to order a thermos of r'hom; the Dorian equivalent of a warm coffee. Then she continued, with a slightly harder edge to her voice. "It would seem that Cealth failed to instruct you two to deliver the Starswallower to us upon arrival. This is most unfortunate- not for her, of course, as she is not present- but for you two. Regrettable in the extreme.

"Now there are three courses of action available to me as a result of your foolhardiness; I could allow you to 'fetch' the Starswallower, but I have a feeling that, even if I were to hold one of you captive, you would not return to this vessel now that you have a chance to be rid of your colleague forever. I could request that Captain Tungsten steers the Nebula to the last known co-ordinates of the Starswallower, but this would place this vessel and all aboard in unnecessary danger of being Galexed, and would, in any case, be a fruitless search, due to the fact that we would be attempting to find a being which can move at light speed and was last seen engaging in combat with the most powerful entity in the Starswallower's half of the Universe. This leaves me with option three- expel you from the air lock as a warning to your employer when she comes looking for you.

"NOPE!" Barked Exath, springing to his feet. "**Not** happening! I need air!"

"Calm down." Snapped Jath, glaring at his colleague and remaining seated, hearing only a meaningless string of gasps issuing from the panicking, now unintelligible, Manicarian in place of speech. "I think she's joking."

Exath, for his part, didn't understand a single utterance from the deep, consonant-heavy dialect that Jath was using either.

The Dorian raised a single fold of flesh above her eye that may, in some parts of the galaxy, have been considered an eyebrow.

"I'm glad we understand one another." She muttered to Jath in fluent Xvzodghorian.

"You speak my language?" Jath frowned. "That's nice to know. It'll be a real kick in the teeth for any linguistics butchers back home."

The Dorian shrugged. "I don't like people challenging the intellect of the Dorians. Your people claimed to have invented an incomprehensible language- we went ahead and programmed it into the Universal Translators. We have received no complaints from them as of yet."

"I'll bet," muttered Jath. "Do you even *have* a complaints department?"

"Not anymore," replied the Dorian with a thin-lipped smile. "It was annexed shortly after the Earthian lawsuit. The other species in our solar system deemed it 'unnecessary'. The majority of Dorians agreed." Auren paused and sipped her r'hom with blatant nonchalance. It was a struggle to keep her expression neutral; one gulp of r'hom enhanced the drinker's sensory abilities to the point where they could read a single speck of dust like a braille novel.

"So, what happens now?" Jath frowned, glancing at Exath's continuing hysterics with obvious distaste. "Cealth would probably know where Galex would take the Starswallower and be able to plot a course to locate him."

"So where *is* your boss?" The Dorian asked casually, her eyes flicking momentarily to Jath's. "I assume she had business which prevented her from being here in person."

"Yeah," muttered Jath. "Something like that."

"You are loyal, and I appreciate that- it is a quality rarely found in these uncivilised times," Acknowledged Auren. "However, you cannot suggest something like this without expecting me to want more details. That would be unrealistic. Don't forget about my third suggestion."

Jath gritted his teeth. "I am *trying* to contain all my organs- something which would be next to impossible in that vacuum," he nodded out of one of the windows overlooking the glorious whitish-blue star that Doria was orbiting. "But I *really* don't want to betray my boss. Look, just trust me enough to go collect her. I'll bring you back the Starswallower, and we can both go away happy."

"How long would this take?" Auren mused, tracing the rim of the r'hom thermos with a single taloned finger. "The space pirates have *other* commitments outside of hovering in orbit."

"You want to find out who detonated Earth though, right?"

"Personally? No, not particularly."

"What?"

"Sam came from Earth, so naturally she would quite like to catch the culprit, and, regrettably, she and our captain are somewhat... close." Auren drummed her fingers on the arm of the sofa irritably (it was after a few moments of this that Jath recognised the tune of *Colossus*, the Space Pirates' latest hit, and internally smiled) then seemed to come to a decision and sat up straighter.

"Ok, Xsovzorite. I-" But she was cut off as the ship abruptly lurched to port, the lights flickered ominously, and the artificial gravity failed. Auren flew backwards off the sofa, the thermos fell open and the r'hom contained within began a leisurely trip upwards, pooling in mid-air into an opaque, vaguely green bubble. Jath instinctively extended his claws and latched onto a surface that, once, might have been the floor. He glanced over at Exath, just to ensure that the idiot hadn't hit his head on the wall- or rather... ceiling. Exath's eyes were closed, his jaw set, and for a horrible, lurching moment, Jath worried that the Manicarian was about to be sick. Then his eyes opened, and the lurching feeling intensified.

Exath's pupils were dilated, and the irises suddenly divided- a hundred rings of varying shades suddenly rolling away from one another as he landed on the floor- the actual floor, not the ceiling- of the spinning vessel and stayed there, anchored by some incomprehensible force as he grinned at Jath with undisputed menace.

Chapter 23

"So... you're Neutroby?"

"That *is* what we just established, yes Galex."

"And... you've been my secretary for the last few decades."

"Correct."

Galex shook his feathered head for a few moments, then ran his eyes up and down Starthur's body. "Why?"

Neutroby shrugged. "Would you've believed me, or told me to shut up?"

"I meant why are you so skinny?!"

The cosmic owl closed his eyes and mentally quashed the headache arising behind his eyes. "I was a secretary, Galex. The salary is *quite* different from what I was used to. Planning meals on a budget is not my speciality."

"Yeah, fair point." Nodded Galex. Then he hesitated, a look of guilt flashing across his face for a very brief moment. "So, if the reverse-Obligons really were telling the truth about the distorted..."

"...Yes?"

"I committed genocide. For no good reason." Galex polished his beak uncomfortably, with a single wing. The feelings of guilt that he'd held down for so long were getting worryingly close to the surface. "I suppose I'll have to live with that now."

"You'd detonated planets before then."

"No, I hadn't." Galex snapped, rounding on the cosmic owl with rapidity befitting one of the only creatures capable of travelling at light speed. "They were all stunts- Starswallower publicity demanded that I be a ruthless tyrant who ruled through fear, so I pretended to conform. I pretended to detonate worlds on a whim for years- but then we arrived on Sandros 6 and everyone expected me to do it out of retaliation for your death. They were shouting it, and I just did it without thinking about... well. I can't change what happened."

"You can make up for it." Neutroby said, quietly. "Cealth's the last survivor of her race, and she's been trying to exterminate every last one of the distorted-Obligons for decades; the least we can do is try to help."

"Where is she?" Galex said, quietly, his wings already out in anticipation of a swift light.

"The exit to the universe." Neutroby said quietly. "She wanted to destroy the last distorted there, so she'd be away from anything else it could possess."

"How the... how did she even get co-ordinates?" Galex spluttered. "After what happened to the Obligons, I had it covered up! Galex knows we didn't need more of those light-mutants running around!"

"We... may have had to kidnap Vedrfolnir and borrow his memory."

"And that was the only reason for his kidnapping?" frowned Galex, folding his wings back unconsciously.

"No. We thought he was being possessed by a distorted."

"And was he?"

"Well... we had really strong evidence, but... well not as such, no in the end. Cealth momentarily drained his mind before dropping him off next to Cygnus, and there was no trace of a distorted in his memories."

"I meant to ask- is that *really* the technical name?" asked Galex. "Distorted?"

"Unless..." continued the cosmic owl, bluntly ignoring Galex as a horrible possibility opened to him. "It transferred itself from the cosmic hawk to something else before we landed on-" he froze, suddenly remembering a tiny detail Cealth had mentioned, when filling him in on how their journey to Cygnus had gone. *'A very smooth journey.'* She'd said. *'Well, apart from Exath's unfortunate failure to go to the toilet in plenty of time. By the time Jath and I attempted to disembark, he was floating beside the cosmic hawk next to the only facility on board. We had to revive him before we could attempt to land.'*

"What if the distorted had transferred itself to Exath?"

"Who?"

"One of Cealth's colleagues. You would've seen him at Bar Aquila."

"The little Manicarian? That seems unlikely," shrugged Galex. "Besides, I spoke to Vedr... Vedrofolnof... Ver... damn it! The cosmic hawk! I spoke to him a few days ago. Didn't you say their minds were deleted when a distorted took possession of them?"

"Well, yes, but *we're* partially cybernetic, Galex. After what happened, the cosmic dove ensured that the biological minds of every cosmic Starswallower perform regular backups to digital storage, so if his mind *was* deleted, the system would've restored it as soon as the distorted left. It's a pity the lower classes like Starthur didn't get the same treatment..."

"Hang on." Galex said, holding up his hands to stop Neutroby going off on a tangent. "You're getting carried away, and I'm *very* confused right now. This is all just speculation, right? This whole 'lackey is possessed' theory only works if the cosmic hawk was possessed in the first place, and I *really* doubt that."

"Like I said," the cosmic owl ruffled his feathers nervously. "We had strong evidence. We saw his irises-"

"Sorry?"

"If you get possessed, your irises multiply. They split- it's a very strange phenomenon that I was hoping to study, if we ever managed to catch one of them." The cosmic owl waved his hand dismissively. "We saw it on a broadcast- I thought it was a trick of the light initially, but Cealth saw it too."

"Hang on," Galex barked. "When would he have even been possessed in the first place?"

"I don't know!" Neutroby sighed furiously. "The first time we saw the irises change was on an illegal Livestream from the Federation half of the Universe- we *wanted* to investigate, but there were a ludicrous number of space police, and Cealth couldn't sneak the Celestelia past them."

"Well we're in the Federation half of space now," Galex grinned at the cosmic owl. "If you're right about the Manicarian, I'll take you to Draconis."

"Counter proposal." Snapped the cosmic owl, muscles tensing as he prepared to take off. " *You* investigate- you're the one who can teleport after that upgrade- and *I* will try to find the Celestelia and Exath before the distorted reveals itself and starts attacking everything. Also... don't take me to Draconis. The service is awful. Take me to S'rou."

"That doesn't sound like fun." Frowned Galex. "Why don't *I* try and find the Cealth-ites?"

"Galex! The Distorted **want** to possess members of authority and, much as it pains me to admit it, **you** are the Supreme Galactic Overlord. I'm just some dust-coloured secretary. If you go showing up around one, it'll jump on you and your mind will be destroyed before you have a chance to realise what happened!" And before Galex could come up with a better argument, the cosmic owl took off and launched himself back towards to Starswallower quadrant of space, aiming directly for Doria.

Galex glanced around the asteroid for a few moments- it was nothing special, just a 16 mile long hunk of ice and rock that'd been floating through space for billions of years. Then he spread his wings, each measuring nine feet in length, and took off, stirring up a tiny quantity of the dusty surface which was then pulled back by the asteroid's miniscule gravitational field.

Chapter 24

The security of the DPEB's headquarters was laughable to a Starswallower. Galex shot through the irregular gravitational fields as though they weren't even there, teleporting a few thousand light years at a time to fine-tune his new ability. By the time he reached the tiny space station that comprised the 'democratic' headquarters, he was almost bored. The laser weapons that had been fired at him would never have been a danger to him even *before* he'd acquired teleportation-the majority of the beams simply missed him (due to the ludicrous speed he was travelling) and the few blasts that actually hit could barely get through the thick atmosphere surrounding him; by the time they did, all he felt was a slightly warm breeze.

He landed on the docking platform, rolled his eyes at the camera pointing at him from what was clearly supposed to be a hidden position, then poked the intercom.

"Have you made an appointment?"

"Yes." Galex said confidently- it wasn't as though the machine would actually check.

"Name?"

Damn. Thought Galex. *A machine that* actually *does its job.*

"Galex Nallim Cam, ruler of about three more sectors than the Federation."

There was a pause *just* long enough for Galex to start feeling uncomfortable, then the intercom responded, "Please proceed to the waiting room on level thirty-six, the Democratic Peoples Elected Bloke will be with you shortly."

"Thanks." Galex nodded, silently making a mental note to destroy the overly efficient AI on his way out- you didn't want them to get too confident, it'd only lead to a robot uprising.

He wasn't impressed with the décor- there was no theme and it looked as though the only design decision had been to find the cheapest furniture in the universe, then buy it *ALL*. He stumbled along pasty corridors until he found himself in an entirely generic waiting room, filled with too many (mismatched) chairs, a plastic plant and, to complete the room of stereotypes, contained a receptionist who never looked up, and continued to type *Star war and peace* into her computer even after he'd cleared his throat. Eventually, he gave up trying to attract her attention and instead started testing each chair in the room- some were overly yielding, others felt as though they'd been stuffed with living Melcharian sludge. Finally, he stretched his wings and accidentally knocked over a decorative vase of coins with a hideous crash. Still the receptionist didn't look up.

After literally three hours, the DPEB strolled into the room, then froze as he saw the looming, eight foot Starswallower.

"Galex!"

"M'ron." Nodded Galex.

"I- uh... didn't expect- uh that is..."

"You invaded Revlar, M'ron." Galex said, strolling over to the two-foot tall DPEB and casting a huge shadow over him. "Now, I'd like to work this out in a calm, reasonable manner, which is why I haven't already detonated this base."

"Look," the DPEB started, raising his hands in a half-placating, half-panicky gesture. "It was a legitimate loophole in the treaty- and you!" he raised a shaky finger. "You invaded Pangol!"

"Yup," Galex said casually. "It's called retaliation. Maybe you should try it some time. Now then, don't you have some sort of office? It's not *polite* to keep your guests waiting. Even in the waiting room."

"And it's not *wise* to invite mass murderers into your home!" barked the DPEB, sounding far braver than he felt. Not for the first time, he wished he was just a few feet taller. Not *that* much, not enough to insult his ancestors, but tall enough to stop half the species he'd met laughing at him behind his back.

"Are you calling me a murderer?" Galex leant closer to the DPEB and whispered, "My universal translator's on the fritz."

"YES!" snapped the DPEB. "Yes, you are a murderer! And your translator's probably failing because you're too stupid to know not insult a Dorian!"

Galex raised a tuft of feathers, which *might* have once constituted an eyebrow. "At least I do my own dirty work. You just swan about claiming you're a great, elected leader. I've never heard a bigger load of rubbish, and I recently heard the Darstday speech you made on your home planet!"

"Let's take this into my office!" snapped the DPEB, his face turning a strange (but visually pleasing) furious shade of heliotrope.

While the two universal leaders were squabbling, several thousand light years away the cosmic owl was nearing Doria- when something smashed into him and knocked him into orbit around a desolate gas giant. Blinking the dazed spots out of his eyes he was became aware of the strange outline of a Glitchis (whose eyes abruptly

129

became visible as the orbit of the gas giant took them to the sunny side of the planet) and whose many irises rolled furiously in all directions.

"*You tricked me!*" Reath hissed, staring at Neutroby in disbelief.

"Yeah, about that," Neutroby swallowed, examining the distorted cautiously.

"*Soulth just told me!*" He said. "*You're not my only ally! We're not the last ones!*"

"Uh... yeah." *Hell.* Thought the cosmic owl. *Exath's a distorted, and Cealth didn't kill the Glitchis. But at least Galex owes me a trip to S'rou when this is all over.*

"*Why are you still in that puny vessel? I was told that you were last seen chasing the supreme galactic overlord- or have you lost him?*" the Reath's eyes narrowed suspiciously.

"I thought you wanted to possess him anyway," Neutroby responded, evading the question clumsily.

"*You lost him didn't you?*" countered Reath, instantly getting the conversation back on track.

"Yeah," glowered Neutroby, trying to give a convincing performance. "But he *was* travelling at the speed of light. Did you have better luck with Cealth?"

"*What do you think?*" Snorted Reath. "*Of course, I did! Even as we speak, her body has frozen in the vacuum of this plain.*"

"Congratulations," nodded the cosmic owl. *Hell!* He internally screamed.

"*We must regroup with our brother and prepare another assault to capture Galex.*" the Glitchis had already turned away from him, its eyes scanning the distant stars for its next location. "*I can only hope that Soulth's remergence is evidence for the survival of others like ourselves. Earth's devastation was... monstrous for us. I'd hoped that she wouldn't blow up such a life-filled planet, but...*"

"Cealth had a tougher shell than we thought."

"*Hmm?*" The Reath glanced at him. "*Have you been picking up Galaxian expressions?*"

"Yeah," nodded Neutroby, scrambling to cover his slip up. "Side effect of living on Cygnus."

The Glitchis looked at him almost pityingly. "*It's a struggle to retain your individuality after passing through so many minds, isn't it? Still, soon enough we will no longer have to worry about that.*"

"Listen Galex, I do NOT know what you were thinking, invading Pangol, but I assure you, the Federation can and *will* sue!" the DPEB was shouting.

"Then I'll hire a Xvzodghorian lawyer." Galex drawled, glancing longingly at the various bottles of liquor artistically arranged behind the DPEB's desk. "It shouldn't take too long to win that lawsuit. Your prosecutor will be throwing in the towel in minutes."

"Well, if you're so confident you could win, then why are you here?" snapped the DPEB, uncomfortably aware of Starswallower's fondness for drink, and determined to protect his personal stash.

"I didn't come here to talk about politics," Galex growled, and the DPEB's heart sank. "Or lawsuits. I've been doing some digging- hardly one of my usual pastimes, but in this case it was necessary- and I discovered some rather incriminating footage of you speaking with a certain... distorted individual."

"What?" snapped the DPEB, adjusting the height of his chair while his brain buzzed in alarm.

"If you don't want people to discover your secrets, maybe don't leave them alone in a room with internet access for three hours!" Galex glared at his 'democratic' counterpart and felt a surge of irritation as his took in the Wex's pitiful form. "You schemed with one of those creatures to absorb the minds of some of my best friends- *and* my own. I like my mind M'ron!"

"Look-" started the DPEB, feeling around under his desk for a panic button.

"No." snapped Galex. "*You* look. Open your eyes! You've been played for a fool. Why would these creatures only want *my* half of the universe when they could easily have yours too?"

"Ah, but *I'm* their ally," smiled the DPEB pompously. "They need me to rule the universe."

"They need your body." Growled Galex. "What makes you think your *mind* means anything to them? As long as they had our faces, they could do whatever the heck they liked!"

The colour drained from the DPEB's face as he took in the truth of Galex's words. "But- we have a treaty!"

"*Do you?*" Galex snorted sardonically. "You mean a treaty like the ones *we* had concerning the three neutral planets?"

"Oh."

"Yeah." nodded Galex. "Now we can either sit here having a delightful chat about the end of our universe, or, alternatively, we could blow them to smoky smitherines."

"B-but for the love of light! This is all conjecture!" laughed the DPEB nervously. "I wouldn't trust you over them!"

"OH, FOR GALEX'S SAKE!" yelled Galex, slamming his fist onto the cheap desk so hard that it cracked like glass. "How stupid are you?!"

The DPEB trembled slightly, adrenaline rushing through him as his anger and terror smashed into one another in waves- but when he spoke it was with forced control. "You have given me no evidence for a pre-emptive strike against beings who have, up until this point, been entirely peaceful! Need I remind you that your usual 'strategy' consists of charging in and detonating a planet before its inhabitants can apologise for whatever imagined transgression they have committed?"

"YES!" barked Galex. "But *your* feeble excuses for armed brutality are hardly any better! Look at what you've already done to Revlar! It's ruined! There's rubbish everywhere and people are too scared to queue! On **Revlar!**"

"We fixed congestion!"

"You terrified people and then stole their booze!" Galex glared pointedly at the liquor arrangement behind M'ron. "Who died for your skullsplitters?!"

"Who died for yours?"

"And there's your problem!" snapped Galex. He gestured to the window, swatting a stream of dust aside as he did so. "You just write a few words on paper, parrot them to a camera and think you've convinced your people that everything's alright. I fly through the stars seeing the messes I've unintentionally made, and I try to fix them!"

"You're a dictator!" shouted M'ron, beside himself with rage and leaping to his feet. "You conquer planets!"

"SO DO YOU!" Bellowed Galex, bolting upright.

There was a moment of total silence as the two leaders glared at each other, then they both sank back into their chairs.

"What do you suggest we do? They could possess us at a glance, and then where would we be? They would win."

"Not me," smirked Galex, tapping his skull. "I've got a memory backup. Plus, if we fought them in *my* sector..." his eyes gleamed momentarily. "I have a certain genetic advantage."

"I can get roughly thirty thousand Yarflargians to the Lumina Brie sector," frowned M'ron, checking his computer. "I can also spare General Starre."

"*General?*" frowned Galex. "I thought it was commander. Please tell me there aren't two of them."

"No, no. I promoted her after her victory on Radelaine the other day."

"Where?"

"Delightful new planet discovered on the outskirts of the Lucidor system."

"Nice." Nodded Galex. *But I'm going to steal it from you later.*

"Thank you." Smiled M'ron. "I believe this most recent victory puts me ahead of you by a sector."

"Probably not. We captured Haulodor last week."

"The bug planet?"

"The very same!" Abruptly, Galex shook his head. "But anyway, we're getting off track. I could probably get all three thousand cosmic Starswallowers to fight them. There're only two Distorted after all."

"This is official then?" The DPEB swallowed uncertainly. "We're allies now?"

"For this one battle, yeah." Nodded Galex. "I don't know about you, but I quite like living."

"Me too." Agreed M'ron. "Then again, you'll outlive me by about four hundred years either way."

"That's biology for you," smiled Galex, although internally, he felt a small squeeze of sadness work its way into his mood. He'd miss having such an obtuse rival.

133

Chapter 25

The distorted within Exath had wasted no time in flitting from body to body, until every space pirate lay slumped on the floor, their minds simply erased from their brains- the bodies' hearts still pumped, they still breathed and blinked, but their memories, personalities, thoughts and feelings- everything that had comprised *them*- had been eliminated.

Jath alone was still aware, staring in panic at the Manicarian that had once been Exath, his irritating colleague and Cealth's only other confidant. He didn't move, but remained crouched on all fours, clinging to the roof and never letting his gaze wander from the distorted below.

"Y'know, it's funny," Soulth finally broke the silence *"I honestly planned to delete you first- but then again, I didn't count on your expression being* so priceless!" He laughed huskily, the intruder playing with Exath's vocal cords experimentally, as though testing their flexibility. *"I think we should probably keep you around for a bit. I've always wanted a pet."*

Jath's claws tightened, scraping down the roof as he clenched them in fury. "What the hell are you?" he snarled.

"Nobody's ever asked that before!" laughed the distorted, clapping its hands in slow, mocking sarcasm. *"I knew that I was right to keep you around, you're so creative!"*

Jath said nothing. He'd just watched that creature, whatever it was, tear through five other entities, all at least as skilled in combat as himself- six if he counted Exath. He wasn't about to destroy his chances of survival by irritating this... thing.

"I'm one of Cealth's- oh there are so many words for this in the Manicarian tongue! I'm an old enemy of hers- a nemesis, you could say. Or could you? I've never really studied your language before. For all I know, Xsovzorites only have one word for their worst nightmare."

"You seem excited."

*"I am! You have no **idea** how long I had to put with this idiot's personality! But I fooled both of you- even Cealth was taken in."* Soulth smiled slyly. *"She's been hunting my kind for years- every person she ever assassinated was one of us. I was honestly surprised you didn't know that- it seems she never thought you were important enough to know."*

"If Cealth's been hunting you for so long, why didn't you just take over our ship?" growled Jath. "I saw how quickly you killed these guys. Why didn't you take revenge on her when you had the chance?"

"*I haven't killed them. I just deleted their minds.*"

"Isn't that the same thing?"

"*Not to me.*" shrugged Soulth. "*I didn't take over your ship because, quite annoyingly, my possession doesn't affect Cealth, and the moment she realised what I was she would've shot me, no matter whose body I was in. That stubborn freak of nature doesn't form attachments any more. But then, you'd know that better than anyone.*"

Jath didn't respond immediately; under the fury invoked by the distorted's words, his brain had started to work furiously. Cealth had been unaffected by the distorted's powers... this thing had the same eyes as the Glitchis, so they were probably the same species... and Cealth had taken the Glitchis away, far away, apparently to kill it. If he could somehow get this thing to Cealth, maybe, just maybe, she could end its miserable life and... maybe get Exath back too.

"*Are you playing around?*" a second voice suddenly hissed it's way through the room, and Jath felt the fur on the back of his neck lift as terrified adrenaline raced through his veins. The Glitchis dropped into the room, glanced at the unconscious Space Pirates, and then flicked its eyes to indicate that a third figure should follow it into the vessel. Jath stiffened as a Starswallower, nearly seven feet tall, with neatly pruned feathers and sinister yellow eyes, followed it in. Their eyes met briefly, and, with a lurching sensation, he recognised Starthur's face.

Reath glanced at Jath briefly and frowned. "*Why is **that** still conscious?*"

"*I wanted a pet.*" shrugged Soulth, his irises bouncing as he moved. "*Call it a souvenir if you like. He had a brilliant expression on his face when he saw me.*"

"*Don't be a moron.*" Snapped the Glitchis- clearly *he* was the one in charge here. "*Cealth's dead. We don't need him for anything anymore.*"

"What?!" barked Jath, feeling a surge of warm blood rise through his veins as the two words punched through his eardrums. Before he knew what he was doing, he was propelling himself through the zero-gravity environment towards the Glitchis, his claws already extended in preparation *to slit the Melchar-wallower's throat!* Starthur tackled him before he could get close, and he hit the cabin's floor with a startled growl. He squirmed, trying to get up, only to be pinned firmly to the floor by the Starswallower's overly-heavy body.

"Stay down." Snapped the Starswallower. The Glitchis was smirking nastily.

"*I see what you mean.*" Reach nodded at Soulth. "*It does have a funny expression on its face.*"

Jath bared his teeth, squirming furiously to try and free himself. Nothing else mattered now- nothing other than avenging Cealth by slaughtering each and every one of these *freaks.* If only he'd had some form of natural poison like Exath had boasted of on multiple occasions, or some weird ability to knock out everyone in the vicinity like Cealth. Heck, he would've settled for his *sunglasses* at this point; at least they had pointed ends.

"We'll have to find some way to lure Galex here; personally, I recommend using Cealth's body. If he thinks she's killed everyone aboard, just like on Sandros 6, he's probably going to be angrier and not think things through." The Starswallower was saying.

"*I just came from her body!*" Growled the Reath. "*Why didn't you suggest this before?*"

"You can teleport." Pointed out the Starswallower. "It would quite literally take you one second."

Soulth poked Jath's face experimentally, then shrieked with laughter as he tried to bite the finger off.

"*Can you stop messing about?*" snapped the Glitchis, glowering at his immature nephew. "*Your laugh is intolerable in that body!*" Then to 'Starthur'- "*Alright, fine. We **are** assuming he still wants the truth about Earth's detonation, right?*"

"Don't worry about it, I sent him a message through the Dorian's universal translator. He said he'd be here 'in force' whatever that means." Nodded the Starswallower.

"*Right.*" Frowned the Reath. "*Well keep an eye on **that**,*" his eyes flicked to Jath, the irises trailing after the pupils. "*And I'll be back in a minute.*"

The Glitchis teleported and immediately Soulth poked Jath again.

"*So, when did you use the universal translator to contact the Dorian?*" the 'Manicarian' asked, casually resting his elbow on Jath's forehead. "*Back when we ejected you? I didn't see you wearing one.*"

"No," agreed the Starswallower. "That's probably because I wasn't." and with no further ceremony, the cosmic owl shot him. Soulth stared at Neutroby in disbelief for a brief second, then toppled over backwards with a resonating crash.

Neutroby released Jath, and for a moment, the Xsovzorite simply stood there in total shock.

"...Why?" he gulped. It was the only thing he could think of to ask.

Neutroby dusted the smoking end of the cellsplitter he was holding, frowning slightly as he spotted a stray particle resting on the barrel. "Because he was being a complete upstart," he shrugged. "Also, the fact that I'm not a distorted might have had something to do with the decision making process."

"A what?"

"Distorted. One of those mind-robbing parasites." He glanced at the Xsovzorite and noticed Jath peering at his irises.

"How can I trust you? Exa- the distorted controlling him- it was able to hide it's weird eyes."

"You mean besides the facts that I just killed it, and freed you?"

"Yeah, okay, fair point." Jath watched the Starswallower warily as he tossed Exath's body into a nearby cupboard. "What happens now?"

"I wasn't lying when I said I'd told Galex to come here," smiled the Starswallower, tightly. "He's heading towards this spot with around forty thousand of the universe's strongest inhabitants. And the majority of the cosmic Starswallowers. They'll kill Reath- that's the last of the distorted- and the universe will finally be rid of the parasites."

"I meant, what happens with Exath and Cealth?" snapped Jath.

"Oh." Neutroby shifted uncomfortably. "Well, your... comrade is... look, it might be easier for you if you remember that his mind had been destroyed long ago by the being that possessed him."

"You killed his body then."

"Yes." The cosmic owl frowned slightly, unsure of the guilt pooling up in his chest. "Look, that creature *had* to be destroyed! You do understand that? You saw the devastation it wreaked while simply on this ship- if it were to escape onto a planet..."

"Yeah, whatever." Snapped Jath. He forced an unexpected surge of pain away- he'd hated that dumb little Manicarian like a brother. There was no reason for his stomach to feel like lead. And there was still an even worse matter to discuss. "What about Cealth? Please tell me that freak of nature was lying when he said she was dead."

"I wish I could."

Jath felt as though he'd just hit an asteroid while travelling at light speed. Suddenly he understood what the Obligons felt on a daily basis, as the pain in his chest vanished; he felt numb, empty, damaged in a way no sensor could detect. This wasn't right. It **couldn't** be right. Cealth was still alive- she was just somewhere else; somewhere so, so far away he couldn't even reach her if he travelled at the speed of light for a million years. The Starswallower was still talking, although he didn't know why. What else was there to say? "-didn't see her myself, but Reath seemed... confident. I'm sorry. She was my friend too."

"*Was she?*" Jath's voice was a harsh bark- hurling at the cosmic owl all the sarcasm that he'd planned to unleash on Exath once they'd got home, to the Celestelia, his beautiful ship, where Cealth would be waiting, slightly irritated by his lateness, already with some other, distant mission in mind for them...

"As I say, I haven't *seen* her body. Don't delude yourself though. She's... probably been dead for a while now."

"But there's a chance she's alive?" Fire was burning through the rock lodged in his stomach- bright, pure flames melting despair.

"But if the Glitchis went to retrieve her, I doubt that's the case-"

"Then why's he taken so long coming back?" Jath was grinning so widely it hurt- his jaw muscles ached from the strain, but he forced himself to hold onto the hope, to let the fire burn through him- it needed fuel to stay alive. "You said it yourself- he could have done it in a second!"

"I was exaggerating. Look, Jath, it's been barely five minutes." Neutroby swallowed, uncertain of how to act- caught between agreeing with the Xsovzorite to pacify him, squashing his hopes and making him face reality, or urging Jath to wait until *after* the last distorted had been beaten...

And it was at that moment that the decision was ripped out of his hands by the furious, distant war-shrieks of several thousand Starswallowers, flanked by tens of thousands of Federation forces. Even as he glanced out of one of the portholes towards the distant specks, the dignified lines of Federation ships standing apart from the bird-hybrids, all vying for a position on the front line, he felt the half of the ship he was standing in shudder, and knew, with a thrill of irritation, that Jath had just ejected the shuttle and was now planning to hurry across the stars to find his employer- or, more realistically, to find her body.

Chapter 26

"HELLO!" Roared Galex, his whitish-grey plumage glowing, and his silver armour reflecting the powerful blue glow of the star that Doria orbited. Among the bland hospital-room-yellow of the Federation ships, the Starswallowers' array of colourful armour stood out like a rainbow over a dormant volcanic island, the furiously competitive cosmic beings having gathered alloys from all corners of the cosmos to forge the armour that now protected their heads, necks, spines, the crests of their wings and their arms. The cosmic Starswallowers were out in full force, each with a magnificently unique atmosphere surrounding them- the faint shade indicating the daring- and by extension, personalities- of their owners, with the explorers having obscure pale greenish or blue gasses circulating them, while the more 'classy' were coated in bold shades of pink or even orange, their personal atmospheres swirling with gases likely poisonous to any lesser creature. Then there were the cowards- the very small minority of cosmic Starswallowers that had squatted on Cygnus in their luxury spires for so long that their atmospheres were entirely comprised of the same gasses as their home star, who hovered in isolated, ruby groups.

Galex soared ahead of the rest of the flock, closely followed by the cosmic hawk and swan, who paused as Galex stopped to grin at the cosmic owl.

"Hi." Neutroby said, glancing around at the assembled Starswallowers- and then, in an undertone to Galex, *"Please* tell me they know who I really am."

"Neutroby!" roared the cosmic dove in delight, hurling himself, with alarming ferocity for such a generally reserved bird, at his cybernetic predecessor. "Why on Melchar did you leave me to rot in the bio-lab for so long?!"

"Because I've been busy being dead?" blinked Neutroby in alarm. "Anyway, we can talk about your less than perfect work later. The Glitchis could be back at any moment-"

"What do you mean 'less than perfect'?"

"You forgot to upgrade Galex's biological stamina after you increased his speed." The cosmic owl admonished, pedantic in spite of the situation. "Honestly!" Then he turned to the cosmic swan and blushed slightly beneath his feathers. "Hi Sunsanna."

"Hello."

"You look... well."

"Mm." She said, tilting her head to one side. "You don't look dead, so that's an improvement."

"Thanks. You're looking radiant as ever. I'm sorry it took so long-"

"However, you *do* look like Starthur, which isn't brilliant either."

"Ah."

"You're having a complete biological transplant once this is all over, correct?" She sniffed distastefully. "You *really* don't suit that idiot's body."

"If you're all done with the pleasantries, we've got a battle to fight." General Starre had driven her personal galaxy cruiser right between the cosmic owl and the other Starswallowers. "Now, where's the parasite?"

"He- it- left to go retrieve Cealth's... body. I convinced it that doing so would lure Galex here, so it could possess him."

"And, knowing this, he's here anyway." General Starre's expression was exasperated. "Galex, if you want to act as bait, then do it in a situation *where something can't possess you!*" She thought for a moment, ignoring the indignant spluttering now issuing from the Supreme Galactic Overlord's general direction, then nodded. "Right, you'll have to keep to the centre of your flock. Stay out of sight and for the love of light *get rid of that atmosphere!*"

Galex, surrounded by the pulsating yellow of TL-IF-H's bioluminescent atmosphere, cocked his head in confusion. "What's wrong with it?"

"It would be visible from the other end of this galaxy!"

"That's in fashion at the moment! What's your point?"

"That as soon as the distorted returns, it will see you instantly!"

Galex waved his hand dismissively, and accidentally backhanded the cosmic hawk. "Oh, sorry." The hawk winced, his eyes screwed up in pain at the force of the blow, then opened them. Instantly Galex had been pulled into the mass of Starswallowers and General Starre was barking orders, priming her lasers and activating all shields because, a moment before he could disguise them, the hawk's irises had become visible, multiplied, and had momentarily flared in anger. The cosmic swan stared at him, not quite comprehending the danger before it was too late; the distorted jumped, a tiny sliver of darkness, which comprised its entire physical form, streaming from the hawk's eyes to hers. As for the hawk, he floated, seemingly unconscious, for a few moments- before his eyes sprung open and he hurled himself at the swan, punching her squarely in the jaw.

"*What on Melchar*?!" Reath, stared in alarm at the hawk. "*How-*" but his question was cut short by another solid hit from the hawk's fist.

"BACKUPS BABY!" roared the hawk, attempting a roundhouse and feeling almost cheated when the 'swan' ducked it, Reath dipping her long neck. General Starre's forces moved in, their smooth, interconnecting ships trapping Reath into a perfectly spherical arena, the Federation ships moving in perfect formation to encircle the distorted.

"SURRENDER!" General Starre's voice barked from one of the nearby vessels, transmitted through the cosmic swan's universal translator and reverberating through her advanced eardrums.

The distorted darted away, and, a moment later, one of the nearby Yarflargians bellowed "*No!*"

The cosmic swan, now freed of the parasitic distorted, blinked a couple of moments later and righted herself, glaring towards the Yarflargian's ship. Another body switch- but, unlike the Starswallowers, this Yarflargian's mind couldn't be recovered.

"It's on the move." The swan snapped, glancing at her pristine blue armour to double check that it hadn't been damaged by the hawk's initial blows. "Get ready. And Vedrfolnir? You hit like a Melcharian."

"Heavy and damp?"

"Leisurely and weak."

The distorted's ship opened fire, the lasers cutting in perfectly straight lines across the sphere towards the two Starswallowers hovering inside it- only to have the impact dispersed when General Starre's personal cruiser, shields raised and thrusters firing, swept in front of them.

The distorted responded with breakneck speed, and Vedrfolnir saw it slip from a Yarflargian ship towards Starre. It slammed against her shields at the last moment, and the cosmic hawk almost thought he'd heard it let out a quiet sob of pain. Then it moved off again, the shadowy cloud spinning away from the furious blasts Starre's ship was now pumping out towards it. The Yarflargian ships re-organised themselves, this time forming a long, hollow rectangular corridor, allowing the unmanned ship of the deceased Yarflargian to fall through the formation before locking into position. The thing twisted, looking about for a new body, and selected the cosmic hawk's again. Before anyone had realised what was happening, he'd barrelled through the ranks of the Yarflargians and was charging towards the close-knit flock of Starswallowers just outside. He felt their feathered bodies brushing against him and suppressed a shudder of revulsion. What had gone wrong? Where were Soulth and Outh? *They were supposed to be helping him!* He quickly dipped into the body of the cosmic chicken and glanced around desperately, scanning the ranks of feathered cyborgs for a familiar figure- *there!* He allowed himself a grin of satisfaction as he spotted Neutroby- Outh- right next to Galex! It was as if the supreme galactic overlord had allowed himself to be gift-wrapped.

There was a muffled roar of confusion from the Starswallowers as Starre exited the formation of Federation ships and manoeuvred her ship around to face their ranks; to them, it seemed as though Federation commander intended to start attacking them. Galex rose out of the fray for a mere moment, attempting to get a better view of the situation, and the distorted lunged desperately towards him, slipping out of the cosmic chicken's body and away from the searching prow of Starre's flagship, his now fragile, smoky form buffeted by the constantly moving, huge wings surrounding him. He caught a brief glimpse of Galex's pale grey wings between the tawny shades of the other Starswallowers, and forced himself between their ranks, uncomfortably aware that they were beginning to take notice of his presence.

He felt himself being blown through the air towards Galex, and kept himself on course with sheer willpower, as he barrelled towards the overlord, seizing control of the cosmic heron as she spotted him, did a double take and opened her mouth to warn Galex, whose large form loomed over him now- dwarfing even the cosmic heron with her long legs- and it was with a pulse of adrenaline he had not felt in decades, that Reath lunged toward Galex, certain that he'd won, and that the Starswallower would remain under his control until he'd ripped the universe in half...

... The Supreme Galactic Overlord turned at the last moment, his pure gold eyes seeming to momentarily brighten with recognition as the distorted slammed into him, crawling down his throat, looping up into his brain and hi-jacking one of the most powerful beings in existence... General Starre's vessel burst through the crowd of Starswallowers, all of whom were fluttering about in confusion, and Reath heard a garbled message being barked into Galex's universal translator.

Ignoring it, he casually removed the universal translator and crushed it, feeling the unrestrained power in the supreme galactic overlord's grip. Now there was complete silence, the true, total silence of the void, unbroken by the nattering of the universal translators. The cosmic heron swept upwards towards Starre's command ship, yelling something now inaudible to the distorted. Whatever it was, it caused every other Starswallower to rush away from him in panic, and the distorted allowed himself a calm smile, contemplating the best order in which to destroy these buzzing, fly-like members of Galex's race- who, it now seemed, were far too much trouble to possess permanently- before leaping forwards, blurring through their lines with talons that had almost certainly been manicured shortly before the battle had begun.

Chapter 27

Jath's ship landed on a small asteroid roughly four million light years from Doria. He disengaged the engine, prepared a strong mug of tea for the Glitchis who'd been powering his teleportation drive, thoughtfully downing a strong mug of r'hom himself and shuddering as his synapses sparked with the stimulant's introduction. He knocked at the door to the engine room, and the Glitchis called a greeting that he took as confirmation that he could enter. She accepted the tea with a nod of thanks, craning her neck elegantly to sip at the brown liquid. Jath waited until she'd finished before repeating the same question that he'd been asking for months.

"Are we there now?"

"Just about," the Glitchis nodded, her voice ragged with exhaustion. "I tried to get us as close to the exit as possible, but if I go any closer, I can't guarantee we won't just teleport into the wall."

Jath had been looking for the exit to the universe ever since abandoning the allied Federation-Starswallower forces, but had been unable to discover the exact location due to the unfortunate events now occurring throughout the universe, with various species suddenly vanishing and then turning up a few hours later in an almost coma-like state, their minds eliminated by the distorted that had been sweeping through the bubble of life unopposed, ever since taking control of Galex.

He'd passed the possessed Starswallower a few weeks ago and had nearly torn out his engine trying to get away. Inevitably, he'd run out of fuel soon afterwards, and had crashed onto the Glitchis' home planet. He'd retained his mind, for which he was grateful- but the entire engine had been destroyed in the crash. The Glitchises inhabiting the planet had helped him to rebuild his ship, and Gorson, sister of the possessed Glitchis, had agreed to travel with Jath and power his teleportation drive. Even if her brother had been possessed, it still filled her with revulsion and guilt when she learned of the actions the distorted had been able to perform by living in his body.

"Excellent!" Jath forced himself to smile back in the present. "How soon can we disembark?"

"Well I'm going to need forty Galaxian hours of sleep," Gorson yawned, matter-of-factly. "But you can leave whenever you want." her sentence trailed off as her eyelids began to droop. Jath nodded and left quietly. He'd become used to the frankly alarming strain that teleportation put on the Glitchis' bodies; many had to sleep for an average of twenty hours just to recover from a single day's teleporting, so it was unsurprising that Gorson needed to pass out for so long after travelling for thousands of light years at a time.

Before he left, Jath had visited the medical bay again where, still in a coma-like state after all these months, was Exath; his heart, lungs and liver still functioning, but his mind entirely wiped. He lay face up on a bed, strapped down so he wouldn't drift away when the ship entered zero gravity, and wired into a set of bags that provided him with air, water and liquidized food. Every now and then, the Manicarian blinked at the ceiling, but other than that, there were no signs of life. It was incredibly eerie. The space pirates were similarly secured in beds opposite.

Jath steeled himself, clenching his chest against the ferocious tidal wave of emptiness that had swamped him every time he'd seen Exath in his current state, and forced himself to sit down at the small computer beside his friend's bed. He entered one more entry into the log he'd been attempting to compile, should he ever come up with a way to restore Exath's mind, telling his brother about the planets they'd passed on the way to this sector, and how, hopefully, soon Cealth would return and be able to fix him.

When the desire to run became too strong, Jath saved the document and left hastily, avoiding eye contact with Exath- just in case the idiot ever decided to yell "Psyche!" and start mocking him for crying. Not that he *was* crying. Gorson must've been slicing space onions. In her sleep. That was way more likely.

Jath gritted his teeth and activated his atmospheric shield, watching his specialised, venomous green mixture of gasses unfolding around him, and felt the reassuring pressure on his arms and legs telling him that he would now be able to stroll through the vacuum without his vital fluids evaporating off of him. The airlock opened, and he stood in it uncomfortably for a few moments, waiting for the room to empty of air before he entered the vacuum of space. When it did, the second door opened automatically, and he eased himself out and onto the exterior of the ship, cautiously glancing around for any sign of the asteroid that Gorson had mentioned.

There! A tiny speck, barely larger than an engine spark, was visible in the distance- and, as Jath's eyes began to adjust to the sudden darkness, his mouth widened in surprise; the asteroid was literally the only point of colour on the expanse he was seeing before him; the wall of the universe, enormous, ever shifting, rocketing away from the centre even as he watched, was completely blank, and incomprehensibly so- a blunt, sudden end to the colourful, lively universe within its confines.

It was jarring; the surface spread for as far as he could see, above, below, left, right, diagonally, horizontally, extending outwards like the indisputable **fact** that it was. Jath could've simply sat and goggled at the spectacle for the remainder of his fifty-year lifespan, but he knew that, if there was some tiny trace of Cealth's fate here, he *had* to find it. The Xsovzorite shook his head, clearing the "WHAT THE-?!" message from his brain and eyes, and forcing himself to focus on moving towards the asteroid.

He kicked his jet-boots into gear and felt the familiar thrum of energy run through them before he shot towards the asteroid, angling himself by tilting his whole body like a compass needle, jabbing eternally towards his destination. He slowed himself down at the last moment before hitting the rock, and then stiffened as he landed, staring at the lone helmet resting on the dusty surface. Cealth's helmet. He was stumbling towards it before the jet boots had properly disengaged, so, from a distance, it looked as though he'd hopped in alarm at the mere sight of the smooth, cream, ovoid helmet.

The helmet was cracked right down the middle, the electronic view screen inside dull and blank, clearly damaged beyond repair. Jath winced- he'd built the view screen himself roughly four years ago and it'd taken a huge amount of time, effort and money- but he restrained himself from picking the helmet up, instead examining the dust coating the asteroid. It'd been disturbed at one point, the signs of some former struggle clearly visible in the foot-deep dirt- well, at least this proved that the distorted inhabiting the Glitchis hadn't lied about its battle with Cealth. She *had* been here once.

But where is she now? He thought, frustratedly. He glanced into the helmet again, drumming the ground with his hind claws impatiently. *If she survived, she'd have moved quickly.*

The distorted-Obligon hadn't found her body, so either she was alive or, and Jath tried not to think about this, her body had been hurled from the asteroid with such force that it was now orbiting one of the desolate solar systems far below. Jath willed himself to stay positive; he'd located her helmet at least and, providing she'd found some way to survive without it, he could locate her using the connection between her helmet and her universal translator. He'd connected the two together months before, thinking that he could piggyback the translation software of the universal translator into her helmet. He'd had to ask her if she had ears, and she'd simply turned to him with that blank helmet and replied,

"Everyone has ears."

"What about Exath?!" Jath had challenged, indicating his compadre's lack of lugs.

"I thought you were being metaphorical."

"When have I *ever* been metaphorical?!"

"When you said the spurlian spider in your room was, and I quote, 'Like, the size of a Nightstalker'."

"That was simile at worst! And it **was** the size of a Nightstalker! Just...a small one."

"The infants are about twelve feet tall."

"A *really* small Nightstalker!"

"A zygote then."

Jath winced slightly at the recollection, then reached out and carefully lifted the helmet, tossing some dust-like debris from the top, which drifted, almost in slow motion, back to the surface of the planet, settling with an inaudible noise like thunder. Jath kicked his jet-boots back into action, hovering unsteadily on them before turning back towards his ship.

A pair of many irised, aggressively violet eyes met his, and he just had time to swear furiously before the distorted had lunged towards him, claws outstretched, wings spread and irises bouncing about as it moved.

"Galex," Jath said, almost in admiration, as the distorted grappled with him. "You actually managed to possess Galex of all beings."

"*What else?*"

"So, why're you still following me?" Jath bared his teeth in a snarl. "This won't be good for your health!" He snapped at Galex's beak and the distorted recoiled momentarily.

"*Where are my brothers?*" Reath hissed.

"Who?"

"*My brothers! The ones who were with you on the Nebula!*"

"You mean the parasite who stole Exath's body? Or your little double agent Neutroby?"

"*You mean Starthur?*" the distorted hesitated, its irises dilating in momentary panic. "*Outh had possessed Starthur. Not Neutroby!*"

"I have a terrible memory for faces."

"*Neutroby is dead!*" The distorted hissed. Jath grinned and stayed silent. "*Enough of your diversions! I will end your miserable existence unless you tell me where they are!*"

"You can't." smirked Jath. "If you kill me, you'll never learn what happened to them."

"*So why don't I just rip the information from your puny synapses?*"

"Because," Jath said, with the air of a being who knows he's holding all the aces-despite the fact that three have somehow already been played by his shifty opponent. "You can't. You try possessing me, and you're gonna lose control of Galex."

"*I do not need to possess you to find the others! I don't even particularly need them; my species does not form bonds!*"

"And yet here you are." Smirked Jath. "So, how do you feel about a little trade?"

"*What sort of trade?*" hissed the distorted.

"I'll tell you where your brothers are, when **you** tell **me** where Cealth is."

"*Cealth?*" hissed the creature in shock. "*But... I don't- I thought that* you *had already retrieved her body.*"

The two beings stared at one another, the implications of the information they'd just received slowly sinking in.

"She's still alive." Grinned Jath. A sudden burst of strength flooded his limbs and he hurled the distorted off of him- Reath hurtled off into space with an alarmed squawk. (If Galex had been concious, he would have never recovered from the disgrace of producing such a sound.) Before the distorted could teleport back to the rock, Jath had activated his jet-boots and was speeding back towards the Nebula-it looked as though the Glitchis would have to cut its siesta short.

Chapter 28

Cealth's universal translator was unbelievably annoying to track; it seemed to pick a random part of universe to sit in until Jath was a few mere galaxies away- then it skipped away to the other end of creation while the Nebula crawled through sector after sector towards it. However, Jath wasn't dispirited by this; the initial roar of victory at discovering Cealth's fate was still powering him like a fusion reactor- hell, even visiting Exath wasn't as depressing as it had previously been.

Now he took enormous pleasure in quite literally everything he did- he was so jubilant in fact, that the normally level-headed Gorson felt quite unnerved by the dancing retreat Jath had performed when she'd requested a cup of r'hom. Another time, she had to double check that he'd heard her correctly when she asked him to empty the lavatory and he'd scampered, *actually scampered*, away to do it.

Immediately after the encounter at the exit to the universe, Jath had clambered into the Nebula, legs tumbling over one another as he'd rushed to wake Gorson- and even as she was sleepily grasping the essential points of the situation, he'd already prepared the ship for teleportation, firmly strapped himself down and given the order to teleport as far away as possible.

They'd ended up staying in a rarely visited part of the Laran Sector while Jath repaired Cealth's helmet- fortunately the Dorian that had previously inhabited the ship had a truly impressive array of technology which Jath had enthusiastically cannibalised, once he remembered that Auren was lying unconscious beside Jath and was therefore unlikely to suddenly awaken and come for him in revenge.

The helmet was now wired into the ship's computer, transmitting a constant flow of data into Gorson's room, which doubled as the teleportation drive- a device similar to a human's cycling machine, except that it captured the energy normally expended in Glitchis teleportation and used it to teleport the entire ship, instead of generating a small trickle of electricity to fuel a light bulb for a couple of seconds. Jath had fitted a small screen above the machine which showed the coordinates and location that the ship needed to transport itself to next. Gorson was blinking lazily at it when Jath burst excitedly into the room, threw back his head and yelled,

"I'VE WORKED IT OUT!"

"Good for you?" Gorson let out an enormous yawn and shook her neck aggressively. "What is this?"

"I WORKED OUT HOW SHE'S BLIPPING AROUND!"

"Good."

"ASK ME HOW!" Jath was practically running up the walls, so pent up was his energy. "GO ON! ASK!"

"How-"

"COSMIC WORMS!"

Ok. Thought Gorson. *He's actually gone mad now. Poor guy, I s'pose that's what happens when everyone you love dies...*

"I was just watching one on the bridge when it hit me!" Jath had started clawing his way onto the ceiling as he talked- luckily, hanging at a ninety degree angle seemed to calm him down. "Cosmic worms know things, right? That's what everyone says. So, I was watching one that'd just exited a wormhole, and I was fiddling with some audio to see if I couldn't tell what it was saying while it was in the vacuum."

"And I suppose it told you exactly where Cealth is?" Yawned Gorson. "Had it given her a lift to Revlar recently?" *Poor sap doesn't remember you can't hear sound in the vacuum... he really has cracked.*

"OF COURSE NOT!" Snapped Jath, so abruptly that Gorson's next yawn stopped midway through, leaving her feeling irate and more than a little cheated. "That'd be ridiculous! No, I didn't pick up what it was saying, *but,*" and here his face split into a grin worthy of the toothsome nightstalker, "I did pick up on some waves coming through the wormholes. It's really similar to your teleportation emissions! That's how Cealth's been getting around the universe so quickly- she's using the wormholes!"

"Wut?"

"You do know what a wormhole is, right?" frowned Jath.

"Of course, I do!" cried Gorson, staggering to her feet. "I use small ones on a daily basis! But the cosmic worms are on a whole other level- to be able to keep a tunnel that long and that large open while they travel through is one thing- and they've had to evolve some pretty exotic biology to do that- but to take another being through with them would be practically impossible! What species is Cealth?"

"An Obligon if those distorted are to be believed," said Jath. "I overheard them talking when Exath... y'know. When I got captured."

"Well there you go!" shrugged Gorson. "Obligons would be crushed, even in an atmospheric shield, if they went through a wormhole- the worms only survive because they can control their own gravity!"

"Ah," smirked Jath, feeling immensely superior all of a sudden. "But what if she was **inside the worm?**"

"In- what? Well... I mean... I *suppose* that *might* protect her- but how on Cygnus would she get inside a worm? They're vegetarians, aren't they?"

"They eat rocks." Shrugged Jath. "Big rocks. Planet-sized rocks. All kinds of rocks. They're technically univores if you want to be specific- but that's beside the point. They're so huge, I doubt they'd notice if they swallowed a small ship."

As a matter of fact, Jath was almost entirely correct. At the moment that Jath and Gorson had been talking, Cealth had been harvesting some small plants from the mountains that the cosmic worm had eaten that day. Her shuttle was lodged into the side of one of the more pleasant ranges- and if it hadn't been for the constantly billowing orange flesh that flowed above her instead of the sky, and the seas of stomach acid that lapped at the peaks of smaller mountains, she could almost have forgotten that she now lived in the belly of a cosmic worm. Almost.

His name was Ni, and Cealth had made an arrangement with him after he'd rescued her from the exit of the universe. She was allowed to live within his stomach on one condition; she had to listen to his life's learningsas they travelled and shout an essay she had written about them once per week. While, at first, his teachings had given her a headache as he reminded her about the scale of the universe and the inherently pointless nature of life, she'd gradually realised that these early topics were *easy* to argue against- and the worm seemed to enjoy the verbal sparring matches that erupted between himself and Cealth whenever one of the essays was being read aloud.

"Do we have the right to define the boundaries of our universe?" he intoned one day. "How are we to know when our universe ends, and where the next begins? Supposing all so-called 'universes' are, in actuality, mere specks of dust within the true 'universe'?"

"Then that larger universe would **also** be our universe," Cealth replied. She never needed to raise her voice to be overheard by the worm- simply placing her hand on the wall of his body was enough for him to feel and interpret the vibrations into language. "And the problem of relative size would still apply- according to your argument, this 'super universe' would in turn be a speck of dust within an even larger one. I still say that all universes are just reflections of one another- distorted variations on the true universe. The utopian universe."

"You, of all beings, should know that a utopia is impossible," hummed the worm. "Every single being has a different concept of a perfect universe. They cannot all be correct."

'Then every universe would be perfect for a different person." Shrugged Cealth.

"In that case, whose utopia is this?"

"It depends on who can best shape their reality." Cealth closed her eyes. "I once believed that all I needed to do to create my utopia would be to destroy the ones who destroyed my life and distorted my family- but that was very small minded, I see that now. My foe enslaved the universe because I couldn't see what he would do until it was too late. He nearly killed me, and, I suppose, he did so for the same reasons that I slaughtered his brethren. He thought killing me would've enabled him to make his utopia."

"You don't believe he succeeded?"

"No," Cealth said. "I've heard time and again of people like Reath; they're born, told to improve the world for sole gain of their species, and they eat up the life on their planet to do so. It's parasitic. I have always found such behaviour abhorrent- but I was actually engaging in it by attempting to kill distorted. I allowed the Earth to burn in exchange for my revenge. I didn't destroy the distorted Obligons to stop Reath's plan. I'm not a selfless person- but I don't think that's a bad thing. It's just the way I think. And yet I was killing my species for my own selfish revenge."

"And so, the wheel of hatred turns." The worm said, a little sadly. "Few people notice the sheer enormity of a cosmic worm's lifespan- my kind slip through the voids and leave no trace behind- but we see the traces that others leave. People are, inherently, flawed- and usually too lazy to fix what they know is wrong within themselves. They bicker and squabble, destroy planets out of some sense of revenge- and there are always innocent bystanders who swear revenge on the former for the destruction of their home and, in turn, destroy their enemy's planet, once again fuelling the hatred of another child of war."

"The wheel turns?"

"The wheel turns." Nodded the cosmic worm, and Cealth felt the ground shift as his body rippled.

"What do you think is the solution?"

"To war?"

"To us. All life forms. What do we do to fix ourselves? Not everyone is willing to be a pacifist- many beings would consider such behaviour weak or foolish. And we can't keep going like this- sooner or later we'll run out of room to battle."

"Slow down." Advised the worm. "Watch the galaxies turn. And don't despair at the thought of fading from history- that's foolish, and an insult to all those who died in peace, unnamed but satisfied."

"The universe needs a quick resolution now." Cealth replied. "We can't watch the galaxies turn as our- as my enemies are burning them."

"Then, there's only one more solution."

"Aggression," Cealth said, reluctantly. "I'd hoped that you would be able to show me a different path."

"And yet earlier, you said that whoever was able to shape the universe would be the one who would find within it their utopia. You would be willing to let me shape it for you, with my opinions?"

"Do you object?"

"You know I do. Utopias aren't created through pain, or through laziness. But then, for all we know, they may not be 'created' at all."

"You're saying that they can't exist?"

"I'm saying that they may already exist- they do not need to be created or shaped. Without entities in it, would this universe function the same?"

"Yes..." Cealth said, doubtfully. "In essence."

"Well then, if there isn't something fundamentally wrong with our universe, then there's only one thing holding this universe back from being perfect for us, isn't there?" the cosmic worm's body rippled again, and Cealth sat down heavily as the ground was whipped out from beneath her. "You know what to do. Break the cycle. Slow the wheel- stop it if you can. And don't let hatred ruin this utopia anymore."

Cealth stood again, walked to her shuttle and dislodged it from the rubble. "Thank you." She said gravely, engaging the engine. "You've helped me more than I can say."

"You are very welcome," the worm responded, and Cealth thought she heard a smile in its voice. "Now, I would very much appreciate your compliance in leaving my digestive cavity; your friend is here, and he isn't being terribly gentle or, for that matter, civil in his efforts to gain entry."

Chapter 29

"OPEN UP!" barked Jath, hammering on the worm's second set of jaws with the prow of the Nebula. "Get your dumb mouths OPEN!"

"Most impolite."

It was the shortest utterance Ni had ever said, and Jath was so surprised at the brevity of the philospher's response that he momentarily stopped his attack. Then he blinked firmly, engaged reverse gear with a dexterity rivalled only by an octopian, and prepared to ram into the mouths one final time- when they suddenly opened, and a sleek, elliptical vessel exited through the jaws.

Cealth's ship cruised towards Jath's and stopped, smartly, alongside it. Jath's mouth gaped open as he stared at the tiny vessel- the worm was so large that he'd barely noticed the ship at first. Then his fingers began manically dancing over the controls, broadcasting a hail to the ship and preparing to open the airlock.

"Jath?" Cealth's usually impassive voice actually held a note of surprise as she responded to the hail and saw the Xsovzorite's beaming grey face staring back at her. She had expected the 'friend' that the worm had mentioned to be a certain distorted Obligon.

"You're not dead!" Jath whooped.

"Naturally." She smiled dryly. "I approve of your choice of vessel- but I can't say the same about your speed. If you've been conscious for all this time, I would have expected you to arrive far sooner. I see you've acquired a personal teleporter."

Jath glanced at his wrist, where the teleporter he'd been constructing from Gorson's leftover energy in his spare time sat, wedged in place between two of his leg-spikes. "It's only got enough juice for a single jump- and you weren't exactly easy to track down!" he grinned. "Gorson and I- oh, she's my co-pilot by the way-"

"Co-pilot?" Cealth smiled. "I'm surprised that you've learned to share the controls with anybody- although it does appear that you still can't do so with Exath."

The smile melted off Jath's face like an ice sculpture hitting a star. "You- uh, boss, you should probably come aboard."

"What's wrong?" she asked, eyes narrowing under her hood- but she already had a horrible feeling swirling in the pit of her stomach, consuming the delight she'd previously felt.

"I-" Jath swallowed down a lump of emotions. "It- uh- it's best if I show you." And, before he could make a bigger fool of himself, he ended the call and opened the airlock, slumping into his chair and re-arranging his face before Cealth could see it.

Cealth stood rigidly as she reached Exath's bedside, taking in the medical equipment that was keeping him- or at least, his body- alive. Her head jerked around, and she stiffly reached for his life support, finger moving towards the off-switch.

"No!" yelled Jath pulling the control out of her hand. She was so numb, she didn't even move.

"Why bother?"

Jath blinked, unsure of who Cealth was talking to. He'd never seen her lose control before and did **not** like it; it was unnerving in the extreme. "I **have** to keep him alive." He said, urgently. "If there's any way of sav- of helping him, I have to."

"You didn't even like him." Cealth said harshly, turning to Jath. "Nothing can be done for him now. It's kinder to let his body pass on."

"But- the Starswallowers- I saw them at the battle! They were able to recover from possession-"

"That's because they can create backups of their minds." Her words were flat, but at least they came more easily now. "They were never in the slightest danger of... this." She waved a hand towards Exath- she could barely look at him now.

"You've moved minds around before now." Jath said cautiously, glancing towards her hooded face.

"I have never absorbed Exath's mind," she said, relaxing her posture slightly, but still maintaining clipped tones. "I can't restore something that I never possessed in the first place. I'm sorry Jath, but he's gone for good."

Jath turned away and closed his eyes bitterly. "You'd absorbed my mind before now. If I'd been eliminated instead, you could've..."

"Exath was an idiot." Cealth sighed, cutting across Jath gently. "He would never have been able to find me, and I doubt he would've had the sense to keep *your* body alive." Then she straightened. "But in any event, we have to keep pushing forwards. I need to know what happened after I left you two- and, most importantly, what happened to Neutroby."

Jath nodded, relieved to see Cealth finally acting somewhat like herself again, and filled her in on the events that had transpired after they'd left the exit to the universe. She listened for a time, then nodded thoughtfully, asking him to prepare a room for her on the ship, which he did- repeating the gases that made up her unique atmosphere in his head as he moved. It wouldn't do to have a room comprised of even 1% too much carbon dioxide.

Cealth, meanwhile, sat down and thought. The space pirates were lying unconscious in the medical bay, and she started slightly at the sight of the Dorian,

Auren, whose eyes opened momentarily to stare blankly into space; like a derelict house whose windows are being blown open in breeze. Tungsten watched the dorian for a moment longer, then allowed her gaze to wander onto the human figure lying next to Auren, pityingly. To lose your planet and then lose yourself... it was unthinkably painful. If only the human had been a little more intelligent; perhaps then she could have prevented the destruction of Earth, helped Tungsten to hunt down the distorted. Then again, even if she *did* remember Sandros 6 from her time, she hadn't been there when it fell- Sam wouldn't remember the distorted.

Remember them. Cealth frowned- she had the sudden feeling that she had just forgotten something... something that was important, something vital. Something hopeful.

Remember them. The distorted. Sandros 6. Her mind raced as she began to construct a plan.

The Starswallowers had forced her to erase the entire universe's memories of the planet- decided it would be better if nobody knew the true reason they'd detonated it- to hide the evidence of the sheer, devastating power of the reverse Obligons, and stop any attempts to reproduce their frightening power.

Thinking back on it... she *had* absorbed the memories of the entire universe, hadn't she? Cealth closed her eyes and lowered her hood, allowing the emotionally empty air of the medical bay to wash around her, letting it dull the raw emotions she felt at Exath's brain death, so she could instead focusing on searching her own mind. It was cavernous in there; a place of whispers and of towers, pillars- mountains even- of information. She ignored most of it, although she was tempted to examine a couple of more exotic memories from a holidaying couple- actually, they seemed rather similar to Sam and Captain Tungsten...

She pressed on and eventually she felt it- the tugging of an irritatable purple memory; a small Manicarian in school, who'd become bored listening to the teacher drone on and on about working hard for the sakes of everyone else in their galaxy, and was instead daydreaming about Sandros 6, the jungle of life where he would one day go, to avoid his 'hardworking' classmates, to get away from jabbering teachers... he'd battle Nightstalkers and hack through vines with only his claws to defend him from the beasts within the sprawling mass of plants, he'd build a hut in the trees and maybe even create a new drink from the juices of the exotic fruits surrounding him...

Now he was older, and Cealth almost smiled as she glimpsed the end of a news report on the Starswallower-Obligon summit that was to take place on Sandros 6. The reporter had fluffed up his lines and his ears had gone purple as he repeated them. A woman was laughing on the sofa in front of the television, and the Manicarian smiled too, pleased to see his mother laughing at the interview he had filmed. Sooner or later, those bigwigs would tell him that he could go to Sandros 6 to film the summit itself... and then, maybe, he could finally become a wildlife cameraman, and document all the life on the planet...

His boss had never given him the job. He'd slouched away, feeling numb, as he replayed the conversation in his head... '*We're looking for a more... experienced cameraman to film this encounter. Now you're new at this, it's not entirely your fault, but you really* should *have cut away during that report last week... poor Jarg's getting no end of hate on social media after that mess up...*' -but it had made his mother laugh, hadn't it?

He had been fired only a few weeks later.

Then again, what was he thinking, trying to become a wildlife cameraman? His mother would have nobody to look after her if he left for Sandros 6; his three sisters had already left their planet, and were all incredibly successful in the Lucia Glassias sector, and his father had passed away only an hour after he had been born, as most Manicarians did after giving birth... no, much better to stay on Revlar and get a job in one of the bars. He had daydreamed for long enough; if he continued to obsess over that planet, he'd never earn any money, and would be unable to look after his mother- the only option left was to get a new job in one of his planet's many bars- he could work his way up into Bar Aquarius, maybe even into Aquiline, and earn his way back into favour- because otherwise, he could never face her again.

Cealth had met him in Bar Aquila decades later- still as buoyant as he had been in these memories, but with a certain atmosphere of regret about him; his mother had passed away some weeks before. He couldn't even remember, by then, why he had ever wanted to leave Revlar- and how could he, when Cealth had taken these memories- but he remembered how he had felt when he was younger, and had readily agreed to the proposition that Cealth had offered him, so eager to get into space and off of Revlar that he hadn't even really cared that the job she offered was to be an assassin...

Cealth finished watching, then gathered up every single memory, forced them to the forefront of her face, stood, walked over to Exath's prone body... and expelled them in a burst of light.

Exath's body blinked, as it usually did by itself, but, for the first time in months, a crease had formed between his eyebrows- a crease which grew as his brain gradually began to knit itself back together again, rebuilding a framework around the memories Cealth had passed on.

Chapter 30

"Credit where credit is due, you truly had me fooled for months. If only your little friend Jath was a bit cleverer. Then you might actually have got away with this deception."

Neutroby didn't respond. He was as firmly bound as a trussed cosmic chicken, lying heavily on his back and squinting up at the looming form of the possessed Galex, dramatically silhouetted against the blazing core of Cygnus.

"You do understand what this means?"

"If you do an evil laugh, I'm going to roll over and crush your toes." Growled Neutroby, trying and failing to think of a better comeback. His eyes felt like they were roasting in the light of the core- but then again it **was** a star.

The distorted rolled its eyes. *"You should know better than anyone- these toes are unbreakable. You engineered them after all."*

Neutroby opened his mouth to spit out a retort- when there was a sudden explosion of noise from the ceiling so loud that it caused the distorted to reel back, clutching at its ears, and Neutroby, squirming in pain, wrenched his arms free of his bonds, so he could protect his face from the eight-foot shards of diamond now knifing downwards- impossibly splintering from the supposedly unbreakable roof now breaking apart like an eggshell.

Through the crystalline ceiling that covered the lower floors of Cygnus glowed a wavering, impossibly long shape which streamed over them, its girth seemingly capable of circling the sphere twice over, its form so sinuous that it appeared, at first glance, to be an infinite, space-bound train. Neutroby's stomach growled in appreciation of the specimen.

Ni paused in his great arc, then proceeded to headbutt the dyson sphere once again. The ceiling, made of a material that was both harder and stronger than diamond or steel, cracked with a second, equally deafening, **bang**. The cosmic owl gaped- he'd designed the surface of Cygnus to be impenetrable; it'd withstood attacks by the Federation, the short-lived Earthian Empire- even an assault by the popular band *Just Panic* after Galex had pirated one of their albums. The sphere had sat, firmly, encircling the blue star at its core for hundreds of years, the blistering heat having no impact on the material. And here it was, being broken apart by, of all things, a cosmic worm; the Starswallowers' favourite prey.

"What is this?" Reath asked, his expression tight and nervous. *"What did you do? This being couldn't have just attacked us out of nowhere!"*

Neutroby didn't respond- he couldn't. He was reeling from the revelation that cosmic worms of all species could have snapped Cygnus in half whenever they wanted to. His only thought, as the cosmic worm's set of double-jaws closed in for another huge mouthful of his home, was how grateful he was that the worms had never attacked before- the real Galex would have never let him live this humiliation down.

"This is the Celestelia." A clear voice suddenly rang out, so massively amplified that it could only have been being broadcast through one of the space pirate's audio relays. "Exit the body, disarm all weapons, and you may be spared."

"*Cealth.*" Snarled the distorted, his face contorting in fury as he recognised the calm tones. Neutroby's heart bounced- *she was alive!*

"I repeat," Cealth said, maintaining the politeness and veiled irritation of an announcer notifying a useless parent that their child had been found. "Surrender or be erased from existence."

"*What a terrible assassin!*" The distorted shook Galex's head, quickly regaining his confidence and glancing around for any sign of the Celestelia's position. "*What kind of moron gives their opponent advance warning of their attack?!*"

"One unwilling to commit total genocide?" Neutroby said, quietly. The distorted span around, staring at him.

"*Don't be ludicrous.*" Reath hissed, his entire being coiling within Galex's supressed mind. "*That thought has never stopped her before! She's killed dozens of our kind- why would she hesitate with me?*" He shifted uncertainly, Galex's feathers rustling as it did so. "*Perhaps we're more alike than I thought- perhaps she also likes to savour the kill. But-*"

"That was your last warning." Cealth's voice cut across the distorted before it could finish speaking. "Reath... make peace with yourself."

Cealth lowered the radio she'd been using to remotely access the Celestelia's audio systems. She raised her Cellsplitter, silently primed it and let out a silent breath in irritation as the distorted leapt aside, Galex's heightened instincts screaming a warning at him before Cealth could fire. He whipped around, irises bouncing and searching desperately for the assassin- but she'd already moved from her last position.

Overhead, the Celestelia blazed into view; a sleek, white and gold vessel that glowed brightly in the light of Cygnus and served as a perfect distraction. The distorted winced and stared around in a confused panic, momentarily blinded by the sheer whiteness of the vessel, as the cosmic worm took another great chunk out of Cygnus and swallowed it with a deafening **crunch.**

While the distorted-Obligon was reeling in panic, Jath leapt from the Celestelia, fell through the hole that Ni had just bitten into Cygnus and landed, all four legs working together to reduce the impact, on the second layer, ducking behind one of the many support pillars present on this level and silently priming his Laserifle.

Far above, the Celestelia shot off into the distance, fire trailing behind it as Cygnus's thick crimson atmosphere momentarily ignited. Gorson was piloting the vessel while Jath and Cealth were away, her eyes fixed firmly on the readings the ship was sending her way.

"He's getting ready to teleport again," she murmured, transmitting her voice directly into Cealth's universal translator. Cealth didn't verbally acknowledge her, maintaining her silent approach towards the distorted-Obligon, but Gorson understood- Cealth hadn't spoken, so all was going according to plan. Moving with the dexterity of a Spurlian spider, the Glitchis shifted the Celestelia out of the lower atmosphere and, making certain that the ship's thrusters fired powerfully every now and again (to prevent the ship from being dragged down by the huge gravitational pull of the encased star), entered orbit, out of harm's way, while still keeping the ship nearby in case Cealth needed it.

The assassin in question darted between the support columns with astonishing speed; she might have spent the majority of her life in space, but she hadn't allowed her muscles to atrophy for one day. She moved with the silent speed that she'd learned to maintain from a collection of nocturnal hunters on Crevas Twelve, and lined up another shot on Galex.

The distorted's eyes darted around- he could hear movement, his advanced hearing was picking up definite footfalls, the sound of a light step smacking against the diamond floor echoing like an explosion in his sensitive ears- the only problem was that he couldn't quite tell where it was coming from. Whoever- or whatever- was walking seemed to switch direction every step. He felt his heartbeat gradually increase as the footfalls persisted and, in desperation, grabbed Neutroby and hauled him to his feet, holding him like a living shield against any attacks.

Disgusting. Jath's nose twitched, scenting the air like an Earthian bloodhound. He could smell every bead of sweat that rolled down the distorted's neck. His senses were strained to breaking point, amplified by adrenaline, and he had to physically control his claws to prevent them extending; it was possible that the faint 'shhck' would give his position away.

The seconds dripped away like syrup, one moment lengthened until it was unbearably long.

Each of the four beings waited, in total silence, for *something* to happen, for some signal that the dance of death was about to begin.

Neutroby sneezed.

All hell broke loose; the distorted flinched, his concentration broken, and he dropped Neutroby, who rolled behind a support column and bumped into Jath. The Xsovzorite flinched and fired, his aim wild as his muscles locked together in panic. After a few moments he stopped and glanced towards Galex, tense expectation clouding his vision, until he realised that the distorted-Obligon had moved, blurring with incomprehensible speed, and vanishing out of the way of the laser blasts before they could hit- one had struck a diamond support column and singed it, with a blinding burst of pure red light, a clear ringing, and a revolting smell.

Throughout all this, Cealth's position remained unchanged, her breathing regular and steady. Jath staggered away from his prior hiding place, his retinas seared by the refracted light of the inaccurate blast and tripped over the writhing form of the cosmic owl, still thrashing as he attempted to free his arms.

Engineer he may be, assassin he is not. Thought Cealth, icily.

Reath re-emerged, and, letting out a short bark of laughter at Jath's incompetence, hurled himself at the Xsovzorite, landing on top of him and knocking the air from his lungs.

"*You moron,*" snorted the distorted. "*Did you honestly think-!*"

Cealth calmly walked up behind the Obligon, aimed her gun at the back of his head, and fired.

At the last possible moment, Reath teleported away, the laser missed Jath's head by a hair and he yelped in indignation. Above them, Ni, who Cealth had convinced to aid them in the assault before they'd left for Cygnus, continued to crunch up the surface of the dyson sphere, and with every bite more knife-like stalactites thundered downwards.

"Galex's instincts are too good." Cealth muttered to Jath, her free hand clenching momentarily as the distorted re-appeared and turned back towards them.

"Yeah." Jath agreed. "Uh... ideas?"

Reath charged, and Cealth grunted as he slammed into her shoulder first, taking her momentarily off her feet. "You're the engineer!" she barked as they thundered on towards another of the pillars. "Figure something out! He's not going to be processing all this information biologically!"

"Right!" Jath barked, tapping his universal translator and connecting to Gorson's. "HEY!" he yelled as another gigantic chunk of diamond crashed to the floor, the splinters missing him by millimetres.

"No need to shout." Gorson responded grumpily. "What's happening down there? Who's winning?"

"Um... could go either way." Jath glanced nervously at Cealth and Reath, who were still battling with animalistic ferocity; even as he watched, the distorted clamped Galex's beak firmly around Cealth's cellsplitter and tore it from her hands- but then a moment later she had chopped at his neck with her hand, eyes fixed onto her target through her personal atmosphere. Her helmet was still broken.

"Look, can you grab my holopad quickly?!" Jath glanced at Cealth and gave her what was meant to be a reassuring smile. "I have a plan."

"Where is it?" Gorson barked, although from the pounding footsteps thrumming through the translator, Jath could tell that she was already moving off in search of the holopad.

"I think I left it under my bed? When you grab it look for a file labelled 'contingency'. And be really quick!" he added as the distorted elbowed Cealth in the stomach. She let out a bestial roar and headbutted Reath even as she doubled over.

"No need to be rude!" Gorson growled. "Right, I've got it. What's your password?"

"What? You shouldn't need a password!" Jath grabbed a nearby chunk of diamond the size of his forearm and jabbed it under Galex's armpit as the duelling Obligons passed. The distorted howled and Cealth took the time to reclaim her Cellsplitter.

"Well it says I need one!"

"Try Xsovsorite9, capital 'X', lower case everything else!"

"Thought you hated that name?" Gorson grinned. "You were always complaining about how annoying it was to spell-"

"I still do, but it's a *really* good password! Are you in?!"

"Yes. I've got the file, but it's just a bunch of numbers and letters."

"That's good! Send it to Cealth's translator!" Jath let out a tense huff of air before yelling, "HEY BOSS! Ram your translator into Galex's ear!"

"*What?*" The distorted blinked as Cealth slapped the side of his head, ramming the translator into his ear as she did so. "*Have you lost your mi-*"

"Now!" shouted Jath, and Cealth fired a solid stream of red laser right into the Starswallower's chest. The distorted fell, his gloating abruptly cut off. And the star fell silent.

Cealth glanced at the body, then turned to Jath, smiling. "Well done."

"Is he dead?" Jath's voice sounded oddly quiet in the sudden peace, and his legs shook from the leftover adrenaline still coursing through his body. Cealth leant over and prodded the Starswallower's back cautiously. He didn't move, but she thought she felt the huge body stir momentarily- her heart leapt horribly, but, after a moment had passed her heart rate calmed itself; she'd fired at point blank range; she'd destroyed countless distorted-Obligons that way. There was no conceivable way for the creature to have survived. And, in any case, Galex's heart was still.

"It doesn't look like it." She smiled tightly, a sense of sheer relief and exhaustion washing over her. She had done it. Decades of hunting her own kind had finally paid off. There was a tightness in her wrist and she glanced at it, momentarily confused at the cold, clammy sensation; only to realise that Jath was hanging onto it, presumably for support as his legs shuddered. She almost laughed- but then spotted his irises.

Galex, the true overlord, no longer Reath's puppet, leapt up, unharmed, his own eyes restored to normal; his thick atmosphere had deflected the laser blast, and the distorted was gone from his mind.

"What-?" He staggered, alarmed at the weakness in his limbs; his technological enhanements had been disabled by Jath's 'contingency', and he only managed to blurt only a syllable before Reath's grip on Cealth tightened, he activated Jath's personal teleporter, and the duo vanished.

They were standing on an icy rock around a hundred billion light years from Cygnus. Behind them, a wall of complete, unchanging blackness stretched away in all directions, enclosing their universe in an ever expanding sphere. Cealth kicked the distorted firmly in the stomach, then wrenched her arm free as his grip loosened. The next moment, she'd raised her gun and was pointing it at his face.

"*Wait!*" he cried. Cealth's jaw tightened at the sound of Jath's distorted voice. "*Please, just listen to me!*"

"You've just killed my best friend." Cealth said, her voice edged with anger. "I'm not about to pass up this opportunity."

"*You'd shoot him?*" The Xsovzorite raised his grey hands in surrender. Under his pathetic façade the brain worked furiously- it was a downgrade from Galex's practically immortal, technologically enhanced body, but even so, a strategy was forming, slowly, in the tiny mind.

"I'd shoot **you**, yes." Said Cealth. "And don't think you can try that little teleportation trick again- Jath only powered his personal teleporter with enough energy for one jump, and you've just emptied it. Now, I believe it's customary to ask for last words."

"*Do you have any last words?*"

Cealth fired a single warning shot, which missed Jath's face by a hair. "Consider these final words **very** carefully."

"*Oh, don't you worry.*" Hissed the distorted, smugness oozing from every pore in its face- smugness, and something else. "*I've thought of nothing else for thirty years.*"

Cealth's eyes widened in surprise as she saw her uncle's true, smoky form drifting from Jath's face, through his atmospheric shield with sinister rapidity. "Are you trying to make yourself an easier target?" She barked, firing at the incorporeal cloud- a moment later she stepped back in alarm; her shot had passed right through the being without harming it. Now operating almost entirely on instinct and on its desire for revenge, the distorted-Obligon latched itself firmly onto the closest presence it detected; Cealth.

Within the normally orderly library of her mind, chaos reigned. She pushed against the invading force with a pressure that would've caused any corporeal being to crumple like a sheet of wet paper. As it was, the distorted had to exert every ounce of force it had just to stay in one piece; it had once said that possessing Cealth against her will would be near impossible because of her furiously effective biological defenses, and, before it had latched onto Galex's mind, this would have been true.

Galex's mind had been filled with defences similar in design to Cealth's own- it seemed that whatever moral problems the Starswallowers may have had with the reverse-Obligons, taking their biological mental defences had not been an issue. They'd been careless, however; Galex remained the only Starswallower to have had the defences installed, for the simple reason that the cosmic dove had found the procedure too insanely complex to recreate for anyone other than the Supreme Galactic Overlord- and, in typical Galex fashion, the leader of the Starswallowers had been too lazy to actually activate the defences, allowing the distorted to easily steal the layout and use it against Cealth back in the present.

Cealth threw up another mental block, startled when the distorted simply slipped around it. Her defences failing, she instead faced the being and inhaled, a huge vortex dragging it towards a flaming, mental projection of herself that she'd just created. In response, the distorted enlarged itself, growing bigger and bigger, spreading beyond the reach of the vortex with alarming speed.

Break the cycle. Slow the wheel- stop it if you can- but don't let hatred consume this universe.

There's more than one way out of this. Cealth thought, her flames flickering and changing into a wall, which bluntly sectioned off part of her mind, protecting it, at least for the moment, from the invading distorted-Obligon. **There has to be.**

The distorted burst past the wall with such force that she staggered back a step, tripping distractedly over a stack of memories which she'd forgotten to replace on a mental shelf. No, hang on a moment... Cealth tossed half a dozen sharp spikes toward the distorted to keep it busy, and glanced through the memories, eyes widening as she did, a plan starting to form once again in the unnocupied crevices of her mind.

The Celestelia, teleportation drive powering down, had arrived at the exit to the universe a mere five minutes after Cealth and Jath had been taken. Gorson yawned expansively, then glanced at Galex blearily.

"You're sure they're here?"

"Yes!" snapped Galex. "There's a reason we outlawed personal teleporters- they're so easy to trace, you can't go anywhere in space without being tracked by the damn Federation! I didn't want them to have any more data on us! Viva la Galaxian Empire!"

"Good," Yawned Gorson, oblivious to Galex's posturing. "Because that was a huge jump. If you need me, I'll be in a coma." And with that, she slumped onto the floor and fell fast asleep.

Galex grunted, ran the length of the ship and leapt from the airlock, spreading his massive wings and soaring over to the icy lump of rock embedded in the wall of the universe, squinting at it. Even with his exceptional eyesight, he was barely able to see the two figures on the rock; an unconscious Xsovzorite, and the reverse-Obligon, standing bolt upright, rigid, her eyes closed but moving rapidly beneath the lids. Even as Galex watched, the eyes burst suddenly open and stared straight at him; they were dark blue, and possessed neither whites, nor irises. Tiny stars seemed to thrive within the orbs- separate universes unto themselves, whispering of forgotten things.

Give up. The distorted was moving lazily now- it coiled and uncoiled itself as it twined toward her.

And what then? Compared to the distorted's rasping, Cealth's throughs were clear and sharp. **You have nowhere to go. You can do nothing now- the Starswallowers know of your existence, and they will not simply allow you to roam free again, Reath.**

The distorted sneered. They have no say in the matter. By the time that idiot Galex realises what became of you, it will be too late for him. I will finally possess a body which can feel again- and it- you- will help me to bring about the demise of the Galaxian empire!

I offer you an ultimatum. Cealth continued, as though she hadn't heard him speak. **Leave my mind. Hide yourself away in some forgotten part of the universe, and do not trouble us again.**

Or what? The distorted was gloating now. It sounds to me as though you're begging, little niece.

Or I will tear you apart. Cealth was glowing now, the white vortex of her face brimming with a blinding light. The distorted hesitated, sensing a genuine threat

164

behind her words. **What you have done is madness. You deserve oblivion. However, I am willing to offer you some compassion- something my brother would have wanted.**

Compassion? Laughed the distorted. *I don't need your compassion! It is your mind which shall be torn apart- stripped of all I want- emotions, memories- and then discarded! And you are weakening!*

Then I hope for your sake that, if there is a hell, you find some way to redeem yourself in time.

Cealth's body stood, unsteadily, closed the eyes that had gazed on the universe for such a short time- and released an enormous shockwave that paralysed Galex mid-flight and then continued throughout the universe- a pulse comprised of jumbled memories that Cealth had stolen all those years ago, on the orders of the Starswallowers, and the minds that the distorted-Obligon had supressed and stolen.

Jath's eyes opened and he groaned in pain- his mouth was dry, and his eyes felt incredibly scratchy.

On board the Celestelia, Exath, who was wondering around in a state of considerable confusion, widened his eyes as the shockwave passed through, and, gradually, the space pirates opened theirs.

What are you doing?! The distorted's form billowed, a cloud caught by a tornado. *You'll kill us both!*

Perhaps. Cealth's smile was determined, yet sadness tinged her voice. **But it does not matter.**

Tungsten groaned and sat up, blinking blearily, only to be tackled by a beaming Sam, who hugged her tightly and ignored the captain's stuttered protests- her ribcage was very sore from where she'd been lying on it. On the other side of the ward, Auren watched them through half-closed, slightly cynical eyes while Pho and Nix let out simultaneous, deafening yawns from their linked respiratory system.

It matters a great deal to me! Howled the distorted, lunging desperately away from Cealth even as the memories he had stolen were stripped from him- with each retrieved mind, its smoky form came apart in wisps.

Why? Cealth asked. The distorted twisted to look at her in its panic. **All you have done since attaining your power is to seek power or revenge. And I'm finished with being selfish like you.**

You don't get to take the moral high ground here! You destroyed the Earth, just as the Starswallowers destroyed Sandros 6! You're just as monstrous, if not worse, than us!

I went to a very dark place. Cealth's voice became sad. **I destroyed the Earth to destroy all distorted.** I thought, at the time, that it was justified- that destroying you monsters made up for the deaths of all those other trillions of beings. You're right- I became our enemies for a brief time. I sought revenge when I should have tried to help you.

Still trapped in a small compartment in the bio-lab, along with almost all of the other Starswallowers who'd been imprisoned by the distorted-Obligon, the cosmic hawk frowned as the shockwave hit him.

"Oonaer." He muttered, glancing upwards, towards the bio-lab roof. "Not a good place for a summer home..."

For a brief time? Sneered the distorted, squirming to free himself from Cealth's pull- but it hadn't lessened, even with the distraction. Her will was as iron as ever, even if her mind was elsewhere. *You still act just like the Starswallowers with your assault on our kind! That hasn't changed! It won't ever change!*

I agree that I am a terrible being. I destroyed the Earth just to kill a few thousand beings. But I see now that I am different from the Starswallowers. I have taken another path.

And what's that? Spat the distorted, its form becoming thinner by the second.

The Starswallowers hid their mistakes. Refused to acknowledge them. But I won't run from my fate- whatever it may be. Cealth took a patient breath and stared pointedly at the distorted-Obligon. **Reath- if that really is still you in there, know that I am sorry for my inability to help you.**

Liar. Your last minute compassion does not make you any less of a mass murderer!

I never said it did. Cealth's voice became fainter, and for the first time the distorted noticed that she too was fading- even as the distorted's form dissapated, Cealth's skin was becoming translucent. **But, unlike the Starswallowers, I at least tried to fix my mistakes. And I have just fixed yours.**

Jath looked at Cealth in alarm- her skin, previously an opaque cream, was now almost transparent- he could practically see the blood pounding through her- and her eyes had become little more than glassy spheres. A surge of regret hit him as

166

his memories of being possessed returned, and he stared at Cealth with a sudden, terrible understanding of what she had just done.

"You'll have to apologise to Sam for me about the Earth."

A smile had spread across her face- a half contented, half unbearably sad smile. A second shockwave ripped past Jath as the final stolen memories began winging their way back to their owners.

A moment later he heard a scream of unnatural potency and venom. Cealth fell backwards onto the exit to universe, her eyes fixed onto a single, lonely star, which curved elegantly in its own, exquisitely unique orbit... and then both Obligons were gone.

Epilogue

"THANK YOU AND GOOD SUNRISE!" Roared Sam, ending the concert to the bellows of the surrounding crowd, and an echoing chord from Tungsten's bass. Behind the giant stage, the first rays of S'rou's blazing red sun fell through a small hole in the thick black clouds and perfectly illuminated the platform on which the five space pirates stood, revelling in the cheers as their forty-eight hour countdown concert concluded.

The cosmic swan grabbed Galex by the scruff of his neck to stop him from leaping into the rays of light- and onto the stage- along with the rest of the audience, and firmly steered him out of the crushing crowd and towards one of the many stands selling merchandise, where Jath was casually watching the rays of light- and making the vendor whose stand he was leaning on ever more uncomfortable.

"I... um... I owe your captain- boss- whatever- my thanks." Galex said gruffly to Jath, who glanced up at him and raised an eyebrow. "If she hadn't- well- anyway, it's thanks to her I'm not possessed. And... Sandros 6. We were wrong. I just wanted to... apologise."

"She's dead." Jath replied unenthusiastically. "It means a *lot* that you're actually deigning to thank a puny mortal such as myself though."

"Hey, you finally learnt to use sarcasm!" Sam came bounding towards them from out of the crowd, flashing a toothsome smile at Galex. "Hey big bird, you find out how my planet was destroyed yet?"

"Big bird?" spluttered Galex. "If I hear one more Earthian comment about that-"

"Did ya find out, or not?"

"Yes." Galex nodded reluctantly. "It was Cea-"

"It was the distorted." Jath blurted. Then he directed his words towards Sam. "It blew up Earth to get Cealth's attention. Wanted to make her attack the Starswallowers, lure Galex into the open so it could possess him. And we saw how badly that went for us. I'm sorry."

"Yeesh." Growled Sam. "He destroyed my world just for a distraction? If he weren't already dead, I'd introduce him to my cutlass! By the way," she added, remembering something. "Have any of you seen Tungsten? She was meant to meet me backstage, but she's vanished."

"So, um, would any of you guys like a t-shirt?" the vender asked, uncomfortably.

Sam glanced at him and then frowned thoughtfully. "Hey... don't I know you?"

Jath jerked her aside, quickly.

"Yeah, that's Exath," he muttered in an undertone. "After he got hit by the memory wave his all memories came back- but his personality is weird. I blame those Sandros 6 recollections. His entire childhood revolved around the planet, so when it just disappeared from memory, he lost all motivation to do anything other than annoy me and impress Cealth." Jath heaved a sigh and glanced at the beams of light shimmering down on the stage for a moment- Nix and Pho furiously defending their place in the sunlight with a double-necked guitar, while Auren reclined back on her drumkit, surveying the battle with the detatched nochalance of a well fed cat.

"Wow," Sam whispered, glancing at the Manicarian curiously. "What, so he's just working here now?"

"Pretty much," nodded Jath. "He's a complete wet blanket. I'll miss our arguments, but at least he's alive now. He's saving up for a university course on film making- wanted to make a documentary of Sandros 6- the truth of what happened this time." He glanced back towards the Manicarian, who was desperately trying to find a tour shirt in Galex's size while the eight-foot bird loomed above him.

"And what about you?"

Jath frowned. "What **about** me?"

"Well, you're unemployed now, right? What're you gonna do?" Sam glanced over her shoulder as though looking for someone before continuing. "I was going to wait for Tungsten to get here before I asked- but this seems like the right kinda time. D'you wanna come with us?"

"What, join the space pirates?" Jath almost smiled. "I thought you had to like metal music to do that."

"You do. Besides, Gorson mentioned that you can play the keyboard? We need someone who can do that." Sam cocked her head slightly. "So that's a yes? *Just Panic's* fans are aggressive- we've stolen their place in the charts at last and they ain't happy about it- but that's just part of the fun. It'd get boring otherwise, right?"

"Uh- I'm sorry- but I have to say no." Jath swallowed uncomfortably. "It's just... I'm more of a country and western person."

"Ugh."

"What d'you mean ugh?!"

"Nothing. Everyone's different I suppose. Even so, you'd better change your mind- and your taste in music- before she gets here," Sam jerked her head towards Tungsten, who was storming across the sandy ground with an expression that would have cracked solid rock and forced volcanoes to expel their innards. "One of our amps blew in the middle of the concert- and she's *not* happy about it."

Countless lifetimes away, a reverse-Obligon opened her eyes.

Surrounding her was a light brighter than anything else she'd ever seen- purer even than the beams that had transformed her friends so long ago.

They were here now- surrounding her, not angry or resentful, just peaceful. Free.

They all burned as one now- a star that glowed white hot and ignored the petty battles that sparked around it, content to drift through the cosmos on the edge of their galaxy.

Cealth smiled and closed her eyes.

<u>The End.</u>

Printed in Great Britain
by Amazon